"Who are you really, Donovan?"

When Erin felt his body harden against hers, she looked into his eyes and saw a stranger she didn't know. "Something is happening to you. Far as someone in a role you're playing. And I feel I scarcely know you."

His expression softened, changing him into the man she recognized. He drew her into his arms. "We've only been together a few days," he said. "It's natural to have feelings like that."

With his body hard against hers, Erin couldn't force herself to move away. "If you're a true undercover agent, your name probably isn't Dan Donovan," she whispered. "Who are you really?"

"I'm the man who loves you," he whispered back, his voice thick.

Dear Reader,

They're rugged, they're strong and they're wanted! Whether sheriff, undercover cop or officer of the court, these men are trained to keep the peace, to uphold the law. But what happens when they meet the one woman who gets to know the man *behind* the badge?

Twelve of these men have been on the loose...and only Harlequin Intrigue has brought them to you— one per month in the LAWMAN series. This month meet the last sexy Lawman—Irish rogue Dan Donovan.

Vickie York has served as a commissioned officer in both the U.S. Army and U.S. Air Force. After an assignment to the Defense Language Institute, Vickie served as an intelligence officer for the rest of her military career. She was awarded a Bronze Star for service during the Vietnam conflict. Beginning with the publication of *The Pestilence Plot* in 1982, her novels have often been based on her intelligence expertise. The author now makes her home in Tacoma, Washington.

We hope you have enjoyed all the books in the exciting Lawman series. After all, there's nothing sexier than the strong arms of the law!

Regards,

Debra Matteucci
Senior Editor & Editorial Coordinator
Harlequin Books
300 East 42nd Street
New York, New York 10017

Sworn to Silence
Vickie York

Harlequin Books

TORONTO • NEW YORK • LONDON
AMSTERDAM • PARIS • SYDNEY • HAMBURG
STOCKHOLM • ATHENS • TOKYO • MILAN
MADRID • WARSAW • BUDAPEST • AUCKLAND

For PEG AND LARRY McCOOL
Who enjoyed Ireland with me

And for LYNNE AND MICHAEL GRAHAM,
our Irish hosts

ISBN 0-373-22421-4

SWORN TO SILENCE

CAST OF CHARACTERS

Erin Meyer—She knew Dan Donovan was a dead man.

Dan Donovan—This undercover Irishman had something special in mind for Erin.

Margaret Sullivan—Why had Erin's mother fled her palatial Dublin home in the dead of the night?

Patrick O'Shaughnessy—Was Margaret's new husband an innocent victim or the leader of a global conspiracy?

Jean Magee—Did she know where Margaret was?

Colonel Byrd—What was his real reason for firing Erin from the Pentagon Intelligence agency?

Brian Cairns—Where had the clerk at Ballyshannon Lodge disappeared to?

Mrs. Flaherty—She could find anybody in Westport.

Michael Riley—Erin's uncle would do anything to protect his family.

Chameleon—This assassin had many disguises that mirrored his devilish heart.

Prologue

Final instructions for the assassin's next contract arrived early one morning at an elegant old brownstone house in Falls Church, Virginia. Alone in the high-ceilinged gold-and-white reception room, the killer known as *Chameleon* studied a printed copy of the terse radio message.

> Neutralize Dun Aengus's Man At Noon On Green Day. Meet Him On The Left Side Of The South Entrance To The Federal Shrine.

Though decoded, the words remained obscure—a testimonial to his employer's caution. But Chameleon had already received a letter translating the key terms—*Dun Aengus's man, green day,* and *federal shrine*—so he understood the instructions clearly. After memorizing the message, he tore it up and tossed it into the blazing fire.

THIRTY MILES AWAY at Fort Meade, Maryland, a National Security Agency analyst stiffened as he skimmed through a printout of the same radio message, intercepted and decrypted that morning by the secret agency. Did *neutralize* mean *kill?* he wondered, reading the words more carefully.

Probably not, he decided. *Neutralize* might well refer to some mind-changing act rather than assassination.

Even more of a puzzle, there was no way to determine the date and place for the scheduled action, whatever it was. Without additional information, the message was meaningless.

"More nonsense from Dublin," he muttered to himself. With a few strokes on his computer, he ordered distribution of the message to the intelligence officers working the Irish section of the State Department, Central Intelligence Agency and Pentagon. Maybe they could figure out what was going on. He sure as hell couldn't.

But as the message flicked off his screen, the NSA analyst couldn't help wondering if some unsuspecting person had just been targeted for murder.

Chapter One

By the time Air Force Lieutenant Erin Meyer reached Washington D.C.'s National Cathedral, she was already wishing she hadn't come. *There's not one chance in a thousand somebody's going to be killed here today,* she chided herself as she wheeled her car onto the access road.

Yet here she was on the other side of the District, squandering hours of precious time on what was probably a noble fool's errand. And all because of a few cryptic sentences she'd read yesterday in an intercepted message from Dublin.

Driving slowly in front of the broad stone steps to the cathedral's south entrance, Erin carefully scanned the portico. Although this St. Patrick's Day was cold and blustery, the usual throng of visitors trooped up and down the staircase.

Off to the left at the top of the stairs, her searching eyes focused on a tall, lone man, briefcase in hand, glancing to his right and left as though looking for someone. Even as she watched, he yanked up his coat sleeve to peer at his wristwatch. Her breath caught in her throat. Could he be the one? He was standing on the left side of the entrance, just as the message had specified.

A chill swept through her. Though he leaned casually against the stone edifice behind him, the alert way he studied the faces of the crowd told her he was waiting for someone.

Quickly Erin searched the knots of visitors, looking for someone else—anyone—who might be a possible target. No one stood alone the way this man did.

Nervously, she checked her watch. Almost twelve. The message had stipulated *noon* as the time for the *neutralization*. If she was going to act, it had to be now. At this very instant the man at the top of the stairs could be the target of a marksman's weapon.

Erin's muscles tightened. Could he be *Dun Aengus's man?* If so, what was his relationship to her new stepfather, Patrick O'Shaughnessy? Patrick's nickname was *Dun Aengus*, a childhood term of endearment bestowed by his mother who'd compared her four-year-old's strength and fortitude to that of an ancient Irish fortress.

If someone associated with Patrick was targeted for assassination, did that mean Patrick was, too? And what about her mother?

Lord, Erin hoped her mother's impulsive marriage to the Dublin millionaire—less than six months after her first husband died—hadn't put her in danger. Erin's intelligence training had heightened her already keen instinct for trouble. The instant she'd read the message she knew something was wrong in Dublin.

She'd tried to ignore her feeling, called herself paranoid, and told herself *Dun Aengus* must refer to somebody or something else—perhaps the stone fortress where Patrick's nickname originated. Maybe the fortress was the *federal shrine* mentioned in the message as the place for the neutralization. If so, it couldn't be the National Cathedral—the first place that had popped into Erin's mind.

But last night Erin had had horrid dreams about someone—was it her mother?—being killed at the National Cathedral. The dreams convinced her she had to act. No matter how cryptic the words in the message, her gut instinct couldn't be ignored.

But she'd have to go to the cathedral alone. Her commander would think she was a nut if she asked for Pentagon help based on such a nebulous intercept. Worse, he'd probably suggest she'd be wasting valuable time by going to the cathedral herself on a wild-goose chase—in effect, ordering her to stay at her desk.

Slowing her car to a crawl, she surveyed the man standing alone at the extreme side of the steps. There was an air of isolation about his tall figure. In his black overcoat, against the cathedral's light-colored limestone wall, he was a perfect target.

If her interpretation of the message was right, he was about to be killed. How could she help? She was only an intelligence analyst who wrote reports and prepared briefings. Swallowing hard, she tried to force down the beginning of panic welling in her throat.

Behind her, somebody honked, urging her to hurry. Quickly she turned in front of an oncoming car into the no-parking area in front of the stone stairway and braked to a stop without turning off the engine. The man at the top of the stairs glanced toward her and then away, still searching the crowd.

Erin got a quick first impression of big bold features and curly black hair. Not a handsome man, but powerful-looking.

An Irishman, she guessed, afraid she'd been right about the message. If this man was associated with Patrick, he would logically be Irish. Erin's parents had been born in Ireland, and she could spot a fellow countryman from a hundred paces.

Leaving the engine running, she shoved her door open and scrambled out of the car. Cold wind whipped through her gabardine uniform, chilling her to the bone. She raced across the sidewalk toward the massive man at the top of the stairs. He stared directly down at her. Frantically she motioned him toward her. A look of momentary interest crossed his rugged face, but he didn't move.

He was a big man, and she admired the way his black overcoat clung to his powerful shoulders, the way his white scarf framed his broad chin. In another place and time she might have flirted with him. But not now. Now she had to get to him in time. Breathing hard, she started up the stairs.

He's massive, all right, she thought, her gaze fastened on him. *A great target.* She had no idea what she'd say, knew only that she had to get him away from here without mentioning the highly classified intercept.

"Come here," she yelled at him, but still he didn't move.

Hurtling the steps two at a time, she was halfway up when he finally took a step toward her, a frown on his face. A heartbeat later she heard it, the sharp crack of gunfire. Two shots. One right after the other. Limestone splintered on the wall where he'd been standing only an instant before. Thank God she'd come. If he hadn't moved, he'd be dead or seriously injured.

Beside her on the steps, a woman screamed, her terror piercing the air like a dreadful sword.

A man yelled, "Watch out. That guy's got a gun." There were more screams and a child cried out.

Heart pounding, Erin whirled around in a desperate attempt to spot the assassin. Someone grabbed her arm from behind, iron fingers wrapped around the dark fabric of her uniform suit sleeve. In sudden panic she jerked around, her free arm raised to defend herself. It was the man she'd come to save.

"Quick. Run for your car." His controlled baritone vibrated with authority. "This way. Down the side stairs to the grass." His hand, massive and strong, turned her away from the direction of fire to the curve in the steps.

Icy fear twisted around Erin's heart. Could they escape an armed assassin? Running in her high-heeled pumps, she had to take two wobbly steps to every one of his. His hand moved from her arm to her waist, and she felt him close beside her, partly shielding her with his big frame.

They crossed the grass at the foot of the stairs to the

concrete sidewalk. People were still screaming, and Erin got a vague impression of bodies hurtling away from them. They pounded down the concrete to her waiting car, the door still open, engine running.

"Get in," he barked.

Lungs bursting, Erin leapt inside and slid across to the passenger seat. He bounded in behind her and slammed the door shut, putting the briefcase between them.

"Down on the floor," he ordered, glancing over her head through the passenger window. Outside, a solid line of vehicles inched toward them. Since she'd driven her car across traffic to get to the steps, they were locked-in tight. Erin gulped air into her suffocated lungs. Were they trapped? Would the assassin try to shoot the man—and her—while they were inside the car? Erin's mouth felt dry, and she had a hard time swallowing.

"Down! Now!" With one quick movement he grabbed her arms and swung her down and around so she was on the floor facing the front seat. His huge hands had lifted her as easily as if she were a child.

An instant later he jerked the transmission into reverse and shot backward across the sidewalk and lawn. Swiveling the car around, he shifted again, blared the horn, and lurched ahead toward the bumper-to-bumper traffic.

Crouched on the floor, unable to see, Erin expected to hear the grinding rasp of metal on metal and braced herself for impact. Instead she felt the car turn and move steadily ahead, apparently merging with the line of vehicles on the access road leaving the cathedral grounds. She smelled exhaust fumes from the slowly moving cars, heard the approaching scream of sirens—but no more gun shots.

Erin poked her head up. Instantly his paw of a hand pushed her back down. A tremor swept through her. Was the assassin behind them now, determined to deliver on his contract?

"Stay down until we get away from here." The authority

in the stranger's baritone voice matched the steely strength in his hand. "Then we'll talk."

WHO THE DEVIL IS SHE? Dan Donovan glanced down at the silky smooth, flame red hair beneath his hand and from there to the silver bars on her shoulders. Whoever she was, she'd done him one hell of a favor. How she'd managed to show up exactly when she did was the first thing he needed to find out—after she told him her name. From her car's parking tag, he figured she worked at the Pentagon.

Lifting his hand from her head, he turned right off the access road, heading north on Wisconsin Avenue. The sirens screamed much louder now. In a minute the authorities would be at the cathedral. Thank God he wouldn't have to talk to them. The last thing he wanted to do right now was lie to the police about his business there.

Glancing away from the street, Donovan checked the rearview mirror. No one appeared to be following. With one quick motion he tossed his briefcase onto the back seat next to her uniform cap and overcoat, giving her more room to sit down.

As soon as his hand returned to the steering wheel, she peered up at him from the floor. Her oval face with its high forehead, sparkling blue eyes and prominent features glowed with vitality. Framed by that shining mass of red hair, her face was distinctive, one he wouldn't soon forget. Too bad she wore her hair tied back. Loose, it would swing luxuriantly around her shoulders. Donovan felt a stab of remorse that he'd never see her with her hair down, would never meet her again after this one brief encounter.

"Is anybody after us?" In spite of the fear in her voice, it sounded lilting, musical, more like a girl's than a woman's. But she was no adolescent. When she was running up the stairs toward him, his discerning eye had noticed the gentle swell of breasts and hips in her fitted uniform. Now, seeing her up close, she looked older than he'd first thought. Though she had a flawless, scrubbed-clean complexion, he sensed a maturity beyond her years in the confident tilt of her head, in the direct way she met his eyes. Midtwenties, he estimated. Closer to thirty.

"We're okay. Nobody seems to be tailing us," he said, flashing his friendliest, most congenial smile. Donovan was well aware of how that smile affected women. He used it purposely so she'd trust him enough to tell him what she was up to. If that meant turning on the charm—well, he was an expert. And, if the truth be known, he rather enjoyed it—especially when he ran into a woman with such obvious assets.

Her eyes widened, but otherwise she seemed unaffected by his smile. Gracefully she managed to twist herself up onto the seat and fasten her seat belt without showing a hint of thigh.

Too bad, he thought, imagining her long slim legs bare to the hip. With her sylphlike figure, she was built for speed, a Thoroughbred who'd come racing to his rescue.

How the hell had she managed to appear on the cathedral steps in the nick of time the way she had? The sooner he found out, the better. If she knew about his noon appointment, she was probably connected with whoever had tried to rob him of the cash in his briefcase. That must be what the two shots were all about: someone in the crowd wanted him out of action so an accomplice could grab his case. Maybe *she* was the accomplice and had backed out at the last minute. Since she was so noticeable in her uniform, that seemed unlikely, but it was too soon to rule out any possibilities.

Had something other than robbery been the motive for the shooting? Not likely, he told himself. In spite of Donovan's impressive enemies list, only a few people knew he'd be at the cathedral today at noon. One of them must have decided to steal the cash.

Donovan felt the woman's eyes on him but kept his gaze trained on the street ahead of the car. "I owe you one, Lieutenant," he said, flashing her another appealing smile.

She didn't smile back. "Who are you and why was somebody shooting at you?"

Her directness caught him by surprise and, for half an instant, he hesitated. He started to make up a name, intending to tell her a few lies and walk away after he tried to find out who she was and her connection to the thieves. She probably wouldn't tell him, but he wasn't worried. With his resources he could probably find out about her in short order.

But he decided not to give her a false identity. Sometime in the past few minutes he realized that, to his chagrin, he'd changed his mind about seeing her again.

"My name's Donovan," he replied. "As for the rest of your question, I was hoping *you'd* tell *me* what was going on at the cathedral. I haven't the faintest idea. But since you arrived in the nick of time to warn me, you must know something I don't."

Her eyes widened and, though she tried to hide it, he heard her quick gasp for breath. He was right. She must be connected with the thieves and was scared he'd find out.

"You've got it all wrong, Donovan." Her voice quivered with what he interpreted as forced sincerity. "I wasn't heading toward you. I was picking up a friend for lunch. She was standing behind you under the portico." He could tell she was lying no matter how hard she tried to sound sincere.

"Why couldn't your friend walk down the steps to the car?" Though he knew she was lying, Donovan kept his tone carefully neutral. She'd been calling to him, not someone else, when she'd run up the stairs toward him. But the last thing he wanted was a confrontation.

To his surprise, she smiled convincingly. "She couldn't walk down the steps because she's nearly blind—works in the cathedral gift shop. She's probably worried sick about me right now after what happened."

"Then it was just a coincidence that you appeared when you did?" Donovan tried to act as if he believed her. He'd studied every person who came near the cathedral entrance that morning. No woman, blind or otherwise, had stood anywhere in his vicinity.

She let her breath out in a small sigh. "Of course it was a coincidence. How in the world could I know somebody was going to shoot at you?"

He shrugged. "Lots of ways. You might have a friend who knew somebody was gunning for me and talked too much. You might have planned the robbery yourself and changed your mind. You might—"

"Oh, stop," she interjected. "Do I look like the kind of person who would be involved in an assassination?"

"Is that what it was? An attempted assassination?" He eyed her shrewdly, suspicious of the rosy blush coloring her cheeks. She knew more than she was telling, that's for sure, and had probably used "assassination" to throw him off the track.

"As for what kind of person you are—how would I know? I don't even know your name."

Her flush deepened. "Erin—Erin Meyer. Sorry about that, Donovan. I should have introduced myself sooner."

"I'm glad to meet you, Erin," he said, really meaning it. The vitality in her face attracted him the way no woman had in a long while. If the attraction continued, maybe he'd put on the charm and find out what kind of woman Erin Meyer was…

After flicking the car's turn signal, he swung off Wisconsin Avenue onto the scenic Rock Creek Parkway that paralleled the Potomac. On this blustery March day, skeletal trees along the roadway showed no sign that spring was only a few days away.

"Of course, I'm just guessing about the assassination," she went on. "If you don't agree, who or what do you think was behind the shots?"

"Robbery," he declared flatly, deciding she already knew about the money. If he leveled with her, maybe she'd level with him. "I'm carrying a lot of cash in my briefcase.

Somebody must have decided to steal it, even if they had to kill me.''

"But you said you had no idea why you were attacked." Bright blue eyes stared at him quizzically.

Donovan grinned. "That was before we were introduced. A man has to be careful what he says when he's carrying a lot of cash."

She hesitated a moment. "If this was an attempted robbery, shouldn't we notify the police?"

As she made the suggestion, Donovan sensed she wasn't any more eager to involve the authorities than he. Why? he wondered.

"No," he said. "If I report this, the police would want to know to whom I was giving the money."

"Is that what you were doing at the cathedral?" Erin glanced toward the back seat where the briefcase lay next to her flight cap and overcoat. "Waiting for the person getting the money?"

"Right," he said cheerfully. "Since you just saved my life, I'll let you in on my secret." He pulled over to the side of the road. Ignoring the four lanes of traffic whizzing by them, he turned off the engine.

"I'll take these keys," he said, putting them in his overcoat pocket.

"What are you going to do with them?" The thread of tension in her voice told him she was wondering if his *secret* posed a threat to her. He smiled to himself. Keep her guessing. It would serve her right for lying to him.

Opening the car door, he looked at her over his shoulder. "I stopped so you could drive. After all, this *is* your car."

Jingling the keys in his pocket, he walked around the front of the Buick to the passenger's side and got in. "And a lovely car it is, too."

She stared at him from the driver's seat. "It's my one extravagance. I couldn't afford it on a lieutenant's pay, but my father left me some money when he died."

She sounds defensive, he thought, even more certain she

was linked to the thieves. *Must be afraid I'll think she got the car illegally.* If she was involved in robberies like the one against him, that would explain her timely arrival at the cathedral and her lies about why she was there. But why warn him instead of snatching the briefcase?

"Your father died recently?" he asked, hoping to catch her in another lie.

Her clear blue eyes narrowed.

She's like a beautiful Thoroughbred filly with a luxuriant red mane, he thought. But his Thoroughbred was getting impatient.

"Let's cut the chatter, Donovan. You've made sure I'm not going to drive off with your briefcase full of cash, so give me the keys." Erin stretched out a slender hand.

Silently he handed them to her, deliberately letting his fingers slide slowly across her palm. Startled, she jerked her hand back. After a quick glance at him, she started the engine and glided into traffic.

"Since you've told me about the cash, why not let me know the whole story," she said, her voice as steady as a TV news anchor's. "Who were you giving the money to and why?"

ERIN GLANCED AT Donovan's rugged Irish face. She could practically see the wheels spinning in his head trying to come up with a believable answer to her query.

He was lying about the cash, she thought, and was not above exerting his considerable charm to make her believe him. His stunt with the keys had been a transparent attempt to convince her he really was carrying a large amount.

A disturbing thought assailed her. What if he was telling the truth? Maybe she was sitting next to a criminal who'd just robbed a bank. She couldn't dispel the notion, much as she tried to convince herself that men in cashmere overcoats didn't run around with briefcases full of cash from a bank robbery.

But whatever he was up to, she doubted he'd tell her, no

matter how grateful he was to her for saving his life. Thank the lord he hadn't wanted to call the police. She'd never have been able to explain her timely arrival at the cathedral—not without revealing the top secret intercepted message, something she could never do.

"I'd planned to give the money to a congressman," he said, finally answering her question.

Another lie. "Congressmen have offices," she said sharply. "Why the cloak-and-dagger act in front of the cathedral?" The shiver of apprehension running down her spine was on the verge of turning into outright fear.

He lifted a dark bushy eyebrow. "You've heard of baksheesh? The money in this briefcase represents my employer's gratitude for a favor rendered by said congressman. For obvious reasons he didn't want the cash delivered to his office or picked up by an aide."

Aghast, Erin stared at him. In her book, anybody who bribed congressmen was a crook. Why was he admitting the crime? And where had the money come from?

"I suppose he chose the cathedral because he figured a church at high noon was the least likely place to stumble upon a colleague," Erin said sarcastically, swallowing her fear. Donovan didn't sound threatening, but she couldn't relax until she figured out what he was up to.

"Exactly." The roguish smile on his face was reflected in his eyes and voice.

Seeing his smile, Erin suddenly wished she were back at the Pentagon where she belonged. The sooner she got rid of him, the better.

With an effort she tried to concentrate on driving but could still see his face in her mind while watching the traffic on the parkway. His hair was too black and curly, his teeth were too white, and there was a rampant sexuality in his lusty gaze. If she didn't watch her step she'd find herself falling for another egotistical Irishman.

To Erin's surprise, she found herself half believing his story, and berated herself for being conned. The intercepted message had said nothing about a robbery, only a *neutralization*. And where was the assassin? Could he be somewhere behind them right now? Anxiously she glanced in the rearview mirror but saw nothing suspicious.

"The congressman must have done your employer an awfully big favor," Erin began slowly, masking her fear. "Your briefcase is pretty large."

He pulled thoughtfully at his earlobe. "My employer's in heavy construction. The congressman got him a contract worth millions."

Erin stiffened, her hands clenching the steering wheel until her knuckles turned white. Though she tried to hide her reaction, she couldn't help herself. Her mother's new husband, Patrick, operated a global construction company out of Dublin. Could he be bribing politicians for lucrative contracts?

Beside her, Donovan chuckled. "Don't act so surprised. Paying baksheesh is part of doing business these days."

"It's also illegal," she protested hotly. Though Erin had met Patrick only briefly in Washington before her mother's wedding two weeks ago, she'd been drawn to the beefy, charismatic Irishman on sight.

"That's why I didn't wait around for the police." Donovan winked at her like a fellow conspirator. "Bribes may be illegal for a congressman but not for my employer. If he wants to give away a little spare cash as a present to a friend, that's his business."

"And just who *is* your employer?" As soon as Erin asked, she wished she hadn't. She didn't want him to suspect she had more than a casual interest in his answer. Worse, she hadn't needed to ask. She could easily find out if a man named Donovan worked for Patrick by calling her mother in Dublin.

"With a little digging, you can find out who my employer is with no help from me," he taunted. "But I'll tell you and save you the trouble if you come clean with me. Tell me why you showed up when you did and why you thought the shooting was an attempted assassination instead of a robbery. Then I'll tell you who my employer is.''

Erin could feel his eyes on her face, gauging her reaction. She didn't turn toward him. There was no way she could tell him about the message without revealing *special* or *communications* intelligence. This would be a crime punishable by jail and a big fine. Besides, her self-protective instincts were urging caution until she learned exactly who Donovan was and what his relationship was to Patrick.

''I already told you the truth,'' she lied. ''I was meeting a friend for lunch.''

''We both know that's not true,'' he said easily. ''No woman was standing behind me. If she'd been there, I would have seen her.''

''Then she must have stepped back inside to get out of the wind.'' Sucking in her breath, Erin turned off the parkway and onto Wisconsin again. They were in Bethesda, Maryland, a suburb of Washington, where expensive motels and businesses lined the street. She headed back toward Washington.

''Where's your hotel, Donovan?'' she asked, determined to change the subject. Now that she'd done her noble duty, she wanted to get away from this arresting man and back to her secure Pentagon cubicle before she revealed something she shouldn't.

Hearing his smug chuckle, she realized she'd *already* revealed something she shouldn't.

''How did you know I was based out of town?'' he asked. ''There are a couple of big construction companies with offices right here in Washington. How did you know I was staying in a hotel?''

''You look like an out-of-towner,'' she lied, her temper rising. Why did he have to catch every tiny mistake she made? ''If you'd like to question everything I say, go ahead. Maybe I'll answer and maybe I won't.''

''Hey, I'm sorry,'' he said, sounding instantly contrite.

Erin didn't believe him for an instant. Men like Donovan

didn't say they were sorry unless they wanted something from a woman.

"You saved my life and I'm grateful," he acknowledged. "If you don't want to tell me the whole story behind what you did, so be it." Shrugging his shoulders, he held his hands out, palms up. "I'm sure you have a good reason."

Though mollified, Erin kept her eyes on the street, not daring to meet his direct gaze. He had a way of seeing through her that both attracted and frightened her. This whole situation frightened her—the intercepted message, the aborted assassination, the possible connection with her stepfather, and not being able to report what happened to the authorities for security reasons.

Just who was this roguish man by her side? Who wanted to kill him and why? Until she had the answers, Erin wasn't about to confide in him. She desperately needed to be alone to think things through.

"I really was meeting a friend for lunch," she insisted, determined to stick to her story. Even though he suspected she was lying, he would never know for sure.

Half an hour later, after Erin dropped Donovan at a five-star hotel in downtown Washington, she felt strangely let down when he didn't ask for her telephone number. If her mother confirmed that he worked for Patrick, she'd simply have to take the initiative and arrange to see him again. As her only link to possible danger threatening her family, Donovan might be hiding information she could use. She had to find out more about him.

IN HIS SEEDY HOTEL ROOM, the slender, wiry actor surveyed his prominent chin and bulbous nose in the bathroom mirror. Nobody who got a good look at that face would ever forget it. It was a true masterpiece. But then all of the actor's faces were unforgettable masterpieces. With good reason the press had dubbed him *Chameleon*, and the name had stuck.

Without removing the disguise, he returned to the bedroom and carefully loaded two cartridges into the empty chambers of his .357 Magnum revolver. He'd missed his target by a hair, squeezing off only two shots before the crowd panicked, blocking his aim.

How that fool female lieutenant managed to show up when she did, he had no idea. But he intended to find out. With her car's model and license number, he'd obtain her name and address in short order from his information broker. Through the woman, he'd find his target again. She'd made him miss this time. He wouldn't again, even if he had to kill both of them.

Chapter Two

Inside the hotel's luxurious peach-colored marble lobby, Donovan went directly to a pay phone. Without identifying himself, he asked for Mr. Owens, a code for Donovan's operation.

A moment later the familiar voice of his in-house contact, Michael Essinger, came on the line. "Owens here."

"We need to get together ASAP," Donovan growled.

"Did you have problems with the congressman?" Even though this call was highly unusual, Essinger's voice showed no emotion or curiosity, only cold-blooded interest. Good old Mike. Always the professional, a man Donovan could count on.

"I nearly got blown away by someone trying to rip off the cash. An air force lieutenant—a woman—warned me in the nick of time, or I'd be in a drawer at the city morgue right now."

"How did she know?"

"That's what I want you to find out. She wouldn't tell me." Out of habit, Donovan surveyed the phone alcove, keeping a watchful eye on the stocky man and teenage girl who were the only other occupants. Lowering his voice, he raised his hand to shield his mouth before he spoke again. "Her name is Erin Meyer. She's a first lieutenant working at the Pentagon. Get me the entire story on her from the day she was born. I want to know how and where she fits."

An image of Erin's tall slender form flashed in Donovan's mind. For a luxurious moment he let himself dwell on the gentle swell of her hips, on her rich glowing hair.

"You think there's a connection between her and your current assignment?" For the first time, Essinger's voice showed a flicker of interest.

"Got to be. She *had* to know about the robbery to get to the cathedral when she did. There ain't no coincidences in this business, buddy. How long to get together a package on her?" Donovan paused, remembering how slowly the wheels at the agency seemed to turn these days. He was still waiting for biographical material on O'Shaughnessy's new wife, information he'd asked for more than two weeks ago.

"This is an emergency, Mike," he said. "Get your people off their duffs so I'll know who the lieutenant is before she dies of old age."

Essinger sighed into the phone. "Sorry about the delay in that other request, old man. Our research people were hit hard in the last cutback."

"There better not be a delay this time."

"There won't be. I'll have it for you tomorrow if I have to keep somebody up all night. Ten a.m. Lion cage at the zoo."

"I'll be there."

After he hung up, Donovan took another penetrating look around the alcove. A third person had entered, a matronly woman with a load of packages. At the phone next to his, she began dialing. Without being obvious, he left the alcove and went to the restroom. She probably wasn't interested in his conversation, but he was taking no chances. A few minutes later when he returned, she'd gone.

He dialed another number. "Congressman Wiley, please," he told the man who answered the phone.

"The congressman is out to lunch. Can I take a message or have him return your call?"

Donovan knew damned well where Wiley was and it

wasn't *out to lunch*. He was scurrying away from the National Cathedral as fast as his skinny legs would carry him so nobody would connect him with the noon shooting incident.

"I'll call back," Donovan said, hanging up before the aide could press him for more information. Damn! He'd hoped Wiley would have enough sense to go straight back to his office where Donovan could reach him. Obviously that was an optimistic assumption. He'd have to spend the rest of the afternoon tracking the congressman down so he could deliver the promised baksheesh without attracting undue attention.

Donovan reached for the telephone book on a ledge under the counter. Would Erin Meyer be listed? There she was, *Lieutenant Erin M. Meyer* with an address in a pricey condominium building near the Pentagon. She'd said her father left her money. He'd find out if she was lying tomorrow in Mike Essinger's biographical report.

But why wait until tomorrow to learn where she worked? Donovan glanced down at his watch. A mere twenty minutes had passed since she dropped him off. She wouldn't be at her desk yet, even if she went directly back to work. Good, he could call her office without talking to her.

Quickly he contacted the information operator at the Pentagon and got Erin's extension. When he dialed the number, the secretary answered as he hoped she would, by giving the name of the organization instead of the phone number.

"Western European Branch," she said.

A wave of understanding hit him. She worked for the Pentagon Intelligence Agency. So that's how she'd found out about the shooting in time to warn him. She hadn't been involved with the thieves after all. That insight made him breathe easier.

Instead of hanging up without a message as he'd intended, he left his name with Erin's secretary and said he'd call back later. If she'd seen something about the planned

robbery in her traffic—an intercepted message probably—
why hadn't anybody at the CIA seen it and let him know?

And why had she been ready to risk her life to save a
total stranger? Knowing she wasn't involved in the robbery,
he saw no reason to wait until he read the biographical
report to talk to her again. He'd worm the information out
of her over dinner tonight. Since she'd wear civilian
clothes, she'd probably loosen her mane of red hair. He'd
been picturing her with it tumbling about her shoulders ever
since he first saw her. Why not get a firsthand look?

Donovan caught himself whistling a merry Irish tune as
he walked away from the alcove.

GOOD RIDDANCE, Erin huffed to herself as she drove away
from Donovan's hotel. So what if he hadn't asked to see
her again? The last person she needed in her life right now
was a charming Irish rogue, she told herself, but couldn't
deny her disappointment.

And she *did* need to find out if there was a link between
him and her stepfather. If Donovan was somehow a threat
to Patrick and her mother, Margaret, Erin needed to warn
them. And that meant she might have to see Donovan
again.

Annoyed yet vaguely excited at the thought, Erin glanced
at her watch. Not yet two, so it would be nearing seven in
Dublin. A good time to call her mother. She and Patrick
would be having before dinner cocktails with friends. Erin
knew they entertained a lot because Patrick told her he
wanted to show off his new bride. At forty-four Margaret,
an Elizabeth Taylor look-alike, was still incredibly beautiful.

Once inside her condo, Erin headed for the sleek kitchen
with its polished black stone countertops and sparkling
white cabinets. Quickly she fixed herself a cup of tea, settled herself on a stool at the counter, and dialed her mother's number in Dublin.

Through the sliding glass door across the dining room,

she could see the stark outline of the Washington Monument framed against an azure sky. On a hill in the far distance stood the National Cathedral. Erin sighed. From now on, every time she looked out that window and saw the cathedral, she'd remember this day and her traumatic meeting with Donovan.

"O'Shaughnessy residence," said a masculine voice Erin recognized as belonging to the butler.

"Robert, this is Erin. Is my mother there?" Erin had never been to Dublin, never met Robert or the rest of the household staff, but had talked to them so many times, she felt she knew them. Unable to shake the feeling that her mother still needed looking after, Erin phoned her almost every day.

"Yes, Miss Meyer, I'll get her," the butler said.

A moment later she heard her mother's honey-flavored contralto voice. "Hi, darling. Is something wrong? You usually call later."

"Nothing's wrong, Mom. But there's something you can tell me." Hearing her own high-pitched voice, in sharp contrast to her mother's, Erin winced. She hated her voice, had since she was a teenager. Why couldn't she have been blessed with her mother's resonant tones?

"Anything, love. I'm so pleased there's something I can help you with." If anybody else had made such a gratuitous promise, Erin would have doubted their sincerity. But not her mother. She meant every word. Though inclined to be flighty, she was the most honest person Erin knew.

"I was wondering if a man named Dan Donovan works for Patrick," Erin said.

"I'm terribly sorry, darling, but I can't answer that. I don't know any of Dun Aengus's men."

Erin stiffened. *Dun Aengus's men.* It was almost the same wording used in the intercept. Could her mother have known about the message the NSA had intercepted?

Don't be absurd, Erin told herself. *My mom and Patrick*

had nothing to do with that message. Just the same, a kernel
of doubt formed in her mind.

"Could you ask him for me?" she queried aloud.

Her mother hesitated. Was she reluctant to ask her new
husband such a simple question?

"You know how Dun Aengus keeps his business totally
separate from the family," Margaret said, still hesitating.
"I know absolutely nothing about Shamrock Construction
except that Dun Aengus is the president of the board. He
might think I'm snooping if I start asking questions."

Contrary to her mother's assumption, Erin hadn't been
aware of the separation between family and business. She
took a deep breath, trying to be patient. Margaret always
agonized over her decisions, especially small ones like this.

Forcing a teasing lightness into her voice, she coaxed,
"Tell him I met a man who says he's with Shamrock Construction, and I want to be sure he's on the up-and-up before I see him again." It wasn't the exact truth, but close
enough that Erin didn't feel guilty.

"Aha!" Margaret said. "Mr. Donovan sounds interesting."

"He is, but I won't see him again if you don't ask Patrick
about him for me." Erin interjected a forlorn note into her
voice and took a long swallow of tea, knowing her last
comment would send Margaret on her way to Patrick. Her
mother's fondest dream was to see Erin settled down and
having children.

Picturing Donovan's massive frame, Erin sighed, not at
all certain she could handle a houseful of little Donovans.
Her mother was back before Erin could expand on the fantasy.

"Yes, darling, your Dan Donovan told—"

"He's not *my* Dan Donovan," Erin interrupted, annoyed
and pleased at the same time.

"At least not yet," her mother added. "He works for
Dun Aengus all right—is a lawyer on his staff here in Dub-

lin. His parents were born in Ireland, too, like yours. Dun Aengus hired him last year to handle American contracts.''

Erin received this news with a tumble of confused thoughts and feelings. Since Donovan was her only link to possible danger threatening her mother and Patrick, she'd have to see him again. In spite of the warmth coursing through her at the thought, instinctively she knew he was dangerous. *Better not get involved with another Irish rogue,* she told herself. If she was foolish enough to fall for him, she'd wind up getting hurt.

But Erin sensed a darker danger in learning more about Donovan. If he was simply following Patrick's orders when he delivered illegal bribes, that meant her stepfather was a crook.

A cold knot formed in Erin's stomach. Had her mother's impulsive marriage linked her to a criminal?

No. It couldn't be. Her fingers tightened around the receiver.

"Are you still there, darling?" A worried quiver crept into her mother's voice.

Suddenly Erin wanted desperately to see her face, to feel her arms around her. "Yes, Mom, I was just wishing I could see you, talk to you in person. I miss you and want you to know I'm here for you if you ever need me." Erin found herself gripping the receiver with iron fingers and forced herself to relax.

"You sound like you're wasting perfectly good time worrying about me again."

In spite of herself, Erin had to smile at the teasing tone in her mother's voice. She had always claimed that most of Erin's worries were unnecessary.

"Guess I'm still the family worrier," Erin agreed. "But you seem so far away."

"Worry no more, darling. I'm in safe hands with Patrick here in Dublin."

"I'll try not to, Mom. I just wish you were closer."

"Me too, Erin. Have fun with your Mr. Donovan. Patrick

says he's coming back to Dublin tomorrow afternoon so
that gives you tonight. If you like him, maybe you can
arrange to see him when you come to Dublin on leave next
summer." She paused. "I love you, sweet girl."

"I love you, too, Mom." Erin hung up the receiver after
promising to call back the next night with a detailed report
on tonight's date.

Shaking her cramped fingers to restore circulation, Erin
propped her elbows on the countertop, bowing her head
and allowing the shadows she had pushed away earlier to
move in. She couldn't ignore her feeling that something
was wrong in Dublin. Seriously wrong. And whatever it
was might well be linked to Donovan. Troubled thoughts
swirled in her mind while she fixed herself a sandwich and,
a little later, while she drove back to work.

Before she phoned him, she'd better do some checking,
Erin told herself grimly as she hiked in to the Pentagon
from North Parking. Maybe Central Intelligence had a file
on Dan Donovan and on the Shamrock Construction Company. Any firm that bribed to get contracts might be involved in something even more underhanded. A Shamrock
executive working with Donovan without Patrick's knowledge might be behind the bribes. *That must be the explanation,* she thought, refusing to believe her stepfather could
be involved.

"IN ADDITION TO the messages on your desk, a man named
Donovan called. He said he'd call back later." The Western
Europe Branch secretary, a fiftyish woman named Rosealee
Dugan, eyed Erin knowingly. "Sounded like a personal
call."

In spite of herself, Erin felt heat in her cheeks. Donovan
must want to see her again. Good. She wouldn't have to
initiate the date after all. She couldn't help smiling at Rosealee's smug expression. If the secretary only knew. Erin
bit the inside of her cheek. It was best the prey came to
her.

After she'd answered the messages on her desk, she called her counterpart, Maxaline Fallon, at the CIA on the office secure phone. Like Erin, Max was the desk officer for the United Kingdom and Ireland. Asking Max, a CIA analyst, to check the files for her would save Erin the trouble of requesting them through official Pentagon channels. It would also avoid potentially embarrassing questions about why she wanted them.

Erin had met Max when they were both political science majors at Georgetown University. Now they talked on the secure phone almost every day to coordinate articles and briefing items. After exchanging preliminary greetings, Erin got down to business.

"Can you do me a big favor and check out a couple of names, Max? I'd like to know if the agency's got files on them and any info you can dig up."

"Sounds like something personal," her friend returned, a worried tone in her voice. "You know the agency's policy about that."

"Not to worry," Erin insisted. "Since it's about Ireland—our mutual area—nobody has to know it's personal but thee and me."

"So shoot," Max said, with her usual dry wit. "But if my butt ends up in a sling, I'm going to hold you personally responsible."

"No chance," Erin promised, laughing. "The first name to check is the Shamrock Construction Company with headquarters in Dublin. The second is Patrick O'Shaughnessy, who runs the company as president of the board."

Though there was no one else inside the cubicle where she sat, Erin lowered her voice. Checking on her mother's new husband made her feel sour inside, and she didn't want anyone to overhear.

Max whistled softly under her breath. "Your stepfather. Whew, Irish, you're really treading on thin ice."

"Nobody knows this is personal but you and me," Erin repeated firmly. "The third name is Daniel Donovan, a law-

yer who handles American contracts out of Shamrock's
Dublin office.''

"Ah, now we come to the crux of the matter. Mr. Daniel
Donovan must be a handsome Irishman. Does he know
you're his employer's new daughter?''

"I'm not anybody's *new daughter*.'' In spite of herself,
Erin couldn't help snapping her reply.

Max chuckled. "But you *have* met Mr. Donovan and
want to find out more about him. Am I right?''

"No comment,'' Erin said. "Just check the files for me,
will you, Max?''

"Touchy, aren't we?'' Her friend laughed again. "Well,
this is one job I'll enjoy doing. It's about time you stopped
pining for that rat, Brian, and started dating again. Is he
still pestering to get you back?''

Erin didn't like being reminded of Brian, an attractive
navy lieutenant. He'd kept her on the string until she'd
found out about two other women he also claimed to be
serious about.

"I'm through with fast-talking Irishmen.'' Even as Erin
spoke, she knew Donovan was just the same as Brian—
exciting, adventurous and out to get everything he could
from a woman. She almost told Max to forget it, but her
mother's beautiful oval face appeared in her mind. If Patrick was unknowingly involved with crooks, Erin *had* to
find out and warn him and her mother. "How soon can you
get back to me?''

"I'll start checking right now,'' Max returned. "If we've
got anything, I should be able to tell you by tomorrow
morning, but I can't promise. Our research people are really
behind.''

Back at her desk, Erin spent what remained of the afternoon working on another special briefing and trying to get
Donovan's compelling face out of her mind. With his deep
chin and bold nose, he impressed her more as strong and
rugged than handsome. But no sweet-talking Irishman, es-

pecially Dan Donovan, was going to catch her unawares—emotionally or otherwise.

Why didn't he call back? Now that the regular staff had left for the day, time was running out. She couldn't afford to wait much longer before calling him herself. When the phone finally rang, she snatched it up. Her heart gave a little leap when she heard a man's voice.

But it wasn't Donovan. It was the security guard at the agency's main entrance. "Mrs. Fallon is here from the CIA," he announced.

Erin's stomach tightened. Max? Why hadn't she called first? Something must be wrong.

Grabbing her uniform jacket from the back of her chair, she shrugged it on while she hurried to the agency's main entrance.

Max sat in a plush chair facing the entrance. She jumped to her feet when Erin burst through the door. Dressed in a skirt and sweater, she looked out of place in the businesslike waiting area. "We've got to talk, Irish."

"Not at my desk," Erin said, when Max started toward the entrance. "I need a break."

"Good." Max turned toward the nearest corridor. "You can walk me to the River Entrance. My car's parked illegally outside."

"So what's up?" Erin asked anxiously, when they'd reached the corridor.

Max scowled. A small woman with an elfin face, her scowls were as frightening as growls from a toy poodle. But this time when Max scowled, Erin felt shivers of dread run down her spine.

"What's up is our little game," Max spluttered. "You know those three files you wanted?"

Apprehensively, Erin nodded.

"The agency's got files on those three names, but they weren't available to me."

Puzzled, Erin stared down at her friend. "But you've got all the clearances, just like I do."

"Not all," Max corrected. "I've got no idea what the covert operations people are up to. That stuff's off-limits to me."

"Then you think Patrick and Donovan are involved in a covert operation?" Lowering her voice, Erin couldn't mask her surprise.

Max shrugged. "Who knows? My best guess is that they're informants for our agents in Dublin."

"So why couldn't you tell me this on the phone?" There had to be more to Max's story. From the grim look on her friend's face, she guessed the rest would be unpleasant. Today was going from bad to worse.

"Because we plunked our big feet right in the middle of something very smelly," Max said, her high heels clicking on the marble floor. "I'm sorry, Irish. Right after I put in a request for those files I received an order to report to the director's office."

"As in *CIA director?*" Every muscle in Erin's body tightened. Max's summons meant something was very, very wrong.

"Exactly. He wanted to know why I requested the files. Said he'd already talked to my supervisor who told him I wasn't working on anything connected with Shamrock Construction." She paused and Erin saw the contrition in her eyes. "I had to tell him I was getting them for you."

She looked so upset that Erin put an arm around her thin shoulders and gave her a hug. "Don't worry about it, Max. What can they do to me? So it's against policy to use classified material to check up on family and friends. Well, so what?" Erin had never had a lot of respect for the government bureaucracy. If some colonel wanted to give her a slap on the wrist for this minor breach of policy, so be it.

"I'm in the air force, remember?" Erin said to herself as much as to Max. "They can't fire me or put me in jail just for asking to see a couple of files. The one I'm worried about is Patrick. Is he really a CIA informant, doing something so secret the agency has special files on him and his company?''

But walking back to her office after Max left, Erin found herself worrying not about Patrick but Donovan. Now that she knew he might be a CIA informant—a snitch selling secrets to CIA agents—she realized his life might still be in danger. Maybe he was right when he called today's shooting an attempted robbery. But what if he were wrong? Just the thought that this vital man with such a lust for life could have that pulsating life extinguished by an assassin's bullet chilled the very heart of her.

At her desk, Erin studied the message again. No mention of a robbery. Only an order to *neutralize Dun Aengus's man.* Since today's attempt had failed, would there be another? Some way she had to warn Donovan his robbery theory might be wrong—yet another compelling reason she couldn't let him leave Washington without talking to her. Even if he was involved in something shady, she couldn't let him be killed.

AFTER DONOVAN HANDED the briefcase full of cash to its intended recipient, he couldn't wait to get back to the hotel to shower. There was something slimy about doing business with a creep like this congressman. Donovan had to accept the sleaziness connected with his work, but he didn't have to enjoy it.

Too bad he'd told Erin about the payoff, he thought as he rode the subway from Arlington under the Potomac to the District. He'd figured she already knew about the cash, and that telling her the truth might inspire her to tell him how she showed up at the cathedral in the nick of time. He'd sure been dead wrong about that.

In his room, he noticed the message light flashing on his phone. Erin must have got his message and decided to call back. Remembering her vitality, the way the sun glinted on her flame red hair, he smiled to himself.

Quickly he tapped in the two-digit number to collect his

messages. "Four thirty-five p.m.," a recorded voice said. "Call Mr. Owens ASAP. End of messages."

Damn! It wasn't Erin after all. Now he'd have to put off his shower. An order from his contact at the agency couldn't be ignored, much as Donovan might want to.

Downstairs in the lobby, he dialed the agency and asked for Mr. Owens. Obviously waiting for Donovan's call, Mike Essinger picked up the receiver on the first ring. "Thank God!" he said. "I hope you haven't talked to the lieutenant again."

"No, I just got back from the rescheduled meeting with our friend." Donovan leaned closer to the pay phone in the lobby alcove. For Mike to show such emotion, something very definitely was up. And it involved Erin Meyer. Were the lieutenant's pretty fingers as dirty as his own?

"We need to talk before you see her again."

"What makes you think I'd want to see her again?"

"I got a look at her picture."

"Well, well, well. So you got her picture for me, too, did you?" Donovan found himself grinning as the image of his crimson-haired Thoroughbred flashed before his eyes. "You really went all out on this one." Intrigued, Donovan swung around with his back to the phone and rested one elbow on the counter behind him.

"We had good reason to be thorough. Meet me in an hour outside Blackie's on M Street. We'll take a walk around the block and I'll brief you."

"Fine." Hanging up, Donovan swore softly under his breath. He wanted to hear about Erin from her own lips, not Mike Essinger's.

After taking his usual precautions to avoid being followed, Donovan arrived at the restaurant a few minutes before eight. He joined the small crowd of patrons on the sidewalk outside, and, without being obvious, searched for Essinger's big, blond frame.

A moment later a black sedan pulled up at the curb. The back door opened and Mike leaned out and beckoned. Donovan strode to the car and got in. After he shut the door behind himself, the vehicle glided sedately into traffic.

"Change your mind about the walk around the block?" Donovan asked.

Essinger nodded without smiling. For a big healthy male with everything going for him, he had to be the glummest man Donovan knew.

"The car is more secure than walking," Essinger said succinctly.

Without asking, Donovan knew the vehicle had been de-bugged and the driver was clean. He stared at Essinger's unsmiling face.

"So what's the connection between the lieutenant and Patrick O'Shaughnessy?" The question had gnawed at his insides since Erin Meyer had saved him from an assassin's bullet. "It's not enough that she's the military analyst for Ireland at the Pentagon Intelligence Agency."

"So you've already found that out," Essinger said with a hint of admiration. "She's also O'Shaughnessy's new wife's daughter."

"Damn!" Donovan pounded his fist in his palm. He would have known who Erin was if the agency researchers had been on the ball with his request for information on the new wife. "Then why isn't her name Sullivan, like her mother's?"

"Her mother was a hippy back in the sixties. She kept her maiden name when she got married. The daughter took the father's." Essinger paused, fingering the manila folder on the seat beside him. "What do you think of the lady?"

"I've never met the woman," Donovan said, mentally cursing the agency's researchers for being so slow.

"You haven't met O'Shaughnessy's new wife?" Essinger's voice held a touch of disbelief.

"No, and I probably never will," Donovan replied firmly. "O'Shaughnessy keeps his business and family carefully separated."

"Like the mafia?" Essinger said quizzically.

"Exactly." Donovan felt his stomach tighten. "He also delegates authority—like a mafia don—so he can claim ignorance if Shamrock Construction is caught doing something illegal. I'm still not positive he's the man we're after."

"It might be someone else in the organization?"

"Or in the household," Donovan added. "I haven't ruled out that possibility, either."

"What do his family and friends call O'Shaughnessy?" Essinger asked.

"You mean a nickname?" Donovan returned, puzzled by the question. "I suppose they call him *Shawn,* the way we do at work—when we see him. He's not around much."

The car was getting hot. Donovan took off his overcoat and laid it beside him on the seat.

"Ever heard anybody call him *Dun Aengus?*"

"Not that I recall." Donovan stared at Essinger's face, glowing whitely in the reflected light from the oncoming traffic. "Is it important?"

"Here. Read this." Essinger handed him a piece of paper and a pen flashlight. "We think this is how your lieutenant found out somebody was gunning for you."

Quickly Donovan read the paper. It was a copy of an intercepted message sent from a broadcasting entity in Dublin to an unknown receiver here in Washington. After finishing, he felt anger boiling up inside him. Though he tried to control it, it spilled out into his voice.

"If you guys knew about this, why the hell didn't you warn me?" His angry gaze met Essinger's regretful one. "You geniuses at the agency almost got me killed."

Chapter Three

"Sorry." Essinger's voice was so soft Donovan could barely hear it. "We didn't make the connection between you and the message."

"You didn't make the connection?" Donovan slammed his fist into his hand again. "Excuse me, Mike. How many undercover agents does the bloody CIA have in Dublin? How many were planning to be in Washington on St. Patrick's Day?"

"You've got to admit the message wasn't all that clear about the time and place," Essinger said, his voice rising. "Your lieutenant did a lot of guessing to get to the cathedral today at noon."

Donovan bit back an oath. "If that message was clear enough for her to figure out, it should have been obvious enough for your mental giants at Langley."

"She had information we didn't." Essinger's blue eyes met Donovan's head-on.

Donovan could hardly believe his ears. He stared incredulously at his contact. "You mean the nickname? You had a hell of a lot of information she didn't—what I'm doing in Dublin, for starters."

"Maybe she knows more than you think," Essinger suggested, with a sage nod of his blond head. "She's part of the clan now. Both she and her mother are probably in cahoots with the new man of the family."

Sliding away from Essinger, Donovan leaned against the car door. "I've already told you, I've found nothing to incriminate O'Shaughnessy. Besides, if he sent the message, he'd never use his own nickname—too incriminating."

"But it was in code. He didn't expect anyone but the recipient to read it."

"True," Donovan agreed reluctantly. "Since his family nickname was used in the message, the person we want might be part of the household—not the business."

"O'Shaughnessy's the only person who's part of both the business and the household," Essinger pressured, his square face gleaming whitely in the lights from an oncoming car. "Whoever sent this message is gunning for you. Does anybody suspect you're a plant?"

Donovan glanced at the message again, then shook his head. "Definitely not. I'd never have been trusted with this delivery job today if anybody in the organization had the faintest suspicion I was undercover. I still think the motive for the shooting was robbery. Somebody at Shamrock found out about the cash delivery and decided he needed the money more than the congressman."

"Have any idea who?" Essinger asked.

Donovan shook his head. "No, but I'm betting it was somebody in the household, someone I don't know."

"The message doesn't say anything about a robbery." Essinger bent forward and spoke to the driver. "You can start back downtown, Ed."

Obediently, the driver swung the car around a corner and started toward Donovan's hotel.

Donovan shrugged his shoulders. "This message set the time and place. Period. The other details must have been worked out elsewhere. That's why it says nothing about the robbery per se."

"Maybe you're right," Essinger said thoughtfully. "You carried a lot of cash, and stealing it's a damn good reason for somebody to take a shot at you. Was the cash clean?"

"Clean as a whistle. I took it out of a Shamrock safe-deposit box in Washington this morning."

"Whoever's running this operation knew better than to use dirty money to pay off the congressman." Reflecting, Essinger leaned forward, one hand on his hip. "Though it's too late to pull you out now without arousing suspicion, maybe we were barking up the wrong tree by getting you on the company staff. Like you said, the person we're after might be part of the household. Any way you can get an *in?*"

"Not likely, unless..."

"Unless what?"

"The new wife. Since her daughter saved my life, she'll at least want to know who I am."

"And she probably has a good idea what her husband's up to." Essinger studied Donovan's face. "The daughter can give you the *in* you're looking for. How soon do you have to be back in Dublin?"

"My plane leaves tomorrow afternoon."

"That gives you tonight." Essinger frowned as though daring Donovan to protest.

But protest was the farthest thing from Donovan's mind. His anger vanished, and he couldn't help smiling. "Why Mike, old buddy, are you suggesting a reputable CIA agent prostitute himself in the line of duty?"

Essinger didn't smile back. "It wouldn't be the first time." He handed Donovan a sealed manila envelope. "Take a look at this biographical report on the lieutenant. Then do whatever you have to to know her personally. Maybe she'll tell her mother about you and that'll give you an entrée to the household. Even if she doesn't, you'll still have a good excuse to get acquainted with the old lady."

Donovan reached out and shook Essinger's hand. "Thanks, good buddy. I can't think of an assignment I'd like better."

Still smiling, Donovan leaned back, relaxing against the

plush car seat. He visualized Erin's trim form and flaming
hair. Yep. A perfect assignment.

FOR A LONG MOMENT Erin stared at the phone on her desk,
poised to tap out the numbers for Donovan's hotel. She had
to see him tonight, had to find out what she could about
Shamrock Construction and her new stepfather.

If both Patrick and Donovan were CIA informants, as
she suspected, the reason for the assassination attempt
against Donovan became disturbingly clear. Somebody had
found out. And if somebody wanted the snitching to stop,
Patrick was in even greater danger than Donovan. Both
men had to be warned.

She reached for the receiver. Before she could pick it up,
the phone rang. Her heart skipped a beat. Something told
her it was Donovan.

"Lieutenant Meyer," she said quickly.

"Donovan here," he returned. His voice sounded exactly
as she remembered: resonant and impressive with a touch
of laughter. She was so happy to hear him she felt like
hugging herself—or better yet, caressing him. Now that
he'd called her, she was saved the embarrassment of chasing after him.

Though Donovan was a rogue, Erin knew she had to see
him tonight. His and Patrick's lives—and maybe her mother's as well—might depend on what she could find out from
him, and how much she could tell him.

"Have you had dinner?" he asked, his hearty voice
sending an excited ripple down her spine.

"No, just a sandwich. I'd love to have dinner with you."
Maybe she shouldn't appear so eager, but Erin didn't believe in beating around the bush. The sooner they talked,
the better.

"Good!" he exclaimed.

She thrilled at the gladness in his voice.

"How soon can I pick you up?"

Mentally Erin measured the work left to do. Like magic,

the briefing had shrunk to manageable proportions. "Nine o'clock at my condo."

"I'll be there." He was about to hang up.

"Wait!" she cried, suddenly worried that something would go wrong and he wouldn't show up. "Do you know my address?"

"I found it in the phone book." He paused. "Bring a good appetite."

Erin couldn't stop the sudden rush of excitement that shot through her at the thought of an evening together. Too bad Dan Donovan was dangerous...in more ways than one.

WHEN HE LEFT the phone alcove, Donovan glanced around as was his habit. No one was near. He puckered his lips and began whistling as he strode away from the alcove.

Erin was dying to see him. He could hear it in her voice, in the breathy way she talked. In his mind he pictured her long slim legs when she ran toward him up the cathedral stairs. Their date promised to be one of the most interesting assignments he'd had in a long time. Undercover work might have its sleazy side, but occasional rewards like tonight made the business easier to swallow.

Walking across the lobby to the elevators, he resisted the urge to sink down on one of the luxurious silk-covered sofas and rip open the sealed manila envelope Essinger had given him. Erin's bio would have to wait until he got upstairs.

Inside his room, he switched on the floor lamp, settled in a comfortable armchair, and skimmed through the report with the speed of an experienced undercover operative.

Erin was illegitimate, he read with interest, born to Margaret Sullivan, the teenage daughter of Irish immigrants, and a young soldier named Kevin Riley from nearby Fort Benning, Georgia. Riley, who shipped off to Vietnam without marrying Margaret, was killed in action.

Probably didn't know she was pregnant, Donovan thought, forcing down a flicker of sympathy for the two young lovers. He was constantly annoyed with himself for letting things like that get to him.

As he continued reading, Donovan saw no reason to feel sorry for Erin's mother. A year after her daughter's birth, she had married George Meyer, an army major fifteen years older than she. He had adopted Erin shortly after their marriage. While still on active duty as a lieutenant general, he had died suddenly less than a year ago.

Donovan looked up from the report. So that's where the name *Meyer* came from. Erin had taken her adoptive father's name even though her mother had retained her maiden name, Sullivan. With no other children, General Meyer had left Erin an estate believed worth about half a million dollars, mostly invested conservatively. His widow got the rest.

After scanning the report one last time, Donovan tore it up in small pieces and flushed it down the toilet.

DONOVAN HAD TO BE the sexiest man she'd ever seen, Erin decided, settling next to him in the back seat of the taxi. His black overcoat clung to his broad shoulders, and his green tie made his blue eyes take on a buoyant greenish hue. Smiling, he beamed the full Donovan charm straight at her. Even though she suspected he flashed smiles at every woman he met, she couldn't help smiling back. He fairly bubbled with Irish good spirits. His infectious charm warmed her in spite of the blustery March weather and her determination to stay on course.

Seduced by his charm, Erin forced herself to concentrate on her objectives for tonight: warn him yesterday's shooting might be an assassination attempt, find out what illegal activities he was involved in and determine what threat he and his associates posed to Patrick and, by extension, to her mother.

"Where to, fair lady?" he asked. "You're the native in these parts."

"On St. Patrick's day, there's no place like Georgetown," she replied, laughing. "We can barhop until we find a good place to eat."

"A woman after my own heart," Donovan said cheerfully. "Georgetown," he told the cabbie.

The middle-aged driver turned in his seat to stare at them. "That place is a madhouse tonight."

"I know." Erin smiled fondly, remembering her days at Georgetown University. Georgetown was the historic original area of Washington where the university was located. Its main street—Wisconsin Avenue—boasted upscale shops, pubs and restaurants. "You can let us out before we get to Wisconsin."

"You sound like you've been to Georgetown before on St. Patrick's Day," Donovan commented, as the taxi sped toward Memorial Bridge.

"Yes, I went to Georgetown University. We all used the wearing of the green as an excuse for a big celebration— but then almost any holiday was."

You're already having too good a time, she warned herself, fighting the glow of his nearness.

"The cab driver's right," she said, more to dampen her own enthusiasm than his. "The streets around the university will be jammed."

"You must have majored in something like political science to get your job at the Pentagon Intelligence Agency." His tone sounded matter-of-fact.

She nodded, matching his casualness with pretended candor. "How did you find out where I worked?"

"Simple." Something inside her melted when he flashed his broad smile at her again. "From your parking sticker I figured you were assigned somewhere at the Pentagon. So I checked with Pentagon Information. Voilà! They gave me your extension."

"Why didn't you just ask me for my phone number? Wouldn't that have been easier?" Growing more suspicious, Erin struggled to maintain her casual tone. Why had Donovan gone to so much trouble to get her number when he could have had it by asking? Erin had the uncomfortable feeling that he'd been checking up on her—the same way she'd been checking on him. But that didn't make sense. She told herself not to be paranoid.

He assumed a woebegone expression. "But what if you'd refused to give it to me. My heart would have been broken."

"Be serious, Donovan. I really want to know why you didn't ask me." Erin leaned toward him, ever more certain he'd been checking up on her. She'd have to watch her step tonight.

"All right then. Since you insist, I'll tell you." His intense blue eyes stared into hers. "The only reason to ask for your number would be to see you tonight. Not a good idea since I'm leaving Washington tomorrow afternoon. One night together wouldn't be enough for me, Erin. When a lady attracts me as much as you do, I want to see more of her than that—much more."

The not unpleasant melting sensation Erin had felt before flowed downward, pooling in her loins. Embarrassed by his frankness, she looked at her hands, clasped neatly in her lap.

"So what changed your mind about phoning me?" Listening to his seductive voice, she reminded herself he was a scoundrel involved in making illegal bribes.

"After you dropped me off this afternoon, I found out something interesting about you that gave me hope."

Apprehensive, Erin held her breath. "What...?"

"After a little research, I found out you're General Meyer's daughter," Donovan continued.

Letting her breath out in a long sigh, she scowled across the taxi seat at him. "So that's how you spent your afternoon? Checking up on me?" She wasn't sure whether to be pleased or annoyed that he'd gone to the trouble.

"Damned right." Matching her scowl, he tugged his earlobe with his fingers. "I wanted to find out everything I could about the lady who saved my life. Do you blame me?''

Embarrassed by his gratitude, Erin was glad for the semi-darkness in the taxi that hid the flush on her cheeks. "So whom did you ask about me?''

"Nobody," he replied, after a moment's hesitation. "I figured somebody who saved a stranger on the steps of the National Cathedral might have performed other deeds worthy of media attention. So I spent a couple of hours in the morgue at the *Washington Post.*"

Comprehension swept over Erin. Searching newspaper files was so logical, she had to believe him. "And of course you read the article about my father's death. It mentioned both me and my mother.''

"Yes," he said, nodding. "And Margaret Sullivan, the general's widow, just married my boss, Shawn O'Shaughnessy.'' Obviously proud of his detective work, he moved closer to her on the taxi seat. "So there's a good chance we'll see each other again in Dublin when you visit your mother—if things go my way, and you want to see me again.'' His dark blue eyes clung to hers, as if analyzing her reaction.

Erin nodded. She couldn't stop herself. He might be a scoundrel, but she couldn't help reacting to his bold good looks, to the controlled strength she sensed in his muscular body.

"I just found out you worked for Patrick this afternoon myself," she said breathlessly, impressed that he'd discovered the connection between them. "When I talked to my mother.''

"Then you've already told your mother about me?'' For some reason this seemed to please him. Maybe he figured a good word from O'Shaughnessy's wife would give him an *in* with his boss.

"Yes," she said lightly. "I talk to her almost every day.''

"Lo and behold, my employer's new wife turns out to

be your mother. My, my, my. Isn't it an amazing coincidence that we ran into each other at the cathedral this morning?'' His eyes were completely guileless. But Erin heard the teasing tone in his voice and realized he knew her daring rescue was more than a coincidence.

''It wasn't exactly a coincidence,'' she began, an unwelcome warmth flooding her face again. What was there about this man that kept her continually flushed with embarrassment?

''Faith!'' he exclaimed, imitating an Irish accent. ''Then 'twas a tiny fib you were tellin' me about the blind woman in the gift shop?''

In spite of herself, Erin had to smile at his perfect Irish brogue. Sobering, she glanced at the taxi driver. Though his back was to them, she suspected he'd listened to everything they said. Her explanation would have to wait.

''I'm ashamed to say you're right,'' she admitted. ''I'll tell you the whole story when we get to Georgetown.''

THE IRISH AND THEIR admirers—everybody who wore green once a year on St. Patrick's Day—turned out in force in Georgetown tonight. Added to them were the thousands of students who milled in the streets blocking traffic, roaming in packs from bar to bar, drinking green beer from foam cups. This time of night, the area was strangled by total gridlock. The cab couldn't get near Wisconsin Avenue. They got out blocks from where they wanted to be.

''Sure you don't mind walking?'' Donovan eyed Erin's long slim legs and high-heeled pumps. With her red hair bouncing over the shoulders of her white leather coat, she looked even better in civilian clothes than he'd imagined.

''Not if you don't mind slowing down so I can keep up with you.'' She didn't seem put off by the prospect of barging into the huge crowd ahead. In the distance, he heard loud music and laughter as people looking for a good time choked the main street.

With a jolt, Donovan realized he'd been paying more

attention to Erin than to vehicles in their vicinity. Had they been followed? Well, they'd be less obvious targets once they melted into the crowd. Deliberately he set as fast a pace as Erin could manage.

"So give," he said, wondering if she'd tell the truth about getting her information from an intercepted message. *Not if she's a loyal American,* he thought, well aware of the stringent security restrictions that guarded communications intelligence. "What's the story behind your timely arrival at the cathedral?"

She hesitated. He thought she was going to chicken out on him and not answer. "Since you know I'm an analyst at the Pentagon Intelligence Agency, you've probably already guessed," she said in her lyrical voice.

"Why don't you tell me, so we can see if I'm right?"

"I can't give you any specifics about sources," she began slowly. "Most of the material I work with is classified."

Good girl! he thought, unexpectedly relieved she wouldn't identify her source. "Then tell me what you can."

"I saw references in my reports that made me think one of Patrick's associates would be the target of an assassin today near the National Cathedral. When I saw you, alone and obviously waiting for someone, I suspected you were the one."

"Then it was more an off-the-wall hunch than anything definite?" he asked. Though she referred to *reports,* she must have based her hunch on that one intercepted message, just as Mike Essinger thought.

Erin gave a self-conscious little laugh. "It was so off-the-wall that I didn't bother trying to tell anyone. If I'd told my division chief what I was going to do, he would have thought I was a real nut case. The report was so iffy, I almost didn't go."

"Lucky for me you did." He watched an embarrassed smile tremble over her lips and had an urge to embrace her. With her hair curling over her shoulders, she looked unexpectedly vulnerable. Catching her hand, he drew it over his arm so they could walk faster. Erin brushed against his side, and a warm protective feeling washed over him. Damn. If they'd been followed, she was in as much danger as he. Why hadn't he been more alert to nearby vehicles while they were in the cab?

When they reached the milling crowd on Wisconsin, they threaded their way single file through the shoulder-to-shoulder mass of humanity.

"I know the bartender at Mickey's Pub," Erin said over her shoulder. "They've got great steaks. He'll find us a table."

Donovan held tightly to her hand, enjoying the excuse to touch her. He knew if they got separated, they'd never find each other again.

"Let's go for it," he yelled at her back, admiring the way she maneuvered through the crowd. Kids holding sloshing cups of beer stumbled into her, but none of the green liquid spilled on her white leather coat. Donovan's cashmere overcoat already had soaked up two major spills. The yeasty smell made him thirsty and even hungrier than before.

When they finally reached Mickey's, Erin pushed the stained glass door open and they went in. After the bright streetlights outside, the place seemed dark and hot, and the beer smell that had enticed Donovan in the cold March air hung heavily in the jammed room.

People were packed three-deep at the bar. Standing on her tiptoes, Erin waved at one of the bartenders. Grizzled, his hair iron gray, he looked like the Ancient Mariner compared to the other two bartenders—and to most of the tavern's other patrons. Donovan watched him meet Erin's eyes and incline his head toward a half-open door at the end of the bar.

Edging after her through the crowd, Donovan let his gaze swing over his shoulder to the throng behind him. Most were students, if the Georgetown and George Washington logos on their sweatshirts could be believed. He stiffened. Standing near the street entrance lounged a man whose face he recognized. Donovan caught only a glimpse of his profile as the man looked away, but he'd seen that bulbous nose and jutting chin yesterday on the cathedral stairs, only seconds before the shots were fired.

The assassin! It had to be him. The same man showing up at two such different places was too much of a coincidence. Though the man wore a college sweatshirt under an open ski jacket and did his best to melt into the crowd, Donovan knew he wasn't wrong. His sharp eyes and strong survival instinct had saved him too many times to doubt them. Somehow the assassin had managed to follow them here. Sometime tonight he planned to finish his contract.

If Donovan hadn't been with Erin, he would have set a trap for the bastard, one that would have put him in either the morgue or a hospital. But with Erin here, he'd have to wait. He balled his hands into fists. Dammit. The SOB might be after her, too, since she was now part of O'Shaughnessy's family. His clenched fists made him realize he no longer held Erin's hand. He stiffened, his body rigid with fear.

Where was she? Somehow her hand had slipped out of his grasp, and he'd lost sight of her. Then he noticed her standing near the door to what was probably the restaurant section of the pub. A pack of unruly students stood between them.

"Hey, take it easy, man," one said, as Donovan elbowed his way through.

"Sorry," he flung over his shoulder with a broad smile. The last thing he needed was a confrontation with a drunk college kid. He reached the door half an instant behind Erin.

"Is there a back way out of this place?" he asked, as they entered the dining room. With a practised eye, he glanced around. Dark heavy wood furniture. Tablecloths.

Dim lights. Though crowded, it wasn't as chaotic as the bar.

Erin gave him a curious look. "Why? Do we need to leave in a hurry?"

"A big hurry," he said. "The guy who shot at me is out front."

Her eyes widened. "What're we going to do?"

"Run like hell."

Chapter Four

Straight ahead, at the rear of the dining room, Erin spotted a door with an Exit sign. Donovan jerked her hand, pulling her toward it.

"Hurry!" he yelled.

As she started running, her arm hit something solid. A man swore. She heard a tremendous clatter but didn't look around to see who or what she'd struck, only kept her eyes glued to Donovan's broad back. Terror sat on her shoulder like a grinning gargoyle. Gasping for breath, she took the last few steps to the exit door.

Emergency Only, a sign read. Ahead of her, Donovan shoved the door open. Instantly the blaring screech of a security alarm rent the chill night air. Thank God! Now that an alarm had sounded, the police would be coming soon. But would they be in time to save them from the monster behind them?

A heartbeat later, Donovan yanked her through the door and slammed it shut behind them. Then he began to run, pulling Erin along behind him. Her legs felt like chunks of wood, and her feet—in high heeled pumps—had no feeling at all. She stumbled, started to fall, but he caught her upper arm. She gasped, panting in terror.

"I've got you!" he exclaimed, holding her erect.

"Go without me," she screamed. "He's after you, not me." But Donovan held tightly to her arm.

"Keep running," he yelled.

Behind her, Erin heard a door slam and knew instinctively that the assassin had joined them in the dark alley. If Donovan were a CIA informant, maybe he had a gun. If he didn't, they were finished. Mickey's Pub stood in the center of a long block of buildings with no space between them. All the rear doors would be locked from the inside. There was no way they could get out of the alley before the assassin got close enough to aim and fire. In this dark place her white coat would attract him like a beacon.

They were done for. Despair and bone-chilling fright swept over Erin as she realized they had no escape.

Then, directly ahead, a sliver of light angled into the alley from an open door, cracked slightly to let in the fresh night air. Donovan headed for it and yanked the door wide open.

Erin blinked at the brightness. Black images swam before her eyes. Donovan slammed the door shut behind them.

"Hey, you can't cut through here," someone said in a deep bass voice. Erin's eyes focused on a huge man in a cook's uniform. His towering white hat made him appear even more immense.

"Help us," she screamed, her heart beating frantically. "Someone's trying to kill us."

"He's armed," Donovan shouted. Even as he spoke, bullets pierced the door, destroying the lock.

"Move!" the cook yelled at his two helpers who were nearly as big as he. "Get on either side of the door—flat against the wall."

When the door burst open, the three men were waiting, as if they'd done this before. The assassin bolted right into their arms. Erin got a good look at him. Of medium height, he had a wiry build. But his nose and chin were so predominant she knew she'd recognize him anywhere.

Working with easy coordination, the two assistants held him while the head cook delivered a smashing kick to his groin. The assassin let out a piercing scream. His weapon clattered to the floor.

"Damn you," he raged at Erin as he doubled over. "I'll get you for warning him." His odd toneless voice, with its promise of vengeful violence, echoed in her mind like some appalling screech. She'd never forget it as long as she lived.

The cook picked up the gun and tossed it to Donovan. "If you folks want to hold him for the police, go back to the alley. We've got a houseful of hungry people to feed. But we'll get this creep out of here and call 911 for you."

With a mighty heave-ho, the two assistants tossed the injured man bodily through the door.

Certain the assassin was too badly hurt to leave the alley, Donovan paused to shake the cook's hand. "Thanks, friend. We owe you one. That guy was out to kill us."

"No thanks needed," the big man returned. He grinned, showing gleaming white teeth against his dark skin. "We threw him out the way we do drunks who spot our open door. Now, get the hell outa here so we can get back to work." He shoved the alley door wide-open.

Erin followed Donovan through. She expected to see the assassin's crumpled body lying outside, but nobody was there.

A jolt of pure fear shook her body. "Where'd he go? He looked so—so crippled—how could he have got up and walked away? What if he's hiding in the shadows, waiting for us?" She couldn't believe her squeaky voice. "He might have another gun."

Donovan spun around, his back to the wall, and peered up and down the alley. "He's gone. Dammit!" The kitchen door still stood ajar. Taking Erin's hand he pulled her back into the room.

"Our bird flew the coop," Donovan told the cooks, as he and Erin walked past stainless steel counters laden with food.

The head cook's face showed surprise. "Then I won't bother calling the police. I should've kicked him again. He must be one helluva actor. From the way he yelled, I thought the kick I gave him would send him to emergency." He nodded toward a swinging door. Erin and Donovan went through to a dimly lighted hallway.

Glancing nervously over her shoulder, Erin half expected the assassin to come charging through the swinging door. Now that they'd reached relative safety, her legs felt weak. She grabbed Donovan's arm, afraid of falling.

He stared down at her, his eyes wide with concern. "Are you okay?"

"I'm fine," she answered, swallowing her fear, but she still clung to him. They had a way to go before they were home free. She didn't want to slow them down any more than she already had.

"Good girl," he said, but his blue eyes held hers, as though he felt her fear. Firmly gripping his arm, she let him lead her out to the street.

"We really should report this," Erin said, after they'd joined the milling crowd. Though not sure she was ready to face a police interrogation and the publicity that might follow, her strong sense of right and wrong told her the police should be informed.

But when Donovan explained again that he didn't want the bribed congressman involved, she didn't press the point. Civilian authorities would want to know how she showed up at the cathedral when she did. If she lied or refused to talk to protect the top secret message, she'd find herself in legal hot water—something she didn't need right now, and neither did Donovan. Anyway, the assassin was either gone, or had melted into the disorderly throng.

Wisconsin Avenue had become even rowdier and more crowded now that midnight was approaching. Slowly they made their way up the hill through the crowd. Donovan finally flagged down a cab on M Street. With great relief, Erin climbed inside.

They changed taxis twice before heading across the Fourteenth Street Bridge to Virginia. Near Bailey's Crossroads they found an all-night restaurant that seemed strangely empty after the Georgetown crowds.

Once settled in a booth with a cup of hot coffee in her hands and Donovan beside her, Erin felt some of the tension drain out of her. She was aware of his nearness, of the faint wool smell from his jacket now that he'd removed his overcoat. They'd just been attacked by an assassin. They'd had to run for their lives. But with Donovan next to her, she had the illogical feeling that no one could hurt her.

He shot her a piercing glance. "You're okay, aren't you? It's not every day an armed man comes after you."

"I'm fine." She was thankful her voice didn't quiver. "But you owe me, Donovan. Tell me what's going on. Twice in one day that man comes after you. And this time you didn't have a briefcase full of cash—so robbery's out."

He gave her such a quizzical look that Erin wondered if she'd said something wrong.

"I honestly don't know what's going on," he said, his dark eyebrows slanted in a frown. "Before tonight I would've sworn the motive was robbery, but now I'm not so sure."

Doubt deepened the lines on his face. Erin eyed him anxiously, wondering how to warn him he'd been targeted for assassination. She had a sudden impulse to smooth out the creases in his forehead and around his mouth with her fingers. Instead, she put her hand on the table next to his, wanting to touch him, but careful not to let her skin brush his.

"Have you got enemies who might hire someone to kill you?" she asked.

"Every lawyer's got enemies," he returned. "And several of mine would like to see me dead. The trick is knowing which one."

After a quick sideways glance at her, he closed his hand over hers. His warmth seemed to travel up her arm and race through her bloodstream.

Glancing down at their hands, intertwined on the table,

Erin took a deep breath. He was accepting her warning better than she'd hoped, but she had to be sure he understood exactly what she was saying.

"Then you agree the noon shooting might have been an assassination attempt instead of a robbery?" she asked anxiously.

"Is that what your intelligence report said?"

His reply was so quick that she pulled her hand away and took a long swallow of hot coffee to give herself time to think. Did she dare answer him? Yes, she decided, as long as she didn't reveal the *report* was an intercepted message.

"My source used the word *neutralization*," she said. "In my book, that means assassination."

He nodded, his eyes brimming with understanding. "You must have been scared witless knowing a paid hit man was after us in that dark alley."

"Not so much at first," she said, looking down at her coffee cup. "Then I realized you weren't armed."

He lifted a heavy eyebrow and Erin's heart dropped. Had she put her foot in her mouth again?

"What made you think I might have a gun?" he asked quietly. "Did your mother say something about O'Shaughnessy's people carrying weapons?"

"Why—why no, she didn't." Puzzled, Erin stared at him.

"Then why did you think I had one?" Though his smile was as charming as ever, she sensed his uneasiness.

"I—I guess you just look like a man who would own a gun," she said lamely. She couldn't very well tell him she suspected he was a CIA informant who might carry a weapon. That information was sure to be classified.

"C'mon now, Erin," he said in his beguiling way. "After what we've been through tonight, surely you can trust me with the truth." Tilting his head to one side, he waited expectantly.

What harm would it do to tell him she knew he was an

informant? she wondered. Telling him couldn't possibly hurt Patrick or her mother. And it might make him more open with her. She had to take a few risks if she expected to learn anything of value from him. And rogue though Donovan was, Erin yearned to trust him and feel closer.

But did she dare?

CHAMELEON REPORTED his St. Patrick's Day failures after he left Georgetown. Following the usual procedure, he used a pay phone to call Dublin. The number he dialed, reserved for his use only, was answered by a machine that recorded his short message.

Mission unsuccessful, he said into the phone. *First try foiled by female lieutenant who knew time and place. Traced woman and, through following her, located Dun Aengus's man again. Second try also unsuccessful. Request instructions.*

From downtown Washington, Chameleon drove to the brownstone house in Falls Church, Virginia, where he'd received orders for this contract. During the half hour ride, a message answering his phone call had arrived. As usual, he saw no one outside the shadowy building or inside the elegant gold-and-white reception room. Beyond, in the spacious living room, a fire crackled in the marble fireplace.

The message, in an envelope addressed to Mr. Smith, lay on a small table in the high-ceilinged reception room. Chameleon ripped the envelope open.

Mission terminated, read the printed words on the page inside. *Never—repeat—never make second try if first fails. Report to office ASAP.*

From a previous letter, Chameleon recognized *office* as the code word for his contact in Dublin. Humiliated, he strode out of the building to his car. He'd just been reprimanded for tonight's work in Georgetown. And he knew who to blame. Orders or no orders, he'd get even with the lieutenant. There were some things he did on his own, just for the fun of it. Taking care of the woman would be one of them.

But first he had to get to Dublin. Was he finally going to meet his elusive employer face-to-face?

DONOVAN EYED Erin's untouched food. She'd drunk most of her coffee, but hadn't done more than poke at the slice of ham and scrambled eggs on her plate.

Damn! He hoped she was upset by the lies she'd told him and not by their frightening experience tonight. Once Donovan realized his question about the gun made her nervous, he was determined to put on the pressure until she told him the truth. But he didn't want to scare her, not after what they'd just been through. He'd question her in his own uniquely beguiling way, he decided, so she'd end up *wanting* to tell him why she thought he had a gun.

"So you think I look like a man who would carry a gun." He forced a woebegone expression that women found hard to resist. "I'm not sure whether to feel glad or sorry."

She glanced at him without smiling. "I shouldn't have said that, Donovan."

"But that's what you believed." He moved closer to her on the bench seat, close enough to feel her body heat. To his dismay, his own body responded with the beginnings of an arousal he seemed powerless to control.

"What I need to find out now is why you thought so. It could be important, Erin. Since somebody's gunning for me, I need to know everything you can tell me."

Erin's wide-eyed expression reflected a confused mix of dismay and apprehension. Her hair was tousled, her face ruddy in the restaurant's bright lights. Wearing her green silk dress, she looked more like a fashion model than an air force lieutenant.

Donovan reminded himself that, in spite of her alluring appearance, she was a military officer with information he needed. She wanted to talk, he could see that. But something was tying her tongue.

"If you're holding back information because it was in that classified report, just tell me generally without identifying your source," he urged. Forcing himself to ignore the warmth in his loins, he took a long swallow of coffee. "The way you did before."

Since Donovan had read the intercepted message, he knew it contained nothing specific about him personally. Could she have seen something else that identified him as a man who would carry a weapon?

Not likely, he told himself. Central Intelligence received the same reports the Pentagon did. If Mike Essinger had seen anything about Donovan, he'd have mentioned it. Still, the agency researchers hadn't been on their toes lately. Perhaps key intelligence had been overlooked.

"The information wasn't in the report I told you about," she replied. Her voice was so quiet he had to strain to hear her.

"Doesn't matter where it came from." Doing his best to reassure her, he caught her hand again. She didn't pull away. "Just tell me what you know."

From her nearly imperceptible nod, he knew she'd made up her mind to tell him. Though he didn't let his relief show, he could feel it bubbling inside him along with his heightened awareness. Just touching her hand stirred him anew.

"This is more about what wasn't there, than what was." An impish smile replaced her confused look.

Understanding flooded in. "You checked up on me?"

She nodded. "With the CIA biographical people. Don't look so horrified. You did the same thing to me at the *Post* morgue."

Donovan twisted his face into what he hoped was a congenial smile. Damn those researchers if they'd let anything slip. This was O'Shaughnessy's stepdaughter, for Lord's sake. If she knew he was a CIA agent, his cover was blown for sure. Maybe it was discovered already. He couldn't rule out the possibility that someone in Dublin was on to him. Since Donovan had been given today's sensitive delivery to the congressman that wasn't likely. But after two assassination attempts in twelve hours, he couldn't rule out even the remotest possibility.

"So what did you turn up in your fact-finding mission?" He kept his tone bland with a hint of teasing so she wouldn't see how uneasy he was—or how she aroused him.

"I found out you have a CIA connection."

"What kind of connection?" Since he'd promised not to ask about her sources, he avoided asking where she got that notion, much as he wanted to.

"I'm just guessing, of course, but I think you're an informant for the agency." Removing her hand from his, she peered at him, her head tilted, as if expecting him to confirm or deny the charge.

"That's not very flattering," he said with a pretend frown. "An informant is a snitch who tells tales out of school. Do you think I'm ratting on your stepfather to the CIA?"

Slowly Erin cut a small piece of ham and lifted it to her lips. Donovan didn't seem nearly as upset by her revelation as she thought he would be. Was that a tacit confirmation?

"No, I don't," she said honestly. "I think you're informing on somebody besides my stepfather."

"Then you don't think your stepfather knew about today's delivery to the congressman?"

He turned toward his plate, and Erin couldn't see his expression. But if she wanted to get information out of him, now was her chance.

"No, I don't think Patrick knew," she said. "But what I think doesn't matter. You're the one who works for him, so you're the one who knows. You tell me if my stepfather knew about the delivery."

He rubbed his earlobe in a gesture she recognized as something he did when concentrating. Then he looked directly at her. Erin trembled inside at the magnetic power in his blue eyes. Outwardly, she forced herself not to move or look away.

"So, speak," she said.

Still holding her gaze, he nodded slowly. "There'd be hell to pay if the press found out about the bribe. But from Shamrock's view, the money was simply a gift."

"You haven't answered my question," she said. "Did Patrick know? Answer or I'll tell him you're a CIA informant." Erin knew it was risky, threatening Donovan like that. But she held the trump card, and she wanted him to know it.

Though he took a deep breath, his eyes didn't release hers. "If you do, whether it's true or not, I'll lose my job. Maybe a lot more. An unfounded rumor connecting me to the CIA might be behind the shootings. I haven't always worked for your stepfather, you know. Somebody else might think I'm snitching on him or her."

A wave of remorse swept over Erin. Lightly she put her hand on his arm. He'd taken off his overcoat when they entered the restaurant, and she felt hard muscle beneath the fabric of his suit coat. That turned her on even more than the feel of his hand holding hers. Annoyed at the sexual awareness rippling through her, she pulled away. He didn't try to stop her, but his knowing glance told her he guessed her feelings.

"I'm sorry, Donovan," she said, annoyed with herself for threatening him. "I'll never tell anyone about your CIA connection, whether you answer me or not."

He grinned at her and her heart sang at the humor in his eyes.

"In that case, I'll answer," he said, finishing the last of his food. "I work directly under a man named Collins, the firm's lead attorney. He gives me my orders. On the rare occasions when your stepfather shows up, he talks to Collins, not me. I suppose it's possible O'Shaughnessy knew nothing about the bribe, that it was somehow arranged by Collins without your stepfather's knowledge.''

A huge weight shifted off Erin's shoulders. "Patrick would never do anything illegal.''

"Your stepfather's a shrewd businessman," Donovan returned quickly. "I'd bet a year's pay that nothing goes on in Shamrock Construction that he's not aware of.''

"Maybe yes, maybe no," Erin said. "The fact is you can't prove he knew about that bribe—or anything else illegal.''

While Donovan paid the check, Erin slipped into her coat, congratulating herself as she tied the belt securely around her waist. She'd already learned something important, and the evening wasn't over yet. By the time they reached her condo, she'd find out even more about her stepfather's company—and about this enigmatic Irishman.

DONOVAN CALLED THE TAXI from inside the restaurant, but they waited for it outside in the shadows just beyond the brightly lighted entry.

Though after 1:00 a.m., the ever-present hum of traffic on nearby Route 7 and Highway 50 saturated the night air. The wind had died, allowing exhaust fumes to settle over the business areas between the two major thoroughfares.

Donovan was tempted to go back inside the restaurant, but he didn't suggest it. They could talk more openly outside, with less fear of being overheard. And they needed to talk. Or rather, Donovan needed more information, and he didn't have much time left to get it.

How had she found out he was *connected*—as she put it—to the CIA? The agency researchers might not be up to par these days, but they'd never reveal anything so sensitive.

And why was Erin showing so much loyalty to a stepfather she hardly knew? Was there a connection between Erin and Patrick O'Shaughnessy that Mike Essinger hadn't uncovered, a connection that existed before O'Shaughnessy's marriage to Erin's mother?

According to Essinger's report, Margaret Sullivan had met O'Shaughnessy only two months before she married him. Had she known him previously, perhaps even worked with him before? As a lieutenant general's wife, she could have been very useful to a man like Patrick O'Shaughnessy. So could Erin, an air force lieutenant with the special clearances required of an intelligence officer. Because if the mother had known him before, most likely the daughter had, too. Could all three of them be working together now?

It was an interesting thought, one worth following up. Though Donovan had no proof, he couldn't shake his deep-down belief that O'Shaughnessy was a key player in the worldwide conspiracy he'd been assigned to investigate.

He turned toward Erin, standing beside him. In the shadowy semidarkness, her flame red hair reflected the flashing neon sign over the restaurant's brightly lighted entry, giving her an unearthly glow. The awareness he'd felt in the restaurant returned, and a renewed warm sensation coursed through him. If he could inspire a similar desire in her, maybe she'd trust him enough to confide in him.

Moving closer, he brushed her shoulder with his upper arm. The touch, light as it was, aroused an immediate response. Dammit. The contact was supposed to arouse her, not him, at least not any more than he already was.

He beamed his most high-voltage smile. "Even though you've discovered my secret, I hope that won't stop us from getting together next time you're in Dublin."

A triumphant sparkle appeared in her clear azure eyes. "Then you admit you're an informant?"

"You've caught me dead to rights," he lied. Better she thought him a snitch than a bona fide agent. "What I can't figure is how you found out. That kind of info's in the *burn-before-reading* category."

"I've got all the clearances," she said impishly.

"Not that one." He shifted uneasily, wondering just how much she knew.

"You're right, of course. I never saw the files, but I found out they were restricted."

Relief surged through him. *So that's why she guessed I was an informant.*

The headlights from a car turning off Route 7 shone on her face, highlighting her aristocratic nose, her generous mouth, her flawless skin. Too bad they hadn't met in more agreeable circumstances. With an assassin tailing him—and maybe her, too—seeing her again, either here or in Dublin, reeked of danger to both of them.

The car swung into the restaurant driveway and moved slowly toward them. Damn! It was the taxi. Just when she was starting to talk.

"Files?" he asked, wondering who else she'd checked up on.

"Yes." She looked away, acting embarrassed. "I asked to see Patrick's file, too, if the agency had one on him."

"Thought both of us might be up to something, did you?" After her protestations of undying loyalty to her new stepfather, Donovan couldn't resist the dig.

Without meeting his eyes, she answered. "Since you were doing something illegal by bribing that congressman, I'm ashamed to say I was afraid maybe he was, too." Nervously she clasped and unclasped her hands. "When I found out both your files were restricted, I figured you were both informants. What in the world is going on at that company, Donovan?"

The taxi pulled up at the curb. Donovan opened the back door, and Erin slid in, with him behind her. He gave the driver her address.

"Probably nothing," he said, after he'd closed the door. "But be a good girl and keep quiet about this, just the same."

"You have my word," she said. "Scout's honor."

Donovan didn't believe her for an instant. The first thing

she'd do when she got home tonight was call her mother in Dublin to report that both Donovan and her stepfather were CIA informants.

Inwardly, Donovan groaned. With his cover as good as blown, the investigation would have to stop, the two years he'd put into it wasted. Worse, O'Shaughnessy would know the CIA considered him a prime suspect in the conspiracy.

But there was no reason to waste what was left of tonight. He slid his arm around Erin's shoulder. "I know a better way to cement our agreement than with scout's honor."

Her eyes widened and he heard her quick gasp for breath, but she didn't back away. With one quick motion, he pulled her into his arms. A faint scent, like a sea breeze tinged with lilies, swirled around him. Crushing her close, he felt her slender body move against him, felt her arms holding him tightly around his neck.

Intoxicated, he tilted her head up and lowered his mouth to hers. Her lips parted willingly, and he tasted her sweetness. Then he did something so out of character that he would never have believed it could happen. He lost control of himself. His usual carefully managed hunger overpowered him. He drowned in her kiss, in the feel of her against him. Nothing made sense but Erin, the softness of her lips, the smell of her skin, the eager way she clung to him. As her essence swirled around him, he held her fiercely, desperately, as if the world would die if she slipped out of his grasp.

The gentle hum of the taxi's engine slowed as the driver braked to a stop at an intersection. The change of motion brought Donovan crashing back to reality—and apparently, Erin, too. She tore herself away from him, her eyes wide with surprise and warm with pleasure.

"Why—why did you kiss me like that?" Her voice trembled with emotion.

"Because I wanted to, of course." He hoped his own eyes didn't reveal the same shock that hers did. In his thirty-two years, Donovan had kissed many women, most of them forgotten a short time later. But none had affected him this way. He wanted Erin. Lord how he wanted her. He could still feel her arms around his neck, her mouth warm and moist against his. When he closed his eyes, all he could see was her face.

But he couldn't have her. Not as long as he was investigating her family. Even if he was taken off the case he couldn't have her. She struck him as a woman who wanted marriage, children. He couldn't give her that and sensed she wouldn't settle for less. After an overly protective mother and six older, suffocatingly vigilant sisters, Donovan wanted freedom. No more women's apron strings for him, no matter how enticing the package.

"Then that's the way you kiss every woman who attracts you?" she asked, her surprised look changing to a frowning, defiant one.

Donovan forced another quick smile of white teeth and charm.

"Of course not," he denied smoothly. "Only the winners."

She took a deep breath, expelling it slowly. "You're more of a rogue than I thought, Donovan." Disgust—or was it disappointment?—was written all over her expressive face.

"Thanks for the compliment," he said, playing it lightly in spite of a deep down sour feeling in the pit of his stomach.

At her condo she didn't invite him upstairs. They said good-night like two strangers who never expected to see each other again.

Chapter Five

A confused mixture of anger and regret swirled through Erin as she rode the brass-embossed elevator to her floor. Damn Donovan and his hot-cold passion. First he kissed her desperately, rapturously, so she felt like he desired her more than any woman on the face of the earth. Then he blandly told her he treated every woman who appealed to him the same way.

No, not every woman, Erin remembered grimly. *Only the winners.* How conceited could he be?

The elevator hissed smoothly to her floor, and she stepped onto the carpeted hallway. *So welcome to the winners' circle, Lieutenant Meyer.* Erin concentrated on the feel of the plush carpet beneath her feet in a futile attempt to blot out the memory of his arms around her.

Well, maybe Donovan's other women friends put up with such blasé treatment, but not Erin. He could take his winner's roses and throw them around somebody else's neck.

More and more Mr. Dan Donovan reminded Erin of someone her mother had described time and again over the years.

Kevin Riley. Just repeating the name in her mind made her breath burn in her throat. *The Prince of Rogues, himself.*

Though her mother fondly pictured Riley as a charmer who could captivate almost anybody, Erin considered him a cheat and a betrayer, the kind of man who'd walk out on her mother, an innocent teenage girl, after he'd got her pregnant.

Sure, he'd been assigned to Vietnam. Granted, he hadn't known Margaret was pregnant when he left. But in Erin's mind these were phony excuses. No honorable man would take advantage of an innocent seventeen-year-old girl for one weekend's pleasure. At the very least, he should have answered her letters.

Erin still burned with anger every time she thought of her beautiful mother scrubbing hotel toilets to add a few dollars to Grandma and Grandpa Sullivan's dirt-poor existence. Uneducated, the Sullivans earned a meager living cleaning third-rate motels.

Their poverty-stricken situation changed when Margaret met and married Major George Meyer from nearby Fort Benning. But nothing could redeem Erin's resentment of her birth father. Over the years it worsened, festering inside her like an ugly cancer. So why did she have these feelings for a charismatic Irish rogue with a love-'em-and-leave-'em philosophy exactly like her traitorous father's?

Through a sudden veil of tears, Erin found herself standing outside her condominium door, key in hand, staring at the oak panels. Angrily she thrust the key in the lock and pushed the door open. Neither Kevin Riley nor Dan Donovan was worth wasting tears on. Inside, she blew her nose, then flushed the tissue with the steadfast resolve never to shed another tear over either man.

But dredging up the old story about her birth father had made Erin anxious to talk to her mother. She checked her watch. After two, it would be a little past 7:00 a.m. in Dublin. Her mother was an early riser, so this was a good time to call. Half an hour later, dressed in pajamas with two pillows propped up behind her in bed, she dialed her mother's number.

Margaret answered on the first ring. "Good morning, this is Margaret Sullivan."

Hearing her mother's cheerful voice, Erin chuckled at

her greeting. "Hi, Mom. How'd you ever get Patrick to let you keep your maiden name?"

"The same way I did your father—told him there'd be no marriage otherwise." Her husky laugh seemed as clear as if she were sitting on the bed next to Erin. "You have to be firm with men, darling. They're happier if you are."

"That's easy for you to say." Erin settled herself against the pillows. "You've always been able to wind them around your fingers."

"You can, too," her mother said. "After your date last night, I'll bet your Mr. Donovan is counting the days until he sees you again."

"I keep telling you, Mom, he's not *my Mr. Donovan.*" Erin's heart dropped as she remembered his cool goodbye. "We didn't hit it off." Her face burned at the memory of his fiery kiss—and the blasé way he'd acted afterward.

"Tell me about it."

Erin hadn't intended to worry her mother with the harrowing story of the day's happenings, but she changed her mind when she caught her mother's enthusiastic interest. Besides, if Margaret heard the story secondhand, after Donovan reported what happened, she'd be worried sick.

After first emphasizing that no one had been hurt, Erin described the two incidents with the assassin. When she'd finished, there was absolute silence—one of the few times her mother had nothing to say.

"Mom, are you there?"

"Yes. But I'm so scared for you I can't talk." Margaret's usually firm voice sounded shaky. "What did the police say?"

"We didn't report what happened, Mom." She paused. "I didn't tell the police because of my work. It would have jeopardized one of my sources. I'll have to handle the report through military channels."

"Because of your work?" Margaret's voice lowered to a whisper. "You can't talk to the police because of your work?"

"That's right, Mom."

"Darling, you're scaring me. You say this man was after Mr. Donovan? Are you sure it wasn't you?"

In her warm bedroom, a cold chill enveloped Erin's body. She pulled her blankets up higher and bunched them around her. "Why do you say that?"

"Well, I've noticed a stranger watching me from a distance since I've been in Dublin. He walks with a limp, so I can recognize him from a long way off. Maybe there's a connection between him and what happened to you."

Jerking upright, Erin tensed with shock. "You think somebody might be after both you and me?" Her fingers gripped the phone like a lifeline. Her breath felt heavy in her lungs. "Why in God's name?"

"We're both wealthy women," Margaret said, her voice still a whisper. "Maybe someone plans to kidnap one or both of us and blackmail your stepfather."

Slowly Erin expelled her breath. "I'm positive the assassin was after Donovan, not me. But what about this stranger you've seen. Have you told Patrick?"

"I didn't want to worry him." Margaret sounded apologetic. She'd always tried to spare those she loved.

Frustrated and scared, Erin didn't try to hide her alarm. "Tell him, Mom. Today. This morning." She hoped the urgency in her voice would impel her mother to immediate action. "And tell him what happened to me and Donovan. I'm sure Donovan will report everything when he gets back, but this will give Patrick advance notice. I'd die if anything happened to you." Erin's voice wobbled with emotion.

"Nothing will, darling. Remember, we've got lots of family here if I need help. For starters, there's Jean Magee and Bet Ryan, two first cousins."

Listening to her mother rattle off relatives near Dublin, Erin slumped against the pillows. Much as Margaret tried to convince her nothing would happen, Erin couldn't dispel the cold dread washing over her.

A stranger lurking in the distance sounded terribly threatening. Her mother wasn't paranoid. Just the opposite. She was too trusting. If her mother voiced concern about this stranger, she was really worried.

Trembling, she said good-night and hung up the receiver.

THE MESSAGE LIGHT was flashing on Donovan's phone when he got back to his hotel room. For a fleeting instant, he let himself hope Erin had called. He couldn't get her face out of his mind. He could visualize her standing next to him now, her full lips glowing in the rosy light from the bedside lamps.

Annoyed, he shook his head to erase the fantasy. Of course the message wasn't from Erin. After the nonchalant way he'd reacted to their kiss, he'd probably never hear from her again. The message was from Mike Essinger. Cursing under his breath, Donovan went to the lobby phone.

"We've got to talk," Essinger said, waiting for the call even though it was after two o'clock in the morning.

"Damned right we do. I want to know how a certain lady found out about some restricted files."

Donovan heard Essinger's discouraged sigh. "Then you know about that."

"She told me. What I don't know is why your mental giants told her the files even existed."

"They didn't tell *her*," Essinger explained. "They told our analyst who went through the proper channels to get them. Don't worry. The analyst's been warned not to say anything."

Donovan groaned. "Obviously the analyst *did* say something." Using phrases that only his CIA contact would understand, Donovan repeated Erin's assumption that both he and Patrick O'Shaughnessy were CIA informants. Then he reported tonight's attack by the assassin.

Essinger matched Donovan's groan. "Damn! Two years work down the drain. At least we think we know who your unpleasant friend is. The press calls him *Chameleon*. Changes his appearance with every job so he's a hard man to find. Nobody knows what he really looks like. Doubt he'll be after you once you're off this case."

Donovan's heart slipped down to his shoes. "What do you mean *off this case?*"

"If the woman knows you're connected to us in any capacity, your cover's blown. She's sure to pass the word."

"Hold on a minute," Donovan said, as a new thought struck him. "Maybe we can make lemonade out of my lady's lemon. As you say, she's sure to let somebody know about the *snitches* she's discovered. What if I talk to the big man myself and tell him about the restricted files? As far as he's concerned, both he and I are under investigation since both our files are restricted. That puts me in as much hot water as he and, by telling him, I've declared my loyalty."

"It might work," Essinger said, after a moment's silence. "But it's risky as hell."

"It *will* work," Donovan insisted, convincing himself as much as Essinger. If he didn't find out who was behind the conspiracy, his failure would bother him the rest of his life.

But if telling O'Shaughnessy about the restricted files backfired, he could end up dead.

WHEN CHAMELEON RETURNED to his hotel room after his visit to the brownstone house in Virginia, he stood under the steaming hot shower for a long time. The piercing shards of water stung the bruises on his skin, flaming the unspeakable anger that rose deep inside him.

His target had escaped again, thanks mainly to the female lieutenant. She had somehow managed to push her way into the crowded dining room behind the bar, a room Chameleon hadn't known was there. Even then he would have easily killed them both in the alley if they hadn't found that open door to the hotel kitchen. To be tossed out of the place like a drunken bum—such humiliation. Then the rebuke that followed from Dublin. That's what had maddened him most.

Chameleon turned the shower water even hotter. Twice this female lieutenant, Erin Meyer, had interfered with his contract. Did she have any idea of the stakes involved? Whoever she represented, she'd be a dead woman the next time Chameleon caught her with Dun Aengus's man.

And just who was he, this man slated for neutralization? Usually Chameleon preferred not to know. He deliberately arranged his contracts so he'd be aware only of the detailed physical description of the person to be killed, and the time and place for the action. Things were neater that way.

But Dun Aengus's man was different. He'd made Chameleon angry, something that rarely happened. Now Chameleon had to admit he'd failed. More humiliation. He'd have to arrange another contract in the face of his defeat.

Turning off the shower, he stepped onto the cracked tile floor. His hip and shoulder ached where he'd landed in the concrete alley. Ugly bruises were already starting to show, mortifying reminders of the day's failures.

At least he hadn't been seriously hurt by the cook's kick. Thanks to his actor's training, he'd known how to twist his body at exactly the right moment and scream convincingly so he wouldn't be kicked again. If he hadn't dropped his weapon, he would have shot both of them as soon as they entered the alley.

Toweling his wiry body, he reminded himself that anger was a luxury he couldn't afford. At best, this was only a small setback. Though he'd never met his employer in Dublin—had no idea who he really was—he'd worked with this man before and knew he'd be trusted with another contract. Next time Dun Aengus's man wouldn't get away. And neither would Lieutenant Erin Meyer. Chameleon would see to that.

AFTER A COUPLE OF HOURS of anxious tossing, Erin's crisp mauve-and-indigo patterned sheets were hopelessly tangled

with her blankets. Finally she crawled out of bed. There
would be no sleep for her tonight. Every time she closed
her eyes she could see two faces: her mother's and Donovan's. With both etched on her brain, sleep was impossible.

Though it was only four-thirty, Erin decided to put on
her uniform and head for the Pentagon. She could drown
her worries in the ocean of work waiting for her.

A cold mist rose off the Potomac as Erin trudged to the
Pentagon from North Parking in the gray light of an early
dawn. Around the Tidal Basin, Washington's cherry blossom jewels were waiting to burst into luxuriant bloom.
Though spring was less than a week away, the blossoms
were still bound up in their protective wrappings.

Like me, Erin thought, feeling as closed in as the blossoms. Only the trouble with her was that—unlike them—
she seemed destined to stay forever in the bud, never
blooming until some charming cad came along...like Donovan, with his broad shoulders and laughing blue eyes.

An artificial sun makes premature blossoms, she warned
herself grimly, remembering how his insensitive comment
had jolted her back inside her shell. How could she have
let him get to her like that? And why was she thinking
about him now when her mother might be in trouble?

On this early mid-March morning, the Pentagon seemed
almost deserted, its systems humming like a giant machine
running itself. After passing the guard at the River Entrance, Erin saw no one in the darkened corridors until she
reached Pentagon Intelligence, on the first floor.

Though activity was more muted than at midday, indi-
viduals—most in military uniforms—hurried in the corridors, papers and folders in their hands. It was yet another
reminder that the military intelligence agency never slept.

Remembering her own sleepless night, she felt herself
frown. Well, she couldn't let lack of sleep affect her day.
And she couldn't let thoughts of Donovan dampen her spirits.

Taking her uniform coat off, she hung it on the rack near

the office door. Her desk was inside a partitioned cubicle with three other analysts. Nobody else was there.

But at the center of Erin's desk was a scribbled note. She recognized the handwriting. Her division chief's. He wanted to see her. An apprehensive tremor coursed through her. What was Colonel Byrd doing at his desk at 5:30 a.m.? This seemed early, even for him. Had he got wind of the intercepted message and the shooting yesterday at the cathedral? Did he intend to chew her out because she hadn't told him?

She shook her head, dismissing the notion. She'd saved a man's life. He couldn't fault her for that.

Carrying the intercepted message and this morning's briefing in a manila folder, Erin headed for her division chief's office. With his door open, he saw her across the hallway and beckoned her inside. Unsmiling, he watched her enter.

A well-built man with thick white hair and amber eyes, the colonel was said to swoop down on wary subordinates like a diving eagle. Chin high, she resolved not to let him rattle her. At his invitation she sat down in the chair beside his desk.

"You're in early this morning, Erin." He studied her face so intently she felt warmth in her cheeks. But she didn't look away.

"I tried to get you at home," he went on. "When your machine answered, I figured you might be on the way to work." A frown line appeared between his eyes. "Do you usually come in this early?"

Why was he beating around the bush? A flash of intuition told her this early morning summons had nothing to do with the briefing in her folder.

"No, sir," she replied. "I wanted to put some finishing touches on this morning's briefing."

When he leaned toward her, his eyes wide, she sensed he was about to swoop. Hurriedly she went on. "I also wanted to report an incident that happened yesterday."

With a smug nod, Colonel Byrd leaned back in his chair. "Does the incident have anything to do with those restricted files you requested yesterday from Central Intelligence?"

So that was the reason for the summons. Struggling to stay calm, Erin took a quick gulp of air. She should have guessed. If Max had been quizzed by the CIA director, Erin couldn't expect to escape official scrutiny.

"Yes, sir, I requested those files after I received this intercept from the National Security Agency." She handed him the printout of the intercepted message.

He scanned it and shook his head. "It's gibberish, like ninety-five percent of the stuff the NSA picks up."

"Not really, sir," Erin said. "The way I interpreted the message was that a man would be killed at noon on St. Patrick's Day at the National Cathedral."

"Gibberish," the colonel repeated. But he didn't sound as sure of himself as before. "Don't tell me you went traipsing over there yesterday?"

Erin nodded. "If I hadn't gone, a man named Dan Donovan would have been killed."

"So that's why you requested Donovan's file." The frown lines on the colonel's broad forehead deepened.

"Yes, sir. Since somebody was trying to kill him, I thought the CIA might maintain a file on him."

"And Donovan told you he worked for Patrick O'Shaughnessy in Dublin so you requested that file, too?"

"No, sir," Erin replied honestly. "Donovan didn't tell me who he worked for or where. I guessed it was O'Shaughnessy from the message."

Colonel Byrd picked up the message and read it more slowly. When he put it down, Erin caught a perplexed look she'd rarely seen on the division chief's face. "How the devil did you know Dun Aengus was O'Shaughnessy?"

Erin didn't hesitate. "Because he's my stepfather. That's his nickname."

The colonel's face got so red, Erin thought he'd explode.

"Your stepfather?" Standing, he glared at her as though she'd committed an unpardonable sin.

When the colonel rose, so did Erin. "I thought you knew, sir. It was in all the papers."

"What was in all the papers, Lieutenant?"

"My mother's marriage to Patrick O'Shaughnessy two weeks ago. Since she's General Meyer's widow, the marriage got lots of press, especially in the military."

The colonel's amber eyes narrowed, and he leaned across his desk toward her.

He's starting to swoop, Erin thought uneasily. But what could he do to her for requesting a couple of restricted files?

"You're fired!" he said flatly. "Get your things together and get out of my division."

Unflinching, she met his stare. "I'm an air force officer, Colonel. You can't do that."

"The hell I can't. We may wear different uniforms, but I'm your commander. Even in the nineties, a commander still has some authority." Parts of his face had got so red, he'd begun to resemble a turkey.

Erin's legs went weak. "But I haven't done anything, Colonel."

"You've wrecked a covert operation that's taken years to develop," he bellowed. "And your jaunt to the cathedral jeopardized a major source of intelligence. The communications network that sent the Dublin messages will probably go dark when they figure out we're listening to their broadcasts. And they *will* figure that out. There's no other way you could have got to the cathedral in the nick of time the way you did."

Abruptly he shut up, as though he realized he'd said too much. Slowly he sank back into his chair. When he spoke again his tone changed from hot anger to cool authority.

"Haven't you read agency rules about close relatives in our primary areas of interest? As soon as your mother married O'Shaughnessy, you should have requested a transfer."

Erin's mouth dropped open. What was going on? That agency regulation was loosely interpreted. She knew several analysts who had relatives in their analytical areas.

"He's not a blood relative," she returned, her spine stiffening.

Colonel Byrd leaned back in his chair. "Your mother is, and I presume she's in Dublin with her new husband. For God's sake, Lieutenant. Nobody's closer than that."

Erin swallowed the sharp retort on the tip of her tongue. She'd worked hard on this job, put in hundreds of extra hours at night and on weekends. And now the colonel was tossing her out for an insignificant breach of regulations. She couldn't believe he'd take such drastic action for so little reason.

"But where...will I go?"

His scowl softened. "Take thirty-days leave. By the time you get back, air force personnel will have you reassigned from the Pentagon."

Erin managed to walk out of his office without flinching. She numbly cleaned out her desk before any of her fellow analysts arrived. Humiliated, she trudged back to her car in North Parking. Feeling as though she'd been kicked in the stomach, she lay down on her freshly made bed as soon as she got home. What had just happened...and why?

BRIGHT SUNLIGHT STREAMED through the sheer curtains on Erin's bedroom window. Fighting the brightness, she reached for a blanket to pull over her head. There was no blanket.

She opened her eyes. Fully clothed in her uniform, she found herself lying on top of her neatly made bed, her cheek on a comforter.

Now she remembered what had happened. She'd been fired. With that on her record, she'd never make her next promotion. Her career was ruined. She'd disgraced the name of the man who had adopted her, and she wasn't sure quite how or why.

Lifting her head, Erin glanced down at her rumpled uniform, at the nylon hose sagging around her ankles. She sat up. The clock on her bedside table read after noon. Quickly removing her wrinkled uniform, she hung it in the closet. In its place she put on freshly pressed jeans and a blue long-sleeved sweater with a red-and-yellow pattern. Something cheerful, that's what she needed, she thought, vowing to put this morning's clash with the colonel out of her mind.

But try as she would, the scene kept repeating itself. Why had he taken such drastic action for a minor infraction of the agency's rules? Why had he got so heated and angry?

As she busied herself making a tuna sandwich in the kitchen, Erin heard his words over and over in her mind: his words about being fired; about requesting a transfer after her mother's marriage.

But he'd said something else, something significant she'd overlooked in her dismay about her career. What was it? Suddenly she remembered. That a key communications network would probably go dark—stop broadcasting—presumably because her trip to the cathedral would clue the operators that someone was listening to their messages. Even more interesting, he said she'd wrecked a long-time CIA covert operation.

With her sandwich half made, Erin plopped down on a stool to think. How could she possibly have wrecked a covert operation?

By meeting Donovan? By recognizing her stepfather's name in the message? By finding out the CIA files on Donovan and Patrick were restricted? *Or maybe all of the above.*

Unable to sit still, Erin paced back and forth on the Oriental rug in her living room. If there was indeed a CIA covert operation in progress at Shamrock Construction, what did that make Donovan and Patrick? Probably not informants, as she'd first thought. But something else, something far more threatening to Patrick and her mother.

Could Donovan be a CIA undercover agent?

At first Erin fought the idea, wanting to believe she was wrong. But if he wasn't an informant, there could be no other reason for his restricted file. And what about the fact that her stepfather had a file and that it, too, was restricted? Could he, like Donovan, be a covert CIA agent? She shook her head. It was beyond belief that Patrick might be spying on his own company. That left only one answer: Patrick was being investigated by Donovan, a CIA undercover agent.

Hurrying back to the kitchen, Erin finished fixing her sandwich and took a big bite without really tasting it. Was Donovan trying to trap her stepfather in a sting operation? Though Donovan had no proof, he'd seemed certain Patrick knew the most intimate details of Shamrock Construction's operation, details usually left to subordinates. What if Donovan was right and Patrick was a criminal?

Shuddering, Erin remembered her mother's words about the stranger. Could Patrick himself be behind the stranger's scrutiny? Could he be a threat to her mother? The bare possibility made Erin want to dial her mother right then and there to warn her.

But she couldn't. Telling Margaret about the covert operation might expose her mother to even more danger.

Damn! She wished she knew what kind of operation Donovan was running. It couldn't be something as simple as tracking the corrupt bribery of the congressman. He already had the goods on Collins, the man who gave him his orders for yesterday's job. No, this had to be something else, something much bigger.

Thoughtfully, Erin finished her sandwich. One man could tell her what she needed to know. *Donovan.* Was he booked on Aeroflot's flight this afternoon? The airline wouldn't tell her, but the clerk offered to take a short message for Mr. Donovan, if he showed up at the ticket counter.

"Donovan, I'm on my way to Dulles Airport," Erin dictated into the phone. "Must see you before you leave. Meet me at your boarding gate. Erin."

Chapter Six

When the Aeroflot ticket clerk handed Donovan the folded sheet of paper, his heart leapt—just as it had last night when he'd seen the flashing light on his hotel phone. But the message hadn't been from Erin then and it wouldn't be now, he told himself. Essinger must have more last-minute words of wisdom.

After he'd checked his bag at the counter, he unfolded the note. It *was* from Erin.

Instantly his mind registered the significance of her words. She hadn't been as turned off by his comments last night as he'd thought and was coming to the airport to bid him a fond farewell.

After a brief moment of elation, a sense of frustrated helplessness swept over him. Damn! With an assassin stalking him, she was putting herself in danger by coming. Now that he had an *in* with Margaret Sullivan he couldn't afford to jeopardize his investigation by getting involved with O'Shaughnessy's stepdaughter. Nor did he want to. Erin meant commitment, the last thing he needed.

But in spite of his doubts, he found himself grinning at the clerk like a teenager. "Thanks," he said, handing the man a ten-dollar tip.

Still grinning, Donovan stuffed the note in his pocket. When he pictured Erin's radiant face, her luxuriant mane of red hair brushing her shoulders, he couldn't wait to see her again.

But this was a duty day, and unfortunately she'd be in uniform with her hair tied up. Had she left the Pentagon and driven twenty miles to Dulles Airport simply to tell him goodbye? Much as Donovan might like to think so, a sudden gut instinct told him he shouldn't believe it.

Something was wrong. Deep inside he knew. That's why she was coming. Remembering the firm set of Erin's jaw, the way her azure eyes blazed with determination, he knew she'd never leave her desk without a damned good reason. Cursing himself for a conceited fool, he quickened his pace toward the international boarding area. Perhaps she'd already arrived.

Across the mammoth terminal's upper level he caught sight of her, standing near the metal detectors outside the international boarding area. In her jeans and brightly colored sweater she looked more like a teenager than an air force lieutenant. Even from that distance, he could see her flaming hair hanging loosely on her shoulders.

Why wasn't she in uniform?

WATCHING DONOVAN HURRY toward her, Erin felt her pulse leap with excitement. If only he were running because he cared for her and couldn't wait to see her. But that was foolish. He must think she'd uncovered new information about the assassin and was rushing to find out what. His first words didn't dispel that assumption.

"What's wrong?" he asked, not even breathing hard after his run across the terminal. "Why aren't you in uniform?"

"Because I was fired." Erin forced herself to say the words coldly, with no trace of pain.

He stared at her with such an unbelieving expression that it was almost funny. The lump in her throat disappeared. Thank God he hadn't sympathized, or she would have broken down.

"But that's impossible," he said, his eyebrows raised inquiringly.

She shook her head. "Not according to my division chief. He's having me reassigned outside the Pentagon."

"But, why?" Donovan ran his hand along her arm.

Though Erin knew the gesture was an automatic reaction to her bad news, she found his touch comforting. "Colonel Byrd says I can't work the Irish desk because I have close relatives living in Dublin. But I think that's just an excuse to get rid of me."

His blue eyes searched her face, reaching into her thoughts. "Then your transfer must have something to do with the restricted files you asked for yesterday."

Erin took a quick gulp of air. "That's what I think. Do you have any idea why asking for a couple of files should cause such a drastic reaction?"

"Since you're related to O'Shaughnessy, maybe the CIA thinks you'll jeopardize your stepfather's and my status as informants," he volunteered, his startled expression relaxing into a smile.

"That must be it," Erin agreed. While driving to Dulles Airport, she'd decided not to tell Donovan she knew he was a CIA agent investigating her stepfather. That information might come in handy later.

"But I didn't ask you to meet me because I was fired," she said.

"Then, why?"

Erin saw the puzzlement on his face. "Because I'm terribly worried about my mother."

He glanced toward one of the terminal's big wall clocks. "I've got some time before my flight leaves. Let's have a drink, and you can tell me why you're worried."

Erin waited until they were seated at a tiny table in one corner of a small concourse bar before repeating last night's phone conversation with her mother. When she described the stranger lurking in the distance, Donovan leaned toward her, his intense blue eyes absorbing her every expression.

"I'd feel better if you kept an eye on her," Erin said. "Then you could let me know if anything unusual happens—anything at all." She paused, wishing his alert, interested expression were for *her* and not the situation she was describing. "I feel something's going on that's dangerous for her. This stranger watching her is a part of it."

"She doesn't recognize him?" Donovan asked, his voice warm with concern. "Maybe it's somebody your stepfather hired to keep an eye on her."

"That's possible," Erin admitted. "She hadn't told Patrick. But surely he'd realize she'd be frightened by a strange man spying on her. Don't you think he'd let her know he'd hired a guard for her?"

"Probably."

When Donovan glanced around them, so did Erin. The tables near them were empty, and he sat back in his spindly wrought-iron chair, jiggling the ice around in his drink. She noticed that he'd only taken a sip or two. Obviously he, too, wanted to keep a clear head while they talked.

"Level with me, Erin," he said. "Do you think your stepfather's a threat to your mother?"

"Of course not!" she exclaimed, almost before he'd finished the question. Too quickly, she thought. Warmth crept into her cheeks, and she looked down at her drink, away from his knowing eyes.

"C'mon now, Erin," he said. "If you trust me to keep an eye on your mother, you've got to trust me enough to tell me how you really feel about your stepfather."

"All right, then," she said, feeling as disloyal as a Judas goat. "The thought he might be dangerous did enter my mind. Mom had known Patrick only a couple of months when she married him. She was still upset over losing my father—"

"The general?" Donovan interrupted.

"Of course, the general. He's the only father I've..." She stopped in midsentence. A CIA agent could access all available information about the people involved in his operation. Donovan probably knew almost as much about her personal history as Erin herself, including the part about her birth father.

"You know, don't you?" she asked, not sure whether to be relieved or angry.

He jiggled the ice in his glass again, but didn't lift it to his lips. "That General Meyer adopted you? Yes, it was in one of the newspaper articles I read yesterday afternoon."

Erin knew he was lying about the newspaper article. She'd read everything printed about the general's death. None of the articles mentioned that his daughter was adopted. But she didn't challenge Donovan. If he wanted to keep on playing informant, well and good. She'd use his subterfuge to her advantage later.

"Then you know I'm illegitimate?" she asked, controlling her voice so it didn't quiver.

His blue eyes pierced the distance between them. "I thought it seemed likely. But whatever happened was a long time ago, Erin. Let's focus on the present."

"Then why did you bring up my adoption?" She couldn't keep the sharpness from her voice.

"Because I want you to stop worrying about your mom." His gaze lowered as did his voice. "Now that you know I've done my homework regarding her, maybe you'll trust me to keep an eye on things for you."

Taking a card out of his coat pocket, he wrote something on it. Then he handed it to her. "Here's the phone number at my Dublin apartment. Call me any time you're worried."

Confronted with his obvious concern, Erin's resistance crumbled. She found herself leaning across the table toward him. "If only I could be sure—"

"You can be." There was a faint tremor in his voice as though some emotion had touched him. "At the slightest sign of trouble, I'll call you."

Moving his chair closer to the tiny table, he leaned across toward her. Erin felt an eager affection coming from him. He drew so close she could smell Scotch on his breath from the few sips he'd taken of his drink. An unwelcome surge of excitement lurched through her, but she didn't back away. For an instant she was conscious of the table against her stomach, of her hands clasped tightly in her lap. Then all outside sensation faded.

Cradling her face in his hands, he pressed his lips against hers then gently covered her mouth. With the touch of his lips, a divine sweetness unlike anything she'd ever experienced flowed through her. Parting her lips, she leaned even farther forward to meet him.

For a few brief moments their lips joined, and Erin's veins turned to liquid fire. Never before had she felt such an incredible sense of union with another human being. She forgot where she was, and who she was, only that Donovan was sending spirals of ecstasy through her. When he finally released her, she couldn't believe the passion she'd felt for him with only his hands and his warm, moist mouth touching her face.

"That was goodbye," he said, his voice husky. "I've got a plane to catch."

"I'll come to the boarding area with you." Erin stood up, surprised that her legs were so steady.

"No." He stood, too. "Go talk to your mother and make sure she's okay. I'll call you tomorrow morning when I get in, right after I've checked on her."

For a long moment, Erin stood in the crowded concourse, watching Donovan's broad back until he turned away at the top of the escalator. She knew he'd keep an eye on her mother as he'd promised.

If she'd played right into his hands by asking for help, so much the better, she thought, still shaky from his kiss. Let Donovan try to trap Margaret in whatever operation he was running against Patrick. He'd have extrastrong motivation to keep an eye on her. With a trained CIA agent watching her mother—no matter what his reason—she was bound to be safer.

Not until Erin found a pay phone to call Dublin did she

let herself consider the outlandish notion that her new step-father and—even worse, her mother, now that she was married to him—might really be guilty of a crime. Without strong incriminating evidence, why would a secret government agency be devoting highly expensive resources to an operation against them?

DONOVAN LEANED BACK in his first-class seat and surveyed the Virginia countryside hurtling past his cabin window during takeoff.

She played right into my hands, he thought, still surprised at how well the afternoon had gone. With an *open sesame* to O'Shaughnessy's new wife, he had the entrée he needed to the household. Erin would surely notify her mother that he was a friend. Once he'd gained Margaret's trust, she and her husband would be that much easier to pinpoint as key players in the conspiracy he was investigating.

Strangely, the knowledge that he'd outfoxed Erin brought him no satisfaction. All he could think of was the shell-shocked look on her face when she told him she'd been fired.

Much as Erin had tried to disguise her pain, her bland expression hadn't fooled Donovan. With a black mark like this on her record, her career as an air force officer was over. She'd probably never make captain and would eventually be forced out of the service. He admired her fortitude. Most men and women would have broken down in repeating such devastating news.

Neither could he forget Erin's desperate worry as she related her mother's fear of the stranger lurking in the shadows. Was the stranger tied into the Shamrock conspiracy? Probably. When Donovan ran an operation, he ruled out no possibilities.

If somebody on O'Shaughnessy's staff was behind the conspiracy, that individual might have hired someone to do harm to Margaret should O'Shaughnessy refuse to cooperate. That same individual might have hired Chameleon.

With a start, Donovan realized he'd momentarily ruled out O'Shaughnessy as the culprit behind the conspiracy. *Get real, Donovan,* he told himself, disgusted. Even Erin had finally admitted her stepfather might be a threat to her mother.

Even so, Donovan didn't think O'Shaughnessy had discovered he was with the CIA. Carrying cash to the congressman was too responsible a task to be given to a suspected undercover agent. Chameleon must have been hired by someone else. But who? Very few people on the Shamrock staff knew of Donovan's secret mission to Washington to bribe Wiley.

"Something to drink, sir?"

Donovan looked up into the pale blue eyes of a Russian stewardess. They'd reached cruising altitude.

"Coffee, please," he said.

She offered him a cup of steaming black liquid, with cream and sugar alongside, on a silver tray. Next to Donovan a man in a business suit punched out numbers on a laptop computer.

Taking a sip of his coffee, Donovan tried to return to his analytical line of thought, but he couldn't. He kept seeing Erin's face, her skin glowing with color in last night's cold air, or white with worry the way it had been only minutes earlier. Her image tugged at something deep inside him.

Damn! What was happening to him? Something about Erin Meyer spoke to him in a way no woman had before. Maybe it was the proud way she lifted her chin or the confidence in her stride—he couldn't pinpoint exactly what attracted him most. Or was it her smell: the fresh salty perfume of the Irish Sea with a faint hint of lilies in bloom?

He breathed deeply, trying to recapture her fragrance in the stale cabin air. For a moment he had it, then the scent slipped away, a lost figment of his memory. But he couldn't lose Erin's face. Thank God there would soon be an ocean between them. The last thing he needed right now was an adolescent crush on the stepdaughter of the man he'd been assigned to investigate.

WHEN ERIN HEARD Patrick's butler say that her mother and Mr. O'Shaughnessy were out for the evening, tiny fingers of dread crept down her spine. Not that their absence was unusual. Her mother and stepfather often were out when she called. But something about the definite way the butler pronounced the words made Erin wonder if he were lying.

"Would you mind checking, Robert?" she asked, leaning closer to the mouthpiece of the airport's pay phone. "I thought my mother planned to be home tonight."

"I'd be glad to, Miss." His words were even more definite.

Erin heard a muffled sound as he covered the mouthpiece, then a faraway murmur.

"Someone is checking the bedrooms," he said. "But I saw them go out myself. Would you like to wait for an answer?" Clearly, he was trying to make her think she was wasting both their time.

"Yes." Erin drummed her fingers on the platform holding the telephone book. Maybe she was being unreasonably concerned, but the butler's uppity tone bothered her. Erin had always been sensitive to the emotions of others. And right now she sensed Robert was lying. Or was she imagining it?

"Did they say where they were going?"

Again—a hand placed over the receiver and muffled background noise. "No, Miss. The maid has checked and says they aren't in the house."

"Tell my mother to call me at home as soon as she returns," Erin said, hanging up the receiver.

Back in her condo, she warmed a frozen dinner in the microwave but could force herself to eat only a few bites. When her mother hadn't returned her call by seven, Erin dialed Dublin again. Since it was now midnight in the Irish capital, surely Margaret would be home.

But she wasn't. Mr. O'Shaughnessy had returned to the house alone, the maid said.

Alarmed, Erin asked for Patrick. In his cheerful tenor voice her stepfather explained that Margaret had decided to spend the night with her cousin, Jean Magee.

"I suppose you could call her there if it's important," Patrick said, hesitating. "But the family goes to bed early."

Erin wanted to feel relieved that her mother was at Jean's. But she couldn't shake her apprehension. "My mother's never stayed away from home overnight since you've been married. Why tonight, Patrick?"

Closing her eyes, Erin had an image of Patrick shrugging his fleshy shoulders. Unconsciously, she compared his build to Donovan's. Though Patrick was heavier, they were the same height and had similar athletic frames. The image made her lose concentration and she scolded herself for letting Donovan interrupt.

"When we got home from the Abbey Theater," Patrick answered, "she said she needed some country air."

Erin froze. "You let her drive to the country alone?"

Patrick's high-pitched chuckle came over the phone line. "Did you ever try to stop that mother of yours from doing anything she wanted, Erin?" He paused. "This isn't Washington D.C., girl. In Dublin our roads are safe at any hour."

With a stranger spying on Margaret, Erin didn't believe her mother was truly safe anywhere. But surely Jean would have notified Patrick if she hadn't arrived.

Sighing she told her stepfather good-night and hung up the receiver. She'd call her mother at Jean's first thing tomorrow morning. And Donovan would be back in Ireland by then. She fingered his card in her jeans pocket. If her mother so much as hinted anything was wrong, Erin intended to ask for his help and maybe head to Ireland herself.

AFTER ONE STOP AT Shannon Airport on the Irish Republic's west coast, Donovan's flight continued on to Dublin.

It was still early, not quite six. He'd have time to shower and change at his apartment before meeting O'Shaughnessy.

Before he left Dublin Airport, Donovan dialed Erin's mother. The butler answered. According to him, Mrs. Sullivan was visiting relatives in the country. The household staff had been instructed not to give anybody their name or number over the telephone. Donovan resolved to follow up later, after he'd talked to O'Shaughnessy.

Two hours later, dressed in the dark business suit, white shirt and conservative tie that was the unwritten dress code of Shamrock Construction's home headquarters, Donovan was shown into O'Shaughnessy's private office.

A robust man with a shock of graying brown hair, Erin's stepfather leaned across his broad desk, his hand extended and an expansive smile on his round face. When Donovan shook the proffered hand, it felt soft, cushiony, like a woman's. But the grip was strong.

"Collins tells me you had some unexpected adventures this last trip." O'Shaughnessy motioned to a couple of leather chairs near the floor-to-ceiling bookcases across the room. Settling his bulk in the nearest chair, he nodded toward another beside it. "He said there were aspects of your trip you needed to discuss with me in private."

"That's right, sir." Donovan lowered himself to the chair. Like the rest of the room, it was well-worn but comfortable.

"Call me Shawn," O'Shaughnessy said. "You've been on the legal staff what? A year now? Time to call the boss by his first name."

"Thanks, Shawn." Donovan matched O'Shaughnessy's smile, suspecting the other man's was as phony as his own. O'Shaughnessy's cherubic round face and big-toothed smile would charm Godzilla. But Donovan's trained eye spotted a hard insensitivity that most people probably missed on first meeting.

"So what's this between you and my stepdaughter?"

Before he answered, Donovan let his gaze swing deliberately around the room. The door to the outer office wasn't securely closed. He got up and shut it, then returned to his chair.

When he spoke, he lowered his voice. "I'm sure Collins told you what happened at the cathedral and later that night at Georgetown so I won't—"

"Tell me one thing," O'Shaughnessy interrupted. "How did my stepdaughter know about the planned attack at the cathedral?"

Donovan lowered his voice even more. "From an intelligence report. I tried to find out what kind of report, but that's all she'd tell me."

Most of the breath seemed to leave the other man's body as he expelled a mighty sigh. "Of course. Now I remember. She's with that damned military intelligence agency in Washington. That's how she got the report."

His reaction seemed so genuine Donovan almost believed he'd forgotten where Erin worked. But that wasn't logical. A brilliant man like O'Shaughnessy would never forget his stepdaughter was an intelligence analyst. Could he be pretending so he could hide the fact that he knew what the message said?

The alarm button in Donovan's brain flashed crimson. If O'Shaughnessy knew about the message, then he must be the one who had ordered his assassination. Maybe trusting Donovan with the cash delivery to the congressman had been a ploy to cover the real purpose of the trip: his own death. If so, why had the assassin tried again that night, when Donovan wasn't carrying the cash?

"At first I thought the motive was robbery," he said. "But when there was another attack that night, I realized the motive must have been something else—maybe to kill me."

Donovan watched the older man's face redden with anger.

"Damned fool must have made a mistake coming after

you the second time." Donovan's internal alarm screeched even louder. Could the assassin have been acting against orders with his attack in Georgetown? If so, how could O'Shaughnessy know unless he gave the order?

As though he needed time to think, the older man settled back in his chair and busied himself stuffing tobacco in his pipe and lighting it. Fragrant smoke drifted around Donovan's head.

O'Shaughnessy puffed again, then cleared his throat. "The fool must have thought you were wealthy."

"Then you think the motive for both attacks was robbery?"

"Of course," O'Shaughnessy replied. "What else could it be?"

He's trying too hard to make the motive look like robbery, Donovan thought, all his senses still on red alert. Every instinct in his brain was telling him O'Shaughnessy was behind the attack. *Bail out,* his instincts screamed. *Better to fail at this operation than to end up dead.* But he couldn't give up without one last try to gain O'Shaughnessy's confidence.

"Maybe the attacks were tied in with that intelligence report your stepdaughter received," Donovan said.

"She wouldn't tell you what it said?"

"No. But since Erin *is* an intelligence analyst, and a good one," Donovan responded, "she took one more step. That's what I wanted to talk to you about in private."

O'Shaughnessy's alert blue eyes narrowed and his skin crinkled into crow's-feet beside them. They were the only lines on his remarkably smooth complexion. "What'd she do? Run some kind of check on you?"

"Not only on me," Donovan said. "She asked the CIA for your file, too."

The older man's gasp was so pronounced that Donovan doubted it was faked. "What did she find out?"

"The agency's got restricted files on both of us, Shawn."

"No kidding!" Again, genuine surprise. Either Erin

hadn't told her mother yet about the restricted files, or Margaret Sullivan had kept her mouth shut when she learned about them.

"Erin thinks we're both CIA informants," Donovan explained. "My own view is that somebody found out about our payoffs to congressmen and other officials and commissioned the CIA to get the goods on us and the people getting the baksheesh." Donovan didn't believe anything of the sort, but a bribery investigation was a passable explanation for the restricted files, a reason that didn't reveal the conspiracy.

Shawn O'Shaughnessy's mouth dropped open. "Payoffs? What are you talking about, Donovan? Shamrock Construction doesn't have to bribe anybody to get contracts. We're the best damned company in the business."

Donovan couldn't tell whether he was pretending ignorance about the bribes. An hour later, after he'd described the St. Patrick's Day cash delivery to O'Shaughnessy in nauseating detail, he was still uncertain. Finally, Donovan returned to his office across town.

To his astonishment, Jim Collins, the man who'd given Donovan his orders about the cash delivery, was gone. His staff said that he'd been transferred to the Shamrock office in Dhahran, Saudi Arabia.

But Donovan wasn't fooled. Collins had to go, no matter how loyal he was, to prove O'Shaughnessy knew nothing about the bribes. As far as Donovan was concerned, Collins's departure proved nothing of the sort. And it certainly didn't clear O'Shaughnessy of masterminding the conspiracy. The bribes were small potatoes compared to the conspiracy. Nothing O'Shaughnessy could do—short of firing the entire staff and closing the company—would change Donovan's conviction that he was guilty.

Before Donovan left the office, pleading fatigue from his all-night trip, he asked the secretary to locate Ms. Sullivan. He had a message for her, he said, from Erin. When the secretary called the residence, someone told her Ms. Sullivan was staying with her cousin, Jean Magee, for a few days. Ms. Sullivan wanted to rest, the secretary reported, and had asked that she not be disturbed. Anyone who called would probably be told she wasn't there.

With Mrs. Magee's phone number in his coat pocket, Donovan returned to his apartment. Though his instincts were screaming that it was time to bail out of this operation, his stubborn ears refused to listen. He'd never failed at anything important, and he didn't intend to begin now. Maybe his confidential report about the restricted files would be enough to restore O'Shaughnessy's confidence in him, and he could continue with his investigation.

After hanging his coat on a hook near the hall door, he dialed Jean Magee's number. No, he was told, Ms. Sullivan was not there, had not been there for a week.

Was Jean Magee telling the truth, or was she simply protecting her cousin's privacy?

"I've just returned from Washington and have a message from her daughter," Donovan said, hoping this incentive would bring Margaret Sullivan to the phone.

Mrs. Magee's pause was so long, he thought she might have hung up.

Finally she spoke. "I'm sorry, Mr. Donovan. Margaret Sullivan isn't here." The conviction he'd heard earlier in her voice had disappeared.

Donovan kept his voice carefully controlled when he thanked Mrs. Magee. He dialed the O'Shaughnessy residence again and was again informed that Ms. Sullivan had not returned from the country.

Donovan waited no longer. From a pay phone at the O'Connell Street general post office, he called Erin.

Chapter Seven

Erin was still sound asleep when the telephone rang. After tossing and turning fitfully most of the night, she had finally drifted off into a deep slumber. Through a numbing mist, she heard the ringing, like an emergency alarm sounding outside her window.

The phone rang again—and again. Finally awake, she jerked upright. The illuminated face of her bedside clock showed five minutes to five. Quickly she turned on the light and reached for the receiver.

It was the operator asking if she would accept a collect call from Mr. Dan Donovan in Dublin.

"Yes, yes, of course," she said, her nerves tensing with dread. Something must be wrong. If he'd been calling to reassure her that her mother was okay, he wouldn't have bothered to use a pay phone.

"What's happened?" she asked, as soon as she heard his voice.

"I don't want you to get upset, Erin," he said, "but I can't locate your mother."

Taking a deep breath, Erin told herself to stay calm. Donovan must have called Patrick's house, and, rightly, the staff had refused to give him Jean Magee's name and number.

"Patrick told me she stayed with our cousin, Jean Magee, last night," she said, hoping Donovan's failure to talk to Margaret was the only reason he was calling. "I was going to ring her and talk to my mother when I got up this morning."

"Do it now," Donovan said. "Call me back afterward. I'll give you the number of this phone."

Erin's cozy bed suddenly felt cold as the inside of a refrigerator. "Have you already talked to Jean?"

"Yes," he said. Erin pictured his strong chin and the blue eyes that seemed to search her mind. Of course he would have got Jean's number and called her first.

"Your cousin said she hadn't seen your mother since last week," he added.

"*Last week!*" Erin knew she was screeching, but she couldn't help herself. "Patrick said she drove out there last night."

"Maybe she changed her mind en route. Why don't you call your cousin? She might tell you more than she did me."

Promising to call back, Erin hung up. Rising, she put on a blue terry robe and her favorite furry slippers, then hurried to the den. Though the room was intended as a bedroom, Erin had installed bookcases along one wall and placed a desk parallel with the opposite wall so the light from the window shone across her shoulders. At this hour, ominous gray light oozed into the room from the dimness outside. Shuddering, she pulled the draperies, shutting out the bleakness.

At her desk, she found the number and punched it into the phone. Jean herself answered. After Erin explained that she was Margaret Sullivan's daughter and exchanged a few pleasantries with this cousin she'd never met, she asked for her mother.

"Why, she's not here, darlin'," Jean said. "You're the fourth person who's called this morning asking for her."

Familiar fingers of ice crept down Erin's spine again. "Are you saying she did not spend last night with you?" Her words came out sounding squeaky and forced.

"I haven't seen her since last week," Jean said. "Is something wrong? Has she disappeared?"

"I don't know." Erin swallowed the panic rising in her throat. "Who were the other three people who called?"

"Dun Aengus, of course. And two men who didn't give their names." Jean's voice rose. "Tell me if something's wrong, Erin. Dun Aengus didn't think so, but now, talking to you, I'm scared."

Two men called besides Patrick, Erin thought. One was Donovan. But who was the other? "What did you tell them?"

"Same thing I'm telling you. I haven't seen her since last week and when I talked to her on the phone yesterday, she said nothing about spending the night." Jean's voice had assumed the same anxious tone as Erin's. "Dùn Aengus said not to worry, that she'd gone to another cousin's. But I've called everybody, and nobody's seen her."

No longer able to breathe normally, Erin gasped into the phone. "Something's happened to her."

"You may be right," Jean replied. "Come to Dublin, Erin. Your mother needs you." Her words ended in a whisper.

"I'm on my way," Erin said grimly.

Before she could hang up the receiver, Jean spoke again. "Don't tell anyone you're coming."

Erin's heart skipped a beat. "Do you think Patrick—Dun Aengus—had something to do with her disappearance?"

"No, of course not." In Jean's whispered words, Erin heard doubt that made her wonder if her cousin was being completely honest. "But there are advantages in arriving unexpectedly. If you catch Dun Aengus off guard soon as you get here, maybe he'll let something slip about what's going on."

Resolving to take Jean's advice, Erin promised to call when she reached Dublin.

"Come to see me, instead of calling," her cousin urged. "After you've heard what Dun Aengus has to say, we can compare notes face to face." That's when Erin knew Jean was holding something back. The insight clinched Erin's decision to go.

After hanging up, she dialed the number of the pay phone Donovan had just given her. "I'm coming to Dublin," she announced, as soon as she heard his rich baritone voice. "Jean thinks something may have happened to my mother, and so do I."

"You can't come here, Erin," he protested. "It's too dangerous."

She heard a strong note of male authority in his voice, and her independent spirit rebelled. "Don't tell me what I can and can't do, Donovan. I'm coming."

When he spoke again his tone had changed. "Please don't come, Erin. You'll be putting us both in harm's way."

Somewhat mollified, she asked why.

"Because I don't trust your stepfather. He may have hired the assassin. And if your mother's disappeared, he's probably behind that, too."

"I don't believe it," Erin objected, although her trust in Patrick had slipped significantly after her conversation with Jean. "Don't try to talk me out of this, Donovan. I'm coming and there's nothing you can do to stop me."

She heard his tense breathing, but no words. Finally, he spoke. "Then don't tell him you're coming. I'll meet you."

"Deal," she said. "I'd intended to surprise him."

"Good girl." He sounded surprised that she'd already thought of it. "So I'll expect you first thing tomorrow morning on Aeroflot's afternoon flight from Dulles?"

"Wrong," she said, recalling flight schedules to Ireland from the times her mother had flown there. "Aeroflot's not scheduled today, but there's an Aer Lingus flight from New York at nine this morning. It arrives at Dublin around ten tonight."

"You'll never make it."

"Of course I will. The shuttle leaves from National for

New York City every few minutes on weekday mornings. I'll have hours to spare."

He didn't argue. "Look for me. I'll be waiting for you."

She'd see Donovan again later today. When Erin hung up, the fear in her heart for her mother was mixed with eager anticipation.

INSTEAD OF HOURS to spare, Erin found she had only minutes.

Though it was early morning, traffic backed up across Washington's Fourteenth Street Bridge forcing her to take a later shuttle. In New York City, the transfer from La Guardia Airport, where the shuttle landed, to Kennedy took twice as long as she expected.

Rolling her one suitcase behind her, Erin ran all the way to the Aer Lingus gate, desperately hoping Donovan wasn't right with his prediction that she'd never make it. Thank the Lord she'd worn running shoes and jeans.

She bought a first-class ticket at the gate, walked aboard, and the flight took off. Six and a half hours later it touched down at Shannon for forty-five minutes; an hour and a half after that, the flight landed at Dublin Airport, ten minutes early.

Donovan was waiting near a cluster of people by the Aer Lingus off-ramp. Erin's heart swelled at the sight of him. Though obviously trying not to attract attention, he managed to look even sexier than she remembered. In his leather jacket and jeans, carrying a black umbrella, he fit perfectly with her mental image of the ideal man.

Annoyed with such thoughts, she cleared her mind of the image. Donovan was far from perfect. Her face burned every time she thought of his cavalier reaction to their first kiss.

He waved when he saw her, but instead of coming to meet her, he kept to the fringes of the crowd. Hurrying toward him, Erin noticed the way he mingled with the others waiting at the gate, melting in despite his over-six-foot height and linebacker shoulders. Every couple of seconds he glanced from one side to the other, as if watching for someone.

A wave of sheer, black fright swept over her. Donovan was showing classic signs of a man trying to avoid a pursuer. The assassin. Was he about to strike again?

As she drew closer, Erin recognized something different about Donovan tonight. His forehead was creased with lines, and his familiar roguish smile was gone, replaced by a scowl that gave him a concentrated, serious air. She caught her breath. If anything, his darker side seemed even more attractive than the rogue she was determined to resist.

Rolling her suitcase along behind, she threaded her way through knots of people toward where he stood. Would his hello be as passionate as his goodbye yesterday at Dulles?

As she hurried up to him, his frown disappeared and his gaze traveled over her face and searched her eyes. "God, I'm glad to see you."

"Yes," she murmured, feeling like a teenager on a first date. Close enough to see the shadow of his emerging beard, she imagined its roughness against her own skin. For a breathless moment, she thought he might sweep her into his arms, and her pulse quickened.

But after a heartbeat's hesitation, he reluctantly grabbed the handle of her suitcase with one hand and her arm with the other. "Dammit, Erin, we've got to get out of here."

She swung into step beside him, half running to keep up. "What's happened? Is the assassin after you?"

"Somebody is," he said grimly. "My apartment was ransacked while I was out this morning calling you."

"Ransacked!" Her heart skipped a beat. "What were they after?"

"God only knows. I didn't wait around to find out." When he glanced down at her, his expression was tight with strain.

"You mean you've left your apartment for good?" She struggled to control her alarm.

"You bet. I changed cars and don't think I was followed here, but whoever trashed the place might be watching the airport." Though moving rapidly while he spoke, Donovan's eyes constantly swept the terminal.

No wonder he wanted to get out of here. Erin waited until they were past a family with several small children before she spoke again. "You shouldn't have come. I could have got to my stepfather's house on my own." Already breathing heavily from their quick pace, she had to force the words out.

"You can't go to O'Shaughnessy's house." Donovan's voice rang with authority. "I'll take you to your cousin."

"You'll do no such thing!" she exclaimed, annoyed by his bossy tone. "Jean's place is out in the country. They'll be in bed now. Besides, I need to talk to Patrick immediately—find out what he knows." Deliberately Erin slowed her pace, forcing Donovan to slow, too. "With somebody after you, you should have asked someone else to meet me."

"There's no one I trust enough."

Recognizing his subtle compliment, Erin fought the warmth coursing through her. "Not even someone from the embassy?" she asked quietly. It was time to confront him with her suspicion that he was a CIA agent.

They'd reached the terminal's door. Outside a cold, steady rain fell on the road and parking lot across from it. Opening the umbrella, Donovan held it over their heads and started toward the lot.

"The U.S. Embassy?" He managed to appear puzzled, but Erin knew he was faking.

"Yes, of course." She stepped back as a car passed, splashing water near the curb.

"Since I agreed to become an informant, the only embassy officer I know is the man I report to." Handing Erin the umbrella, Donovan quickly led the way through aisles of parked cars. "Other than paying me for information, he's not in the business of doing me favors."

Erin could stomach the pretense no longer. "Come off it, Donovan. We both know you're an agent, not an informant."

"Lower your voice," he whispered over his shoulder. "And don't say anything more till we're in the car."

Silently she followed him to a small station wagon, and let him help her inside. After he'd put her suitcase in back, he got in and started the engine. Half holding her breath, Erin waited for him to confess.

SO SHE'S FIGURED it out already, Donovan thought. For both their sakes he'd hoped she'd be slower to add up the facts. He should have known better. She was one bright lady and with her intelligence background, she'd quickly put the pieces together.

He swung out into traffic. "What makes you think I'm an agent?"

"I don't just *think,* I *know.*"

She sounded so positive he didn't waste time arguing.

"You're right," he conceded, wondering if she'd also guessed his main purpose in life the past few years had been to put her stepfather behind bars—and her mother, too, if she was involved.

"Now tell me how you knew."

Donovan heard her expel her breath in a long sigh. For an unrealistic moment he wished he were close enough to catch her breath, to feel its warmth on his face.

"I knew after I'd talked to my division chief," she explained. "He'd obviously been ordered to get me off the Ireland desk immediately so he fired me for a trumped-up reason."

Donovan heard her voice quiver and knew she was still hurting from the shock of her sudden dismissal. Impulsively he reached out and touched her arm.

After a moment's pause, she continued. "The only logical reason for my agency to get rid of me so rapidly was to protect a covert operation. I put two and two together and came up with you as a CIA agent running an operation against Shamrock Construction. Since I'm part of the family, somebody thought I might give your operation away. The best way to avoid that was to fire me.''

"You're probably right," he agreed, pushing aside an unwarranted tremor of guilt. "My people were trying to protect my operation by having you fired."

"Just what is your operation?" she asked. The swishing rhythm of the windshield wipers accented her lyrical voice. Donovan knew she was watching his every expression.

He didn't hesitate. "I can't tell you about my operation, Erin. For your own sake, it's better you don't know."

"Do you think somebody at Shamrock found out you're an agent?" Her voice lowered. "You don't think I told them—"

"Of course not," he said, giving her a quick glance. "But I'm sure they know. That's why I decided to go to ground."

On sober reflection, he wasn't at all sure she hadn't given him away. Yesterday, after her meeting with her division chief, she'd figured out Donovan was an agent. This morning O'Shaughnessy had appeared hostile. Less than an hour later Donovan's apartment had been ransacked, apparently by someone hunting for clues to his operation. God knows what would have happened to him had he been there.

Had Erin called her mother and warned her that Donovan was a CIA agent? Was that why Margaret Sullivan had disappeared so conveniently? Could Erin's mother be on a secret errand to cover up her new husband's role in the conspiracy?

HE SUSPECTS ME of betraying him. A warm flush heated Erin's cheeks. She prayed the headlights from the oncoming cars wouldn't reveal her hot face.

But why was she blushing? She had nothing to be ashamed of. She'd saved his life. Why would she deliberately put him in danger?

"I said nothing to anybody," she declared defiantly. "Neither about your being an informant nor an agent. Not to my mother. Not to Patrick. Not to anybody."

"Simmer down," he said, obviously hearing the anger in her voice. "Nobody's accusing you of anything."

Erin held her tongue. The more she protested, the guiltier she'd appear. "What's your new phone number?" she asked, to change the subject.

He shook his head. "Sorry, the phone's not connected, and I'm not giving out the address for obvious reasons."

If she'd wanted proof he didn't trust her, there it was. She bit her tongue so she wouldn't blurt out something she'd be sorry for. After all, wasn't this what she'd wanted all along? A barrier between them that couldn't easily be breached? Well, she had got her wish. So why was she feeling so depressed?

"Then I guess I won't be seeing much of you while I'm here." Erin tried to keep her tone light and failed miserably. Until that moment, she hadn't realized how much she'd looked forward to being with him.

"Oh, you'll be seeing me, all right," he said matter-of-factly. "I'll help you find your mother." His gaze challenged hers.

"I don't see how since there's no way to call you." Her disappointment showed, but she didn't care. Between being scared to death her mother was in trouble, and being hurt by Donovan's lack of trust, she was beyond caring if he spotted something as unimportant as her disappointment at not seeing him.

"We'll arrange a signal," he said. "If you need me or have information about your mother, hang a scarf outside your window. I'll get in touch as soon afterward as it's safe for us both."

At first she thought he was kidding, his plan sounded so amateurish. But one look at his sober face told her he was dead serious.

"Patrick has guards and dogs," she said. "How will you get on the grounds so you can see the scarf?"

"Let me worry about that."

Stealing a quick glance, Erin saw that his high-voltage smile was back in place. But now that she'd caught a glimpse of his darker side, she spotted something she'd missed before: a cynical edge to his bold good looks. His smile wasn't so much charming as distrustful; his lifted eyebrow not humorous, but mocking.

He trusts no one, she thought. Not me, not the people he works with, no one. Suddenly the barrier between them seemed as high as the spiked ten-foot-high iron fence Erin saw as they approached Patrick's property on Donegal Road.

LOCATED NEAR PHOENIX Park where both the President of Ireland and the U.S. Ambassador have official residences, Patrick's house was surrounded by several acres of landscaped grounds. Old-fashioned gas lamps matching those in the park lined the lightly graveled road leading to the mansion.

"Sure you want to stay at your stepfather's tonight?" Donovan asked, his question a subtle warning. Concern and caution mingled in the glance he gave her. "I can't drive you up there. You'll have to call and have someone come get you."

"I know." Erin eyed the call box beside the deceptively artistic iron gate across the road. It was probably made of forged steel and strong enough to stop anything short of a tank.

Near the box was a smaller pedestrian gate. Though lighted by gas lamps on either side of the road, the entire gate area appeared dark and forbidding in the cold, steady rain. Suddenly the car's warm interior, with Donovan sitting solidly beside her, enfolded Erin like her down-filled comforter on a chilly morning.

"You'd be safer at your cousin's," he said quietly,

seeming to sense her hesitation. "You could stay with her tonight and call your stepfather in the morning."

Erin took a deep breath to give herself courage. "No. I need to see where Patrick's coming from. If he had anything to do with Mom's disappearance, I'll find out. I swear I will." It was a solemn vow. Erin's throat choked with sudden tears. No one was going to hurt her precious mother. No one.

"Intend to do a little sleuthing, do you?"

Erin heard the kidding tone in Donovan's baritone voice. But now that she knew him better, she recognized a faint hint of approval in the teasing—as well as a desire to lighten a tense moment for her.

"You bet," she returned, inordinately pleased by his unspoken regard. "I'll find out what's happened to her if I have to tear that house apart." Her voice came out strong and assured.

"Good girl." There was an undeniable warmth to his words.

Glancing at him, Erin caught a spark of some undefinable emotion in his eyes. For a brief moment her eyes held his. Then she forced herself to turn away. His eyes were dark blue pools to drown in. If she didn't move now, she never would. She reached for the door handle, but his hand— touching her arm—stopped her.

"Last chance to back out." He caught her arm and held it, the warmth from his hand radiating through her body.

She didn't pull herself away, couldn't—couldn't stop the tremor racing through her at his touch. For a moment she was unable to speak. Then, gathering herself together she said softly but firmly, "I can't back out, Donovan. Too much depends on what I can find out in the next few hours. My mother's already been missing for too long."

Slowly, reluctantly, he released her arm. "Remember the scarf if you want to see me. It may take awhile, but eventually I'll be in touch."

Erin didn't dare meet his gaze. If she did she'd be in his

arms, her fragile resolve damaged beyond repair. He seemed to sense her hesitation. She felt his hands on her face, tilting her head upward, forcing her to look directly into his eyes. Trapped in his gaze, she caught her breath.

"Since I can't talk you out of going, maybe this will change your mind." He pulled her roughly to him. His hand cradled the back of her neck, keeping her near as his mouth met hers.

She tried to back away, and found she couldn't. His lips were soft, but demanding, and she could no more resist than stop her blood from flowing through her veins. Twining her arms around his neck, she pressed against him and returned his kiss, desperately, passionately, knowing it meant good-bye. Much as she wanted to stay with him in the warm, secure car, she knew she couldn't.

Reluctantly she pulled away from him and reached for the door handle. Jerking the door open, she got out. He didn't try to stop her. Cold rain hit her face and sluiced down the back of her neck.

Scowling, Donovan thrust the umbrella out the open car door. "If you must go, take this."

Gratefully, she opened and lifted it over her head.

"I'll get your bag from the back." He jumped out and brought it to her.

For a long minute he stood facing her, his heavy brows drawn downward in a frown. Reading his disapproval, she tightened her resolve.

"We could still go to your cousin's," he said. "Then, tomorrow, she could come with you to see your stepfather. There's safety in numbers, you know."

Tempting though Donovan's suggestion was, Erin knew it wouldn't work. "I'll find out much more staying in Patrick's house a few nights."

"You're probably right," he conceded. "But I hate to let you go."

A car, the first one since they'd turned onto Donegal Road, cruised slowly toward them.

Cursing under his breath, Donovan put his arm around Erin's waist and swung her around toward the gate so the car's occupants couldn't see their faces. At any moment Erin expected to hear gunfire, to feel Donovan's grip on her waist loosen, to watch his big body topple to the ground. She held her breath, waiting.

The car slowed, then continued past, its headlights staring beacons in the rainy semidarkness. Slowly Erin expelled her breath. It was time to say goodbye.

"You've got to go," she said, turning toward the call box.

"I'll wait until someone comes for you." He acted as reluctant to leave as she was to see him go.

"No. I'll be fine." Holding the umbrella over her head with one hand and pulling her bag with the other, she went to the box. She punched a button and a male voice answered. "Glenkillan House. How may we be of service?"

"This is Erin Meyer, Margaret Sullivan's daughter." She glanced over her shoulder. Donovan still stood near the car in the steady rain, his dark hair plastered to his forehead, and water streaming down his leather jacket. Why didn't he go? Lifting a hand, she motioned him to leave. He didn't move.

"I'm at the gate on foot," she said into the speaker. "Can someone come and pick me up?"

"Of course, Miss Meyer." The voice on the intercom showed no surprise at her unexpected appearance. "A car will be dispatched to fetch you. The pedestrian gate lock has been released. You may enter at will."

Uneasily Erin shifted the umbrella to one side and glanced around her. With what seemed state-of-the-art security surrounding the grounds, was a surveillance camera watching her every move? Her apprehension changed to alarm. In the semidarkness, could a camera spot Donovan? She flew to him.

"You've got to leave," she whispered, not knowing if

the intercom system could pick up their voices. "There may be a camera watching."

"There is," he said, in his normal voice. "See it up there on the gaslight across the road to the house?"

Peering in the direction he pointed, Erin made out a small black box designed to blend with the lamp's boxy structure. "Can they see us?"

He shook his head. "It's focused on the gate area. We're out of range."

Headlights appeared through the trees surrounding the residence. "Someone's coming for me right now. You've got to go."

He took her hand in both of his, and gazed into her eyes. Erin caught her breath at the strange eager look she saw in them. Eagerness and something else. Was it fear for her?

"Don't trust him, Erin. No matter what he says."

Donovan's warning sent shudders through her. What did he think Patrick would do?

The headlights burst from the trees and headed down the gravel road straight toward them.

He squeezed her hand again. "And remember the scarf." Releasing her, he climbed into his car. After he started the engine, it moved discreetly down the street, turning the corner just as the house vehicle reached the gate.

Watching him go, ice spread through Erin's stomach. Who should she trust? Donovan, the roguish CIA agent trying to trap her stepfather in some sort of conspiracy? Or Patrick, the man her mother had loved enough to marry?

The gate swung open. The car drove up to her, and Patrick himself jumped out of the driver's side.

With his curly graying brown hair framing his round, good-natured face, he looked every bit as congenial as he had when she'd last seen him in Washington. Only this time he wasn't smiling.

"Erin! Thank God you've come. I've been trying to call you." His tenor Irish brogue seemed hoarse with emotion. "Quick, get in the car. Your mother's been kidnapped."

Chapter Eight

Erin nervously got in the front seat next to Patrick, icy fear twisted around her heart. "Let me see the ransom note."

Turning the car around, he headed back through the gate. "There's been no note, Erin," he replied, his round face grimly distraught in the soft light from the dash. "But your mother was sighted with a stranger yesterday near Mullingar, about an hour's drive northwest of Dublin. I'm sure she's been kidnapped."

"A stranger?" A tight band closed around Erin's chest as she remembered the lurking man her mother had described.

"She was in a car headed west. A man was driving." Patrick's normally jovial tone was edged with anger. "If anything's happened to my Margaret, I'll throttle the beast who did it with my own two hands."

"Who saw them?" Erin gasped, fighting her heart-slamming panic. Had her mother told Patrick about the man watching her?

"A friend." Though his answer was noncommittal, Patrick glowered with rage. "I'm sure 'twas my Margaret. By all that's holy, I'll get her back if it's the last thing I do."

They'd reached the grove of evergreen trees surrounding the mansion. In spite of his wrathful words, Erin sensed he'd dodged her question purposefully. Had he already hired someone to find her mother? But if an investigator was the *friend* who had spotted her near Mullingar, why hadn't he rescued her?

A more frightening scenerio plunged into Erin's mind. Could Patrick himself be responsible for her mother's disappearance? *Perhaps he's lying about the stranger to throw me off the track and make me believe his kidnapping story.* The very thought sent chills racing across her back.

"But your *friend* didn't recognize the stranger?" she asked, unable to keep the suspicion from her voice.

"Of course not, girl. If he had, he'd be behind bars now." He'd barely finished speaking when he turned toward Erin, a half smile of apology on his round face. "Sorry to be so abrupt. I've not been myself since your mother left last night for her cousin's. Then to have her snatched away like this…"

Though he seemed sincerely troubled, Erin couldn't dispel her suspicion that Patrick was somehow responsible for her mother's disappearance. "Did Mom tell you about the man watching her?" she asked, watching him closely to gauge his reaction.

The car lurched suddenly forward, wheels spinning, as Patrick's foot came down hard on the gas pedal. He corrected immediately and the car slowed. "What are you saying, girl? What man?"

From Patrick's nervous reaction, Erin guessed he didn't know about the limping stranger. "The last time we talked on the phone, Mom mentioned that she'd seen a man watching her. I thought maybe he was someone you'd hired as a bodyguard. But she said no, she was sure you'd have told her."

"She was right. But why didn't she tell me herself?" Patrick sounded more puzzled than afraid for Margaret.

"She didn't want to worry you." Erin's eyes filled with tears as she remembered the times her mother had carried heavy burdens alone—like when she thought she had cancer. Not until the biopsy came back negative did she tell Erin or her husband.

"Not worry me?" Patrick's voice rose. "What's wrong with the woman?"

He raved on, but Erin barely heard him. They'd emerged from the grove of fir trees and were headed toward a rectangular mansion that rose above the surrounding landscape like an ancient stone tomb. Through the film of rain on the windshield, the place looked oddly menacing, in spite of its obvious opulence.

Already depressed by what had happened, she felt shivers of dread race through her. With nearly every window dark, her stepfather's house reminded Erin of the luxurious walled-in palace in Poe's "Masque of the Red Death," the tomb no one escaped from alive. She shuddered, half wishing she'd taken Donovan's advice and gone to her cousin's country house for her first night in Ireland. But that would only have postponed her arrival here. Intuitively she knew she'd find the answer to her mother's disappearance in the great house hazily visible through the steady rain.

Patrick drove down the circular drive and stopped in front of the massive front door. "Welcome to Glenkillan House," he said, his round face a sober mask. "I'm sorry your first visit isn't under happier circumstances."

Still shivering, Erin peered up past tall windows toward the flat roof three stories up. It was ringed by a balustrade matching that on top of covered walkways extending from either side of the house. Supported by arches shaped like the windows, the walkways led to outbuildings—presumably garages and servants' quarters.

A uniformed man with an umbrella appeared outside Erin's door. He helped her from the car, doing his best to protect her from the steady rain. On the driver's side, a second servant assisted her stepfather.

"They'll bring your bag to your room," Patrick said, leading Erin to the covered portico, which was supported by four two-story-high columns. A tall, middle-aged man, also in uniform, opened the front door.

"This is Miss Meyer, Robert," Patrick said. "Erin, Rob-

ert, my butler. If you need anything while you're here, he's
the man to ask.''

"It will be a pleasure, Miss Meyer."

Good at distinguishing voices, Erin recognized the nasal
tone she'd heard many times on the telephone. But the butler's congenial words didn't match the cold, hard look in
his black eyes. How had her mother dealt with this man?
she wondered. Visualizing her mother, another sick stab of
loss struck her. *Mom, where are you? What made you leave
so suddenly?*

With an effort, Erin met the butler's gaze. "Thank you,
Robert, I'll be sure to call if I need you."

He bowed slightly, from the waist. Patrick, standing next
to the butler, shrugged off his rain-spotted dressing gown
and handed it to him. Underneath he wore a white shirt,
open at the neck, with navy suspenders and dark pants.

"Bring me a dry robe, Robert," he said. "We'll be in
the library."

Turning away from the two men, Erin pictured her
mother in the house's lush interior. She saw her coming
down the wide white staircase, its walls lavishly decorated
with rococo plasterwork. Or reading in the luxurious blue-
and-white salon. Or sitting at the head of the table in the
immense dining room. The table, with chairs for ten, could
easily have seated twenty.

Fighting tears, Erin handed her coat to an apple-cheeked
maid who appeared from nowhere when the butler beckoned.

"Take the coat to the gold bedroom along with Miss
Meyer's suitcase," Robert told the girl.

Her eyes blurry, Erin followed Patrick through the salon
into the library. Though somewhat smaller than the other
rooms, it, too, had a high rococo ceiling and the spacious-
ness of a so-called *great house*. But the dark mahogany
walls and bookcases gave the room an ominous closed-in
feeling, one that was intensified by the clutter of tables and
red leather chairs and couches. One lamp burned near the

fireplace, its colored glass shade casting grotesque shadows on the inlaid-wood tabletop where it sat.

Mom wouldn't have liked this room, Erin thought uneasily, unable to visualize her mother here. Dark and depressing, the library exuded a sinister ambience, as though evil schemes had been contrived in this place.

Patrick nodded toward two red leather chairs near a marble fireplace with a wood fire blazing within. An acrid smoky smell lingered in the air.

"Make yourself comfortable." Patrick lowered himself into one of the chairs—from its well-worn appearance, his favorite. "Is there anything you'd like to eat or drink? Robert can see to it, if there is."

When she shook her head, he took a Sherlock-Holmes-style pipe from the table between the chairs and filled the bowl with tobacco. "Do you mind if I smoke?"

From the confident way he tamped the tobacco into the bowl, Erin knew he didn't expect her to object. Though her eyes were still blurry with unshed tears, she pasted on as wide a smile as she could manage. "No, my father smoked a pipe. It never bothered me."

Patrick held a lighted match to the tobacco and inhaled, then sent perfect rings of fragrant smoke curling into the air. "Smoking doesn't bother your mother, so I didn't think it would bother you." Lines appeared on his forehead. "I'm glad you've come, Erin. We need to put our heads together and figure out how we're going to get your mother safely home."

He paused, studying her with a puckish expression. Erin wondered what he was thinking, if he were really as worried about her mother as he claimed.

"But first," he said, "tell me about this intelligence work you do. One of our company lawyers, Dan Donovan, tells me you saved his life by interpreting information you read in a confidential report."

Donovan. The mere mention of his name brought sensual memories to Erin of his hands touching her, of his lips against hers: thoughts she'd rather forget. How much had he told Patrick? *As little as possible,* she decided, determined not to betray him. Rogue though he was, he'd trusted her enough to tell her he was a CIA agent. She'd never reveal that to anyone.

In general terms she described her work as a military intelligence analyst and told Patrick she'd guessed someone might be killed from the terminology in a routine report she'd received. When he tried to pin her down, she told him the same thing she'd told Donovan: that the report was classified and she couldn't reveal specific wording.

"And that's all there was to it, then?" His light blue eyes squinted at her through the prismatic glow from the table lamp. The shade's colored glass gave his face an odd greenish cast. "Just a report with some vague clues about an assassination?"

She nodded, withholding information about the restricted files, Donovan's CIA connection, and the fact that she'd been fired to protect his operation.

Robert appeared with a blue robe, and helped Patrick put it on. He went on speaking as though the butler weren't there. "Are you sure you're not leaving something out?"

"Positive." Looking her stepfather straight in the eye, she hoped the reflection from the blazing fire muted the blush on her cheeks. She didn't like lying to Patrick, but betraying Donovan would be much worse.

Thanking Robert, Patrick returned to his chair. His eyes narrowed, giving his face a porcine cast. "We'll never find your mother if we're not square with each other, Erin. Why don't you tell me the whole story?"

Her heart sank. "I—I don't know what you mean." A queer shiver went through her. She stared at Patrick.

"Then I'll tell you." His tone sharpened, and his fleshy face reddened.

Behind her, Erin heard a soft click as Robert shut the door.

Patrick eyed her shrewdly, and suddenly he didn't look

congenial anymore. "Donovan told me about the restricted
files on him and me, and about the CIA connection you
discovered—all the little details you left out. Why don't
you trust me, Erin?"

Resisting the impulse to squirm nervously in her chair,
she matched his scowl. So he knew she was a liar. Well,
so what? She'd had good reason to withhold the truth. From
her three years in the air force, she'd learned never to make
excuses, and she didn't intend to start now.

"Because I don't know you well enough to trust you,
Patrick." Leaning one arm on the table, she stared directly
at him. "Until I do, I'm going to be very careful what I
say."

Obviously caught off guard by her honesty, Patrick took
a long drag on his pipe. After he'd blown more smoke
rings, he gave her an icy stare. "You're a smart girl, Erin.
If you want to see your mother again, you really need to
trust me."

Though he followed the comment with his usual congenial smile, Erin couldn't help shuddering. His words
sounded very much like a threat.

WHEN THE MAID finally showed her to a gilded second-floor
bedroom, Erin said good-night with no intention of sleep-
ing, at least not until she'd explored the library. Just thinking about going back to that depressing room made her
heart beat faster. But she had to do it. Since Patrick probably spent most of his time there, she might find clues to
her mother's disappearance hidden in one of the many
drawers and cubbyholes. If the room concealed secrets,
Erin would find them.

After using the adjoining tiled bathroom, she unpacked
her suitcase, hanging her clothes in the wardrobe at one
end of the room. Then she switched off the lights so anyone
watching her window from outside would think she'd gone
to bed. The only illumination came from glowing coals in

the marble fireplace. Tall windows showed near-total blackness outside.

As she sat in the semidarkness listening to the rain on the windows, Erin saw Donovan's face in the dying embers. She wished he were here with her in this huge golden bedroom to enjoy its thick Oriental carpet, the oil painting of Aphrodite and Adonis over the mantel, the canopied...

Dear Lord! What was she thinking? Her mother was missing, probably in the hands of a kidnapper. Patrick had come close to threatening her. Could he be dangerous? She desperately needed to get some insight into who her stepfather really was: the dangerous criminal Donovan warned her about, or the affectionate husband her mother had married. Thinking of her mother, Erin's sick sensation of loss returned, and she felt a stab of guilt for letting her thoughts wander. Tonight she had to concentrate on her search of the library and not let anything—or anyone—distract her.

Kneeling beside the door to the hallway, Erin listened intently. She heard no sound in the hall, no faint rustling of footsteps over the carpet to signal someone's passing. Quietly she cracked the door and peered outside.

The wide hallway was empty. The lights had been dimmed for the night, but since her eyes were accustomed to darkness, she had no trouble seeing. Silently she slipped out of her room and went to the broad staircase. At the bottom, she held her breath, listening. If someone caught her, she'd never be able to explain why she was out of her room after midnight, and her plan to search the library would be ruined.

In the far distance, she heard the lonesome wail of a train whistle; nearby, the rhythmic ticking of an ornate, nineteenth century grandfather clock seemed soft compared to the wild pounding of her heart. No other sounds disturbed the claustrophobic silence.

Hardly daring to breathe, Erin tiptoed across the darkened salon to the library. The door was closed. But inside, Erin heard muted voices. She pressed her ear against the edge of the door. At first, she couldn't make out the words. But by concentrating and holding her breath, she was able to recognize Patrick's voice and discern enough to understand him.

"Yes, I used Dun Aengus, my own nickname, on the message to confuse anybody who might get hold of it accidentally—on the chance it was traced to my house or company." Obviously certain he was not being overheard, he chuckled, a shallow rasping sound. "No smart judge would believe I'd incriminate myself like that."

The other man spoke. "And I'm sure you had an associate ready to *confess* that he wrote the message."

Chuckling again, Patrick said something in reply, but Erin didn't hear him. All her senses turned off at the sound of the visitor's voice. She froze, her feet rooted to the floor. The blue-and-white salon spun crazily around her.

That voice was one she'd never forget as long as she lived. He'd spoken only a few words in the hotel kitchen back in Georgetown, but those words and the voice that spoke them were etched forever on her brain.

The assassin. He was inside the library at this very minute, talking to her stepfather.

Erin's first impulse was to get out of there as fast as she could. To run out the front door of this horrible house and never come back. To escape before the assassin caught her.

But Patrick's dogs would track her down before she got through the front gate. And even if escape was feasible, she couldn't pass up a chance to overhear Patrick's plans. This might be her best opportunity to find her mother. With her heart drumming wildly, she pressed her ear against the door again.

"They're both right here in Dublin," Patrick said.

They're talking about Donovan and me, Erin realized, shaken to the core. Her concentration was so intense that she didn't hear the man behind her until it was too late. An iron hand gripped her arm. With her heart pounding furiously in her throat, she jerked around to face Robert.

"Can I be of assistance, Miss Meyer?" he asked, so loudly that Patrick couldn't fail to hear. Seconds later, the door opened and Patrick appeared, an angry scowl marring his forehead.

"Erin! What're you doing here, girl?"

Releasing her arm, the butler spoke before Erin could come up with a reasonable explanation. "I was on my way to see if you wanted your usual toddy, Mr. O'Shaughnessy. Found her with her ear pressed to the door, I did."

Patrick's scowl deepened. "You can bring two cognacs, Robert. Don't worry about my stepdaughter. I'll take care of her."

"Very good, sir." The butler left without a backward look.

"I couldn't sleep. Wanted a book," Erin explained lamely, trying to peer into the library where the assassin waited. Patrick's bearish body in the half-open door blocked her view. She couldn't see the chairs by the fireplace where he must be sitting. "When I heard voices I listened to see who it was so I wouldn't barge in on something private," she went on.

"A friend stopped by," Patrick said, his scowl lightening. "We were talking about old times."

"Voices. That's all I heard. Voices." The hair on Erin's forearms prickled with alarm. She had to get away from here before something dreadful happened. From somewhere deep within, she generated a smile and forced her body to assume a relaxed position. "I couldn't make out the words."

"Well, no harm done." His frown disappeared, but Erin knew he must be seething underneath, afraid she'd overheard something important.

"If you don't mind," Patrick went on, "I'll escort you to your room. Wouldn't want you to get lost, now, would we?"

On the long walk back upstairs, Erin attempted to reassure Patrick that she'd heard only voices, not words. Finally she thought he believed her. But when they reached her room, he gave her an odd patronizing scowl, as though she were a misbehaving child.

"For yer own good I'll be locking the door so ye don't go wandering around the house and get yourself hurt," he said. "Mary will be up first thing tomorrow to help you dress." Reaching inside the door, he pulled the key from the lock.

Stunned, Erin faced him. "For heaven's sake, Patrick! My mother—your wife, in case you've forgotten—is missing. I'm only interested in finding her. If you don't trust me enough to leave my door open, I'll leave Glenkillan House immediately."

A tolerant smile spread across his ruddy face. "Fine. If you want to go, I can't stop you. Get your suitcase. I'll have someone drive you to a hotel in town."

A warning bell sounded in her head. Would he lock her in as soon as she stepped inside the room? But what else could she do? If she tried to run, he'd grab her.

"It'll take me ten minutes or so to pack my suitcase." She marched into the room, her back ramrod straight.

"Robert will be up shortly to carry it down for you," Patrick said, before he closed the door.

Erin heard the key turn in the lock. Hastily she tossed her things back into her suitcase and sat beside the door, waiting for Robert. Fifteen minutes passed, then twenty. She became more frightened by the minute as her dismay grew.

Patrick had hired the assassin. He knew Donovan was a CIA agent and had hired someone to kill him. Now her own life was in danger because of what she'd overheard. After half an hour, it was apparent no one was coming to take her to a hotel. She was locked in for the night.

Every hair on her body seemed to stand on end. She had to get out of here at once.

After turning out the light, she went to the three big windows. The two end ones, in spite of their size, were hung in traditional sash frames that latched at midpoint. Twisting the latch, she pulled one window up, half expecting an alarm to sound. But there was only silence and the cold wetness of rain on her face.

Leaning out, Erin looked down. Since the ceilings were so high, there was a drop of at least twenty-five feet to the lawn in front of the house. Her stomach clenched tight. It was much too far to jump, even if she climbed out and hung by her arms first.

She looked to her left and right. A ledge about a foot wide ran below the second-story windows to the balustrade atop the house's covered walkways. From there she could climb down the roof of the nearest outbuilding and drop to the ground, a distance of about ten feet.

Could she do it? Erin had always been good at balancing herself. But she'd have to walk the narrow ledge, slippery with rain, for a good forty feet with nothing to hang on to. Impossible, she thought, shuddering as she glanced down at the ground. One misstep on the slippery ledge and she'd be a goner.

Before she closed the window, she draped a scarf in the jamb so it blew outside. There wasn't one chance in a thousand that Donovan would see it, but he'd told her to hang a scarf outside her window if she needed him. And God knew she needed him now as she'd never needed anybody in her life.

Next, she went to the door and sat down, listening. Was someone on guard outside, someone prepared to stop any escape attempt she made? Barely breathing, she put her ear to the door, alert for the smallest sound of a human presence. When her left ear began to hurt from the pressure, she switched to her right.

Nothing. Convinced no one was outside, she fiddled with the lock using a nail file and a pair of tweezers from her manicure kit. Unlike common inside locks, this one was similar to a bolt action device. Erin had the uncomfortable thought that the beautiful gold bedroom had been specially outfitted as a jail cell. A cold chill ran through her. Had her mother ever been locked up in here?

Not possible, she told herself. Margaret had always sounded so happy and so supportive of Patrick when Erin talked to her on the phone. She and Erin were too close for her to keep such dastardly information hidden.

By now the fire had almost burned itself out. Only a few live coals lay in the ashes. Erin slumped in the chaise at the foot of the bed. At that moment, her chances for escape seemed as dead as the cooling ashes.

An odd tapping noise at the window disturbed her quiet desperation. Her heart pounded frantically. Had Donovan seen her scarf and somehow managed to scale the house wall?

She flew to the window and shoved up the frame. It *was* Donovan. Standing on the narrow ledge below, he poked his head through the open window. He was wearing a gray sweatsuit, and she could barely make out his phantomlike face in the fading light from the fire. But to her he looked better than a squadron of F-16s and the Angel Gabriel all rolled up into one.

He grinned at her with his high-voltage smile. "What's up?"

"Thank God you've come!" She was so glad to see him she didn't know whether to laugh or cry. "The assassin's here. He's going to kill both of us. And—and..." She felt her eyes filling and swallowed hard.

"And what?" Putting one leg over the sill, he bounded into the room.

"And Patrick's locked me in," she whispered thickly. "God knows what he's going to do to me."

"Your stepfather's not going to do anything to you," Donovan said, bursting with confidence. "Because we are getting out of here—now."

After closing the window, Donovan went to the door to examine the lock. "No sense fooling with it," he said, turning away. "We'll have to go out the window."

From the door, he went directly to Erin and caught her in his arms before she guessed what he was up to. He smelled wonderful—like rain washing over a pine forest. When he kissed her, it was done expertly and thoroughly, with a subtle promise of even better things to come. After he released her, all traces of her tears were gone.

"Hello, Erin," he said, in his sexy baritone voice. "Now that we've greeted each other properly, tell me what happened."

Briefly she told him how Robert had caught her with her ear pressed against the library door and how Patrick had reacted.

Donovan's mood veered sharply to alarm. "So we know Patrick's behind the assassination attempt. Do you think he's also behind your mother's disappearance?"

She hesitated. "I honestly don't know. At first he told me she'd been kidnapped. He seemed so upset, I was sure he truly believed it. But something he said later made me think he might be behind her disappearance, or might know where she is."

"He knows," Donovan said, his voice so confident that Erin's warning alarm went off again.

"Do you know something I don't?" she asked, suddenly afraid of what he might say.

"I don't think your mother's disappeared at all," he answered. "I think she and your stepfather rigged her disappearance to serve their own ends."

Stunned, Erin stared at him. "Not *my* mother. You can't be serious." She glared angrily at Donovan.

"I'll explain later," he promised. "But right now, let's get the hell out of here."

DONOVAN USED A ROPE to lower Erin's suitcase, coat and handbag out the window to the ground. Kneeling beside the sill, she watched the case hit the grass below without opening—at least nothing light-colored spilled out. Her black handbag and maroon car coat disappeared into the darkness.

"Are you sure the ropes will hold?" she asked. While she waited inside the room the past hour, he'd climbed to the roof and tied nylon ropes to the balusters so there was a rope about every five feet for her to hang on to.

"They'll hold," he assured her, kneeling beside her at the window sill and putting his arm around her waist. "I'll go first, and you'll see how I use the rope to balance myself."

As he whispered in her ear, the touch of his lips and warmth of his breath gave her new confidence. But that didn't keep the ground from looking a hundred miles away.

Trying to ignore her fear, she nodded. "Don't worry. I'll be fine." She found herself suddenly eager to show him she could do it.

He squeezed her waist, and she was surprised at how much his unspoken admiration pleased her.

"Never let go of the ropes," he whispered, his breath hot on her cheek. "Don't let one go until you've got a firm grip on the next. Keep your face to the wall and don't look down. I'll be right there to help if you run into trouble."

"Piece of cake," she assured him, already dreading the coming ordeal.

"Then I'll see you outside." With the lithe grace of a jungle cat, he bounded over the sill into the dark, rainy night.

And now it was her turn.

Chapter Nine

Apprehensively Erin eyed the slender nylon cord dangling in front of the window. It had swung back into position when Donovan released it. Leaning out she saw him on the ledge about five feet away, facing the house's masonry wall. He turned toward her and beckoned, his features a shadowy blur in the darkness.

At least the rain had stopped. A full moon emerged from the clouds, then disappeared as quickly as it had come, plunging the house's gray stone wall again into shadow. Erin hated to see the moon go, but was grateful for small favors. The almost total darkness made her and Donovan harder to spot from the ground.

Without looking down, she reached for the rope. Even through her lined leather gloves, the nylon cord felt frightfully thin to her fingers. Clutching it, she edged out of the window. The cold damp night wrapped clammy arms around her body, still warm from Donovan's touch, but she didn't flinch.

When Erin's foot touched the narrow ledge below the window, she gingerly pulled her other leg over the sill. Finally, with both feet firmly on the foot-wide ledge, she clung tightly to the rope, using it to balance herself. Her leaden stomach dropped a notch as she took her first small step.

Donovan beckoned again. As surefooted as a cat, he

moved away from her, his light-colored outfit blending perfectly with the house's walls. Since Erin had only dark clothing, he'd insisted she wear his gray windbreaker, leaving him with a sweatshirt. Even so, she felt as conspicuous in her jeans as a black fly against a white curtain.

Where were the wolfhounds? she wondered fearfully. Then she remembered her mother said the animals roamed only the estate perimeter. But one barking dog would be enough to alert the staff—

Stop with the scary thoughts, she ordered herself. Clinging tightly to the rope, she forced herself to take another small sideways step, then another.

To her right Donovan had reached another rope. He let the one he was using swing back into position, ready for her to grab. Patiently he waited while she inched toward it, step after frightening step. Erin's heart was pounding, her hands damp with sweat inside her gloves. The five feet between the window and the next length of rope seemed interminable.

There! Finally she was in reach of the next rope. As Donovan had instructed, she gripped it firmly before releasing the first one. Glancing toward him, she saw that he had already let go of the third rope and was waiting, his body turned toward her, for her to grab it.

They didn't have all night, Erin reminded herself, trying to relax her tense body. If they weren't off the estate before dawn, they'd never make it. Hardly daring to breathe, she forced her rigid legs to move.

Suddenly, excruciating pain shot through her right calf. Her fingers tightened on the rope. Shutting her eyes, she pressed her forehead against the rough stone wall. The pain radiated upward, paralyzing her. She was going to fall. In her mind she could feel the cold air whistling past her, see the ground rushing up to meet her helpless body.

Then Donovan appeared at her side. "What's wrong?" His strong arm gripped hers.

"A cramp," she whispered.

"Rock back and forth on your toes and heel," he returned, demonstrating how easily this feat could be accomplished on a ledge only a foot wide. She did as he said, but it was his firm grip on her arm, his warm breath on her face, that got Erin moving again.

She was within ten feet of the walkway when a third-floor light switched off, and she heard the unmistakable scrape of a window opening above her. Terror ripped through her. Clutching her rope like a lifeline, she froze against the side of the house. Was her rope in front of the window for someone to see? Cautiously she looked up.

No, thank God. The open window was behind her. None of their ropes hung in front of it. While she watched a man leaned out, his elbows on the sill.

The moon chose that unfortunate moment to make another appearance. Halting her slow progress, Erin clung to her rope, wishing she could disappear into the side of the building. Surely the man above would see her. Her stomach clenched tight, and she locked her gaze on the third-story window. Staring upward, she got a good look at his profile.

He had the face of a Greek god.

With his curly blond hair, aquiline nose, and square jaw, he might have stepped off a motion picture screen or magazine cover. Who could he be, this gorgeous man housed on the third floor of her stepfather's mansion? She blinked and looked again, but the moon had vanished behind another cloud. The beautiful face melted into the blackness.

Then she heard his voice. Was he calling to her and Donovan? Hardly daring to breathe, she pressed against the stone wall, listening.

"To be, or not to be: that is the question:
   Whether 'tis nobler in the mind to suffer
   The slings and arrows of outrageous fortune,"

Shakespeare! She could hardly believe her ears. In a low

voice, the man above them was reciting the familiar soliloquy from *Hamlet*. Unaware of them, he droned on.

Slowly Erin released her breath, listening more carefully. Though he was speaking in low tones, with studied feeling, she thought she recognized his voice. Turning her head to one side, she concentrated all her attention on the sounds from above.

It couldn't be, but it was. *The assassin!*

The earth swung crazily on its axis and she clutched the rope with trembling fingers. All the breath seemed punched out of her.

The assassin. But how could that be? The handsome man she'd seen in that brief moment of moonlight looked nothing like the unattractive creature in the hotel kitchen.

An instant later she felt warmth along her hip and knew Donovan was by her side. Glancing upward, he tugged at her arm in an urgent warning that said, "Let's get out of here."

"It's the assassin," she whispered.

Putting his finger to his lips, he tugged again. Above, the killer continued his recitation.

Heart racing, she turned away from the window and once again edged toward their destination: the narrow roof over the two-story-high walkway below. When she finally reached it, and Donovan helped her over the balustrade, she could hardly walk her legs were so stiff.

"It was the assassin," she gasped in his ear.

"I thought it might be." He took her gloved hand.

"But he looks so—so different." She breathed deeply, trying to keep from trembling. Now that they were no longer in danger of falling, she couldn't stop shaking.

For a brief moment Donovan held her close, his warmth renewing her confidence. "I'll explain about him when we're on the ground," he whispered. "Now, we've got to get out of here, before the moon shines again and he spots us."

Donovan tugged at her hand and Erin followed him

across the top of the walkway to the roof of the garage, the nearest outbuilding. From there, she scrambled down the gently sloping surface and dropped the remaining ten feet to the ground.

Donovan was waiting for her. "Good girl," he whispered. "A little more practice and you'll be ready for the Olympics."

"What do you know about the assassin?" she whispered back, unable to get the handsome face she'd just seen out of her mind.

He led her around a corner, out of sight from the front of the house. "The press calls him *Chameleon* because he's so good at disguises. Nobody knows what he really looks like." Donovan's baritone voice sounded grim.

"But he wouldn't wear a disguise in his bedroom at night." A chill of foreboding turned Erin's legs to water, and she sagged against the building.

"No, he wouldn't," Donovan agreed. "If he guesses we've seen his real face, he'll never rest until we're both dead."

THE GARAGE SMELLED like rubber and oil. Erin stared at the five cars lined up side by side, their front ends facing three big garage doors. A sixth space was empty. Did her mother have the car that was usually parked there?

She faced Donovan. "How did you know the side garage door would be open?"

He gave her a smug smile. "Because I jimmied the lock before I went to your room. Thought I might need to get off the estate in a hurry."

Horrified, Erin stared at him. "You mean you were going to steal a car?"

"Since you're coming with me, I mean *we* are going to steal a car," he countered.

She grasped his arm. "We'll be caught for sure."

"It's our best chance." His gaze held hers in a hard

challenge. "On foot they'd catch us for sure. And each vehicle has a gate opener."

Since she didn't have a better plan, Erin started toward the nearest car, the same midsize vehicle Patrick had used to meet her at the gate. Donovan tossed her suitcase and a plastic bag—which they had picked up before they entered the garage—inside.

"Let's get out of here." He motioned toward a blinking red light on a panel near the door they'd just entered. "If that's what I think it is, somebody's on his way here right now."

A cold chill touched Erin's spine. "A silent alarm. Why didn't it go off when you jimmied the lock?"

"Because I didn't open the door." Running back to the panel he punched a couple of buttons. All three of the big garage doors slid open.

"Get in and buckle up," he yelled, running to the front of the car and lifting the hood. In mere seconds he got it started without a key.

Erin smelled burning rubber and heard the squeal of tires on the concrete garage floor as they took off. Swaying precariously, the car took the first turn onto the circular driveway. She clutched the edge of her seat, fearing they might tip over. The second turn was even worse. The vehicle swayed even more, then righted itself as they roared down the main drive heading toward the gate.

Headlights appeared behind them. Twisted around in her seat, Erin watched them come steadily closer.

"They're gaining," she yelled, her heart pumping furiously.

He eyed the rearview mirror. "They've probably got the Porsche. We're no match for them in this Ford." His lips tightened.

The night grew even darker as they entered the grove of trees. Seconds later they burst out of the grove. The gate loomed in the distance, about a mile ahead.

"It's closed," Erin cried. "Press the opener."

Her heart pounding, she watched him manipulate the device.

The gate didn't open.

"They must have switched control to the house," Donovan replied, his voice deadly calm. "Put your head down and hang on." He pushed the gas pedal to the floor.

"No," she screamed, guessing what he intended. "The gate's too strong. We'll be killed."

"Put your head down and hang on," he repeated.

Her heart pounding, she pressed her head between her knees and covered it with her arms. The car turned ninety degrees into the grass beside the drive and skidded to one side, its rear wheels spinning on wet turf. Turning into the skid, Donovan angled toward a section of fence about twenty feet from the gate.

Like most iron fences, the poles between the square concrete foundations barely touched the ground. The Ford easily rammed though and bumped over a concrete curb to the street beyond.

The impact caved in the car's front end and smashed the fenders but didn't break the windshield. Swinging the car in a wide arc, Donovan made an acute left turn onto Donegal Road.

Cautiously Erin raised her head. "Are they behind us?"

"Afraid so," he answered grimly. "But they waited for the house to open the gate so we've bought ourselves a few minutes." Tires screeching, the car swung out of Donegal Road onto a four-lane street paralleling the Liffey River. Tendrils of fog, thick as new smoke, hung over the river and surrounding area.

"Hang on," he yelled, flooring the gas pedal. An instant later he made a sharp left into Phoenix Park. Behind them, headlights drew closer. The Porsche's driver must have seen the Ford turn into the park.

Erin choked back a cry. "They'll catch us for sure in the park."

"Want to bet?" He flashed her his familiar smile.

A second later he switched off the lights and turned into the dimly lighted gravel parking area near St. Mary's Hospital. When he reached the far side, he roared unerringly across the weedy grass toward an unlighted space ahead. In the foggy darkness, Erin could make out even blacker shapes looming in their path.

"Trees!" she screamed. "Donovan slow down! We're going to hit one."

"No, we're not." She could hear the smile in his voice. "Oh ye of little faith, no tree can stop us now." But she noticed that he dropped the car's speed to a saner level.

Behind them, the Porsche had turned into the hospital area, but was no longer following.

"They think we're playing possum," Donovan said smugly. "It'll take them a few minutes to check the cars parked there and figure out none has a caved-in grill. By then we'll be gone."

"The fools," Erin returned sarcastically. "They think we've got enough brains not to drive into a grove of trees in this pitch-black fog at seventy miles an hour."

Erin's attempt at sarcasm failed. Now that they'd escaped she couldn't help admiring Donovan's audacity.

THE SCREECH OF CAR TIRES and the distant sound of men's voices brought Chameleon to his open third-floor window. With his room dark, no one who happened to look up from the ground would see his face.

A chase appeared to be underway below. First one set of headlights and then another raced around the circular drive and headed away from the mansion down the straightaway toward the main gate.

Chameleon watched until the second car entered the grove of trees. When its lights had faded, he turned toward two men near the garage.

O'Shaughnessy and his butler, he observed, recognizing his employer from his lumbering, bearlike gait. The two men entered the covered walkway where Chameleon couldn't see them. He was about to move away from the window when something caught his eye. He focused on it.

A rope. It was hanging a few feet to the left of his window. Leaning farther out, he peered along the side of the house. More ropes, one every five or six feet. They'd been tied to the balustrades on top and now dangled loosely against the stone wall.

Why? Obviously because someone needed the ropes for balance to walk the narrow ledge below the second-story windows.

Suddenly all the pieces fit together. Someone had escaped from Glenkillan House only minutes ago. They'd walked the ledge below, then stolen a car. He'd find out who from O'Shaughnessy.

With mounting apprehension, Chameleon remembered the flashes of moonlight, the sound of his own voice reciting the soliloquy. A sickening nausea ravaged his body. If someone had been on that ledge, they must have seen his face. They could identify him. If they had any idea who he was, they had to be eliminated.

DUBLIN. In the gray light of the approaching dawn, Erin stared out the car's window. Sick with worry, she pictured her mother walking along the broad streets with their elegant Georgian buildings. She'd told Erin of St. Patrick's Cathedral, standing sentinel-like among the surrounding rooftops; of St. Stephen's Green at the top of Grafton Street, with its wonderful scents in the Garden of the Blind; of the city's brightly colored doors with their shiny brass fixtures.

Now, seeing Dublin for herself, Erin knew how her mother must have felt the first time she returned to the place of her birth. Like she'd finally come home. How could anything have happened to her here, in this city she loved and trusted?

In the east a pale rosiness brushed the skyline. The day promised to be bright and sunny, with no trace of the rain that came down so steadily last night. At least they'd have a nice day for their meeting with Jean Magee. Talking to her mother's cousin seemed the logical place to start their search. Patrick might guess they'd go there, but Erin doubted he'd hurt her or Donovan with Jean looking on.

After leaving Phoenix Park an hour ago, they'd ditched the Ford. While Erin waited at an early morning McDonald's, her stomach churning with anxiety, Donovan had picked up an unmarked car at the U.S. Embassy. Then they'd started for Jean's house.

Erin glanced at Donovan beside her. "You never did tell me how you appeared at my window so soon after I put my scarf out. Don't tell me you sat out there half the night watching." She made the comment in a teasing tone, knowing there had to be some other explanation.

"Guilty as charged." His growth of beard gave him a scruffy male look that warmed Erin's heart. The poor man hadn't had any more sleep than she, probably less since she'd been able to nap on the plane.

She swallowed hard. Much as she wanted to believe he cared that much about what happened to her, she couldn't picture Donovan standing guard outside her window all night on the mere chance she might need help.

"Why'd you do it?" she asked.

"I hadn't intended to bring this up right now," he said slowly, "but since you've asked—I want to find your mother as much as you do."

So that was it. Erin kicked herself for her foolish hope that he'd waited outside because he cared for her. "And you thought I might find out something from Patrick about where she is—and would want you to know."

"Exactly." Glancing toward her, his dark blue eyes searched hers. "You haven't asked why I want to find your mother."

Her heart skipped a beat. "All right then, why?"

He didn't hesitate. "I want to find her because I'm sure

she knows something about the conspiracy I've been assigned to investigate.''

"You can't be serious!" Looking straight ahead, Erin tried to disguise the guilty tremor in her voice. Hadn't that suspicion occurred to her also, that her mother and Patrick might be collaborating on something illegal? But no, she couldn't admit such lack of faith to Donovan. Her mother might be in terrible danger. No matter what she'd done, she had to be found and protected.

"I'm sorry to have to tell you this, Erin," he said, "but I'm dead serious." There was a look of implacable determination on his face.

As they'd reached the edge of town near the airport, the fenced front yards had given way to gas stations and flat roofed buildings. Donovan turned northeast on the narrower road leading toward Jean's house. "I think your stepfather knows exactly where your mother is, Erin. I think he sent her to cover their tracks when they found out I was a CIA agent."

Erin heard the sincerity in his voice, and hated herself for what she was thinking. Could her mother be involved in something so illegal that it included murder? No...that wasn't possible. She couldn't let herself consider anything so awful. Without meaning to, she inched as far from Donovan as her seat belt permitted.

Donovan paused when she moved away from him. "I need to talk to your mother and so do you, Erin. We have our different reasons, but I think it'll be easier to find her if we work together."

There, he told himself. His suspicions were out in the open. He didn't like the way Erin's eyes glistened right after he spoke, or the nervous way she clasped and unclasped her hands in her lap. But he had to let her know how he felt if he was to continue respecting himself. In some way he hadn't bothered to analyze, he had to be straight with her, even if that meant rousing her quick temper. Which was exactly what he'd done, he saw to his regret.

"Then this is where we part company." Her lovely chin rose in a determined gesture he was beginning to recognize all too well. "I can't work with a man who's trying to send my mother to jail."

"That's not what I said, Erin." Making sure he could see a good distance in both directions, he pulled the car over to the side of the road and stopped.

"What's—what's wrong?" She looked fearfully out the back window. "Why are you stopping?" Donovan looked, too. At that early hour, the road was empty.

"I stopped so we could talk before we get to your cousin's." He couldn't let her walk out of his life. He needed her help in finding her mother. And, in some indefinable way, deep down in his gut he knew he just plain needed her. Now that he'd tasted her honeyed lips, now that he'd glimpsed her quick intelligence, he couldn't let her go so easily.

"We've got nothing to talk about," she said. "I don't know why I didn't see it before. Your whole purpose in helping me find Mom has been to tie her to this supersecret scheme you keep referring to but never define."

Her wide blue eyes stared into his. "Isn't it about time you told me what she's suspected of doing? Just what is this conspiracy you think she and Patrick are running?"

ERIN'S EYES WIDENED as she saw Donovan's slow nod of acquiescence. *He's going to tell me at last,* she thought, half afraid of hearing what the CIA thought her stepfather and mother were involved in.

He opened his door and came around to her side of the car. "Let's take a walk. The car's getting stuffy."

Her pulse rate doubling, Erin got out of the car. Whatever he was going to tell her must really be bad.

Along the side of the road grew tall thick bushes with bright yellow flowers. When she leaned over to snap one off she smelled a musky fragrance and discovered sharp barbs on the stems.

Like Donovan, she thought. *Charismatic and charming on the outside. But watch out for his thorns.*

On either side of the two-lane blacktopped road, rolling green hills nurtured plump black-and-white cows.

"So what's this big conspiracy all about?" she asked, walking slowly so they didn't stray too far from the car.

"Before I tell you, let's be sure we understand each other." He stood so close she could smell a subtle perspiration scent mixed with the musky fragrance of the yellow flowers. Though he acted cool, could he be as nervous as she about what he was going to divulge?

"If I tell you about the conspiracy," he begun, "do you agree to let me help you find your mother?"

During the past few minutes, Erin had reconsidered her hasty decision to separate. Maybe Donovan was right. They'd find her mother easier together than apart. But she had to be sure he didn't catch Margaret unawares. Her mother might unknowingly incriminate herself if she didn't realize Donovan was a CIA agent out to put her in jail.

Erin stared steadily into his eyes. "I'll agree only if you promise to let me talk to her alone once we've found her."

"That sounds reasonable," Donovan said. "I'm sure I don't have to remind you that what you're about to hear is top secret information." He paused for emphasis, then went on. "We call it the Shamrock Conspiracy because we think your stepfather's company, with its global operational network, is at the hub."

Taking a deep breath, Erin steeled herself for what was coming. "What sort of conspiracy?" Visions of terrorists in black masks blowing up buildings full of innocent people raced through her mind.

"A worldwide counterfeiting ring," he replied.

Erin turned so weak with relief her knees felt like water. "Counterfeiting?" The word brought images of bewhiskered men hunched over printing equipment—not the horrendous deeds she'd imagined. She had to fight an hysterical impulse to laugh.

"This is a serious crime, Erin," he said, his expression sober. "These people are thieves and murderers. You've already seen what they'll do to protect their operation."

He studied her the way a teacher eyes an errant pupil. "The overseas demand for our dollars—along with powerful new optical scanners and advanced imaging software—have created an unparalleled wave of counterfeiting. God knows how many people have been killed to protect this conspiracy."

A car appeared about two miles behind them, moving fast.

"It's probably nobody, but we'd better get going," Donovan said, setting a quick pace back toward their vehicle. "Your stepfather might guess that we're headed for your cousin's place and try to stop us."

Erin matched his long steps. Watching the car come toward them, her breath solidified in her throat. It reached them while they were buckling their seat belts. Its driver whizzed by with only a cursory look in their direction.

Erin let her breath out in a slow sigh. She didn't think her stepfather would risk a confrontation at Jean's, but she'd been wrong about Patrick before. What if his hired assassin was already there, waiting for them?

JEAN MAGEE LOOKED nothing like Erin expected. Since she'd never seen a picture of her cousin, she imagined Jean would look something like her mother who was the same age. So when a middle-aged woman in a plain cotton dress opened the door to the family's rambling two-story country house, Erin thought at first she was the maid. Overweight and sturdy, with glasses and gray hair, she seemed at least fifteen years older than Margaret.

Introducing herself as Margaret Sullivan's daughter and Donovan as a friend, Erin was about to ask for Mrs. Magee

when the woman in the doorway gathered her to her ample
bosom.

"Erin, darlin'," she said, "I didn't expect you so soon."

"Or so early," Erin added, in a rueful attempt to apol-
ogize for their dawn arrival. "But I'm terribly worried
about Mom. Donovan's helping me look for her, and we
want to get started."

"While we talk, you can have some breakfast." There
was an odd insistent note to her cousin's voice. Turning,
Jean showed them into an enormous kitchen at least ten
degrees warmer than the rest of the house.

With a stove the size of two standard American ranges
and wide tile counters, the room rivaled a hotel kitchen. At
the center was a large round table made of the same dark
wood as the cabinets. After she'd seated Erin and Donovan
at the table, Jean turned to the stove and adjoining fridge,
busying herself with thick slices of ham and a bowlful of
eggs. When she spoke, she had her back to the table.

"Where will you be starting your search for your mother,
Erin?" she asked.

Glancing toward Donovan, Erin lifted her eyebrow in
question. Had she come all this way for nothing? He gave
her the A-okay sign with his curved forefinger and thumb,
encouraging her to forge ahead.

"We were hoping you could help, Jean," she said,
"maybe give us a clue—anything at all—that might tell us
where to begin."

Looking over her shoulder, Jean shook her head. "Like
I said on the phone, it's been a week since I saw your
mother." She turned back toward the stove.

Erin felt Donovan nudge her in the side. When she
glanced at him, he pointed to himself, frowned, then inclined his head toward Jean.

So that was it. Jean knew Donovan worked for Patrick
and didn't want to confide in Erin with him present. When
they'd finished eating, he excused himself with a vague
explanation about adjusting something in the car's engine.

He gave Erin a telling glance. "I'll be a while, at least a half hour, maybe longer," he said. "Why don't you and your cousin have another cup of coffee and get better acquainted while I see what's wrong with the bloody motor."

The car was parked in a graveled parking area near the back door. With Erin following, Jean showed him through a changing room with boots on the floor and coats hung on hooks around the walls. Then she watched from the back door while he went to the car and opened the hood.

Returning to the kitchen, Jean peered out the window, obviously assuring herself that he remained outside.

"Erin, I'm so glad you've come," she whispered, as she sat down next to her at the table. Her matronly face glistened with concern. "Your mother desperately needs help."

Chapter Ten

"Where is she, Jean? I've got to know." Erin leaned anxiously across the kitchen table toward her cousin.

"I can't tell you as long as you're traveling with Donovan." Jean Magee's high-pitched voice quivered with emotion. "Don't trust him, Erin. He works for Dun Aengus. Sure as Ireland's a free country, he'll tell his boss where she is."

"He's not working for Patrick any longer," Erin said. "He's quit."

"That's what he says. They're trying to fool you, darlin'." Leaning toward Erin, she lowered her voice to a whisper. "Your mother made me swear on the holy Bible that I'd tell no one but you where she'd gone. You've got to promise you'll keep that confidence, and you can't do it if he's sitting beside you in the car." Jean's determined gaze held Erin's.

For the space of a heartbeat, Erin considered letting her cousin know Donovan was a CIA agent. No. That information would lead to questions about Donovan's top secret operation.

Besides, maybe Jean was right about not telling Donovan, at least not right away. Lord knows, Erin didn't trust him either. As long as he was out to send her mother to prison, he wasn't trustworthy. So Jean's request that Erin not tell might be a blessing in disguise.

"All right," she agreed, clasping Jean's hands. "He's already promised not to talk to Mom until after I have. And I won't let him know exactly where we're going until we get close. That way he won't be able to telephone along the way and tell where we're headed." *Or to ditch me and try to get to Mom first,* she added grimly to herself. "But I *do* need to have him with me."

"Why?" Jean's eyes narrowed. The same dark blue as Margaret's, they expressed doubt. The resemblance reminded Erin of her mother and increased her anxious fears.

"It's his car," Erin said lamely.

"I'll loan you one of ours." Jean gave her such a penetrating stare through her round, wire-rimmed glasses that Erin looked down at her coffee cup. For a moment her mind went blank. She took a long swallow before she answered.

"In exchange for a confidence from Donovan, I promised he could come with me," Erin admitted finally, realizing how weak this must sound to Jean's ears with her mother's safety at risk. "I always try to keep my promises." To her own ears her words sounded sanctimonious, even if they were true.

But deep down she knew more than a promise was at stake here. Regardless of Donovan's motives, she wanted him with her. Her mind acknowledged the fledgling hope nestled in her heart that there would be a bright future for her, Donovan and her mother.

"Besides," she added, "having him with me will let me keep an eye on him."

With a loud rattle, Jean set her coffee cup down on the saucer. "He's truly got you fooled, I can see that." She paused, studying Erin's face.

Something about her expression must have struck Jean's sympathy. Her matronly countenance filled with compassion, and she leaned across the table to pat Erin's hand. "Don't get me wrong, darlin'. I know how worried you are about your mother, and I want to help all I can. It's just that I don't trust your stepfather or anybody who works for him."

Rising, Jean removed the coffee pot from the stove and poured them each another cup.

"Then you think Patrick is behind my mother's disappearance?" Erin asked, vividly remembering the assassin's face staring out of the window above her.

"She didn't say so," Jean replied slowly, staring down at her cup. "Patrick might not have actually kidnapped her, but I can't think of another reason for her to leave in the middle of the night, the way she did. Something he said or did must have made her go." She paused, her blue eyes full of questions. "Can you come up with anything or anybody besides Patrick that might scare your mother into running away?"

Erin swallowed hard to dislodge the swollen feeling in her throat. If Patrick wasn't behind her mother's disappearance, then who—or what—was? "Did she stop here?"

Jean shook her gray head. "No, she called us on the telephone. It was after eleven. We were already in bed."

"Was she alone?"

"Yes." The lines on Jean's forehead deepened. "At least she said she was."

Unable to sit still longer, Erin went to the window. Donovan, hunched over the car fender, appeared to be tinkering with the engine.

"Patrick claims somebody saw her with a strange man the day after she left," Erin said.

Jean joined Erin, peering out at Donovan before answering. "The morning after she called, Dun Aengus sent somebody out here to check on her. Of course, I told him she wasn't here, and I hadn't heard from her since last week."

Erin tensed, a cold knot forming in her stomach. "Patrick said nothing about sending anyone out here. Only that he'd called you to ask about her."

"He obviously didn't tell you the whole story," Jean

declared with fire in her eyes. She led Erin to a row of four upholstered easy chairs at the far end of the big kitchen. Sitting down in one herself, she motioned for Erin to take the one beside her.

"Tell me about this man who came here asking for her," Erin said. "What did he look like?" She held her breath, wondering if he might have been Chameleon in one of his disguises.

"Tall and thin," Jean returned thoughtfully. "Midforties to fifty. Long, angular face. Actually not bad looking— rather like Peter O'Toole in *Lawrence of Arabia*. But the most interesting thing about him was his limp."

"His limp?" The lump in Erin's stomach tightened. Her mother claimed the stranger spying on her had limped.

Jean nodded. "From the way he walked, I'd guess he had a false leg."

Nervously Erin bit her lip. "Mom told me some man with a limp seemed to be keeping an eye on her in Dublin." In a few sentences she repeated what Margaret had said during their telephone conversation two nights ago. Lord! She could scarcely believe it had been that short a time.

"And she was probably driving one of the Glenkillan House cars," Erin said, remembering that the sixth space in the garage was vacant. "No wonder Patrick's spies spotted her so easily."

When Erin finished speaking, Jean leaned toward her, her matronly face taut with concern. "Now that Dun Aengus has sicced this one-legged man on her, your mother may be in even more trouble than I thought. You've got to go to her as soon as you can." She glanced apprehensively toward the window. "I don't trust your Mr. Donovan. But I'll take your word that you won't let him get to her before you do. Or call someone along the way to tell where she is—so *they* can get to her." Jean's clear blue eyes held Erin's steadily.

Erin nodded. At last. Eager to hear Jean's revelation, she sucked in her breath. "You have my word. Tell me where she is."

BENDING OVER THE FENDER, Donovan heard the back door open behind him. Straightening, he wiped his greasy hands on a rag and glanced over his shoulder. Erin stood in the doorway, her stocky middle-aged cousin behind her.

"Did you find out what was wrong with the car?" Erin asked, coming toward him. With her cheeks flushed from the kitchen's heat, she looked as soft and warm as a downy comforter. He had to resist the urge to run to meet her.

"Nothing serious," he said, being purposely vague. He'd spent the last half hour toying with various parts of the engine and wishing he could touch Erin's bare skin instead of metal.

Erin's cousin followed close behind so as not to miss anything. Donovan pegged her as a sharp lady with the combative instincts of a Zulu warrior, particularly when defending her family. His mother was just like her.

"What needed fixing?" Jean asked, in a lyrical voice that reminded him of Erin's—probably a family trait.

"The timing needed some minor adjustments," he said, not caring whether she believed him or not. He'd given her time to talk to Erin alone. If she was as smart as he thought, she'd appreciate it. Apparently she did.

A sunny smile lit her plump face. "Come in and clean up and have another cup of coffee. I tried to talk Erin into staying tonight, but she insists on leaving right away."

Donovan caught Erin's eye and felt an unwelcome surge of excitement at her nearness. Reminding himself to keep his mind on his business, he caught the barely noticeable nod of her head.

Hallelujah! She must have discovered her mother's hideaway.

"I'M SORRY, DONOVAN, I can't tell you where Mom is, not until we get close. Jean made me promise." Erin didn't

feel the slightest twinge of guilt as she refused to answer
his question about where they were headed. They'd barely
driven down Jean's driveway, with Erin at the wheel, when
he asked.

"And, of course, you always keep your promises," he
said dryly.

"If I didn't, you wouldn't be here," she said, matching
his dry tone. "Jean thinks you're a spy for Patrick. It took
all my powers of persuasion to convince her I had to take
you along because I'd promised you I would."

Erin glanced at him. Freshly shaved at Jean's, he had the
air of Jason in hot pursuit of the golden fleece. But the way
his eyes raked boldly over Erin made her wonder if maybe
she was the fleece instead of her mother.

What a silly notion. As usual, she was letting her natural
optimism interfere with her good judgment.

"I'm glad you talked your cousin into letting me come
along," he said seriously. "I wouldn't have missed this trip
for anything."

"Jean was so sure you were still working for Patrick,
she almost had me convinced." Erin had already told Donovan about the one-legged man her stepfather sent to fetch
Margaret home, but was determined not to reveal where
her mother was until it was obvious where they were
headed. Without knowing, he couldn't ditch Erin and get
to Margaret before she talked to her.

Without studying the map on the car seat beside her, Erin
turned west, through County Kildare. The road was rela-
tively free of morning traffic, and she glanced at Donovan
again. Could Jean be right? Maybe he was lying about being a CIA agent the same way he'd lied about being an
informant. Maybe his CIA file and Patrick's were restricted
because the agency suspected both men of illegal activity,
not because one was the hunter and one the prey.

Erin gripped the steering wheel so hard her fingers turned
numb. She had to find out. "Is Jean right, Donovan? Are

you still working for Patrick? If you are, you might as well tell me now. I'll find out sooner or later. And if it's later, I'll make sure you never see Mom, let alone talk to her.''

He recoiled as though she'd slapped him in the face. "Dammit, Erin, I've told you the truth about what I'm doing. If you choose to believe it's a lie, that's your problem."

Suddenly the road ahead looked blurred. She blinked to clear her eyes, annoyed with herself for feeling hurt by his abruptness. "I guess it doesn't much matter whether you're working for the CIA to put Mom in jail, or working for Patrick to bring her back to Dublin. Either way, you're out to take her prisoner."

"You're wrong," he said, his voice inflamed and belligerent. "It matters a hell of a lot who you think I'm working for."

His angry tone made Erin glance at him again. She could hardly believe the furious look in his eyes, the wrathful lines around his mouth. Where was the rogue who played games with her heart? Donovan wasn't playing now.

"Do you know why it matters, Erin?" he asked, his expression grim as he watched her.

"I suppose because you want me to believe you." She felt herself heating up, matching his anger.

"You're damned right I want you to believe me."

But why? she wanted to scream. *What difference does it make whether I believe you or not?*

She'd barely started to ask when a blaring horn interrupted her, and she felt a momentary flash of panic. Unnerved by the left-sided driving, she'd drifted onto the right lane. Quickly she jerked the wheel and the oncoming car roared past, its horn still blaring.

Settled on the passenger seat beside her, Donovan showed no uneasiness. Chalk one up for him, she thought, her anger fading.

"So what difference does it make if I believe you or not?" she asked, unexpectedly troubled by the question.

When he didn't answer right away, she stole a quick glance at him. He met her eyes with such a riveting stare that her pulses leapt with sudden excitement.

Finally he spoke softly, almost as though embarrassed by his answer. "Because I care what you think of me, Erin. I want you to trust me. God knows, I trust you."

Hearing the honesty in his voice, Erin's defenses crumbled. "I trust you, too, Donovan. It's just that I'm so afraid for my mother. Scared of making a mistake that could cause her terrible trouble or even threaten her life."

She passed a car on the two-lane road and went on speaking. "Jean and I think Mom left Glenkillan House on her own. But if she did, who's this stranger Patrick's spies saw her with? Is he the same man who showed up at Jean's asking for her? If so, he might be a kidnapper, out to hold her for ransom, and not one of Patrick's men after all."

"Let's not borrow trouble." Donovan spoke in a firm but gentle tone. "We're going to know soon as we talk to her."

His conviction that they *would* talk to her—and soon—buoyed Erin's spirits. Reaching toward her, he stroked her arm with his fingers. Though his touch comforted her, she couldn't dispel the tiny kernel of doubt about him that remained to plague her. Was he sincere or just conning her?

"I don't blame you for being concerned," he said, his hand resting on her shoulder. "You and your mother are pretty close, aren't you?"

She nodded, glad he'd asked. Maybe if he knew more about her mother, he wouldn't be so quick to link her to Patrick's counterfeiting scheme.

"I always felt responsible for her," Erin said softly. "Even when I was a little girl, I followed her around so she didn't leave packages or her purse anywhere." She paused, savoring her childhood memories. "Then when I was a teenager, I kept her appointment book and made sure she got to places on time with everything she needed."

"That must have made you feel important," Donovan

suggested, a touch of envy in his voice. "Nobody in my family listened to a thing I had to say. I was the original invisible child."

"Did you have brothers and sisters?" Erin asked, hoping he would reveal something about himself. "I always wanted some."

Donovan put on a fierce scowl she suspected was mostly pretend. "I'd gladly have given you my six sisters. All were older and absolutely determined to run my life. Throw in a domineering judge for a father and a mother who clucked over me the way your cousin hovers over you—"

"What do you mean she clucked over me?" Erin interjected. "Jean did no such thing."

"Of course she did." He sounded so matter-of-fact, Erin turned toward him. He was grinning from ear to ear.

"Take it from one with firsthand experience in such matters. Your cousin was clucking, believe me."

Leaving one hand on the wheel, Erin reached out with the other and gently squeezed his arm. "Now that you've told me about your family, I see why you're protective of your freedom."

His hand tightened on her shoulder. "What do you mean?" His teasing tone was gone.

"Well, you've never been married and you're not with someone now. That's right isn't it?" Her ironic tone concealed her embarrassment at analyzing why he was still single.

Removing his hand from her shoulder, he nodded. "So what does that prove?" There was a sudden cool note in his voice.

Erin knew she was treading on dangerous ground, but she forged ahead anyway. "That you're leery of tying yourself down to one woman for the rest of your life."

"Maybe I've just been waiting for the right woman." His teasing tone was back.

Erin kept her eyes trained on the road ahead. Trees just

beginning to leaf dotted the rolling green hills on either side.

"Look here, Donovan," she said, "I don't blame you. If I'd had a bunch of people running my life during my growing-up years, I'd be wary of commitment, too. I had the opposite situation. I was always the one in charge, the responsible one who made sure things ran smoothly."

"Is that the reason *you* avoid commitment?"

His question was so unexpected that a soft gasp escaped her, and she gave him a quick glance. "What makes you think I avoid commitment?" She burned at the thought. Could he be right?

"Well, you've never been married, and you're not with someone now," he said, parroting her words about him.

She chuckled, hearing the illogic of her own argument. "All right, you win. Maybe I *am* afraid of getting stuck with someone who depends on me for everything, the way my mother did."

"You could be wrong about that, you know," he observed thoughtfully. "Seems to me your mom did all right for a single woman with poorly educated parents. Perhaps she deliberately let you take charge to raise your self-esteem and make you feel important."

That thought had never occurred to Erin, but when Donovan voiced it, she realized it might very well be true. "That would be just like Mom," she said thoughtfully. "I was such an ugly child—all gangly arms and legs and stringy red hair. The kids at school used to call me Raggedy Ann. Mom was so beautiful and I was such a mess. I remember how proud I was to watch out for her."

He whistled softly under his breath. "Judging by the way you look now, I don't believe what I'm hearing."

She shrugged. "My mother's always been the beauty in the family."

"Have you looked in the mirror lately? You've got to be as beautiful as she."

At his vote of confidence, a glow of pleasure washed

over her, and she glanced out the window so he wouldn't see her flushed cheeks. Now that they were near Lake Ree, clusters of trees lined the road, giving the landscape a lush appearance.

"You've never seen Mom," she said, wondering if he was conning her. "How can you compare us?"

"I've seen you," he replied quickly. "And you've told me so much about her, she seems very real to me. You're lucky to have a mother who loves you so much."

"I know." Picturing her mother, Erin abruptly pressed her foot down harder on the accelerator, a premonition of impending disaster tearing at her insides. Was she all right? Would she still be there when they reached their destination?

IN A COUNTRY INN near Lake Ree on the Shannon River, Donovan and Erin sat at a rough-hewn table and looked out the window at a couple of fishermen in rowboats taking advantage of the sunny weather. The room was filled with tobacco smoke and the low murmur of voices. Since it was the lunch hour, every table was taken.

Everyone looks so ordinary, Erin thought, meeting Donovan's gaze. Every time his eyes met hers, her heart turned over. Even though he was sitting across the table from her, she could feel his magnetism. The more she knew about him, the stronger her attraction.

Would she be able to resist him when the time came for sex? It was coming. And soon. She could see the craving in his eyes when he glanced at her over his thick potato soup and beef sandwich. But she'd have to say no. She didn't want to let herself get sucked into a one- or two-night affair where the attraction was purely physical.

Refusing to meet his gaze, she looked down at her plate so he wouldn't see the heat in her own eyes. How could she feel this way about him when, more likely than not, his only reason for being here was to entrap her mother?

"It's refreshing to eat with a woman who has a good

appetite," he said, nodding toward her empty soup bowl. "My sisters used to pick at their food. Made my mother furious."

"I was starving," Erin admitted, thankful to get her mind on a less worrisome track. "After that huge breakfast at Jean's, I can't imagine why."

He glanced at his watch. "Because breakfast was nearly six hours ago. And speaking of time, shouldn't we be on our way? No matter how much farther we've got to go, the sooner we get on the road, the quicker you'll see your mother."

He eyed her quizzically. Though he asked no questions, Erin could almost hear him wondering how much farther they had to go.

Donovan peered at her intently, a subtle change in his expression. No longer questioning, his steady gaze bore into her in silent expectation that had nothing to do with finding her mother, she realized suddenly.

After their long talk this morning in the car, he looked different to her—more serious and responsible and less like the rogue she'd first seen in him. As she stared back, Erin realized he was no longer a stranger, but someone she understood: a man with longing and desires like her own, a man she was on the verge of falling in love with.

"Mom's at a lodge in Donegal Town," she said, her heart swelling with newborn trust.

"Thanks for telling me." His eyes darkened with emotion. Suddenly Erin wished they could spend the rest of the day and tonight here together, in this charming country inn. A hot ache grew in her throat as she imagined his hands caressing her skin, his hard body heavy on top of hers. Instinctively she knew Donovan would be a considerate lover who would do his best to please her. But would she be able to satisfy this charismatic man of the world?

As though reading her mind, he reached across the table and took her hand. "When we've got this mess straightened

out, let's come back here, Erin. What a perfect place to get
to know each other better.''

Startled that they were both thinking the same thought,
she blurted out, ''It's so beautiful here.'' A rush of pure
happiness washed over her.

He squeezed her hand. ''I hope that was *yes*.''

''Yes—no—I don't know.'' Her mind whirled at her
mixed feelings.

This couldn't be happening. He didn't want commitment,
and she didn't want a one-night stand. She reminded herself
that he was with her for only one reason—he suspected her
mother of involvement in a worldwide conspiracy. Of all
the men in the world, why did she have to fall for the man
who wanted to put her mother in jail?

''Please don't play games with me, Donovan,'' she said
quietly.

His eyes held hers. ''I'm not playing games, Erin. I don't
want to lose you. Promise me you won't take off as soon
as we've found your mother.''

Suddenly his motivation was as plain as the nose on his
rugged face. He didn't trust her and wanted to be certain
she wouldn't try to elude him when they'd reached Donegal
Town. That's why he'd been exchanging confidences with
her and sounding so affectionate. What a silly little fool
she'd been to think he might care for her.

Without answering she swallowed hard, feeling her
fledgling hope die a sudden death. The room spun around
her in a dizzying circle of faces and brightly colored sweaters and big splotches of sunlight. Blinking away her sudden
tears, Erin bolted to the door. The crisp March air splashed
against her face like a cresting wave. She heard Donovan's
steps behind her before she'd managed to wipe the tears
off her face. He was running after her.

Grabbing her arm, he whirled her around, then caught
her other arm, too. They stood on a gravel pathway leading
around the weather-beaten old inn to the parking area. Be-

side the path the grass glowed emerald green in the sunlight.

"What's wrong? What did I say, Erin? Tell me." There was a puzzled frown on his face and a note of uncertainty in his voice as he stared anxiously down at her. His voice was thick, choked.

"You don't trust me worth squat, do you Donovan?" She tried to jerk away from him, but he tightened his grip on her arms. "All you care about is letting me lead you to my mother." Tears spurted from her eyes. "The things we talked about this morning meant nothing to you."

"They meant everything to me." He glared down at her.

Before she could resist, his hands locked against her spine, and she found herself in his arms. Erin heard her heart pounding in her ears, and the scene around her fused into a riot of greens and blues and browns. But Donovan's face was crystal clear, his blue eyes gripping hers. She could feel his uneven breathing on her cheek as he held her close.

Erin felt as though she were drowning, falling into a deep blue ocean with him beside her. His mouth tasted warm and moist with a hint of the mint tea he'd had for lunch. Against her will she locked herself into his embrace, wrapping her arms around his muscular neck.

"Don't doubt me," he said, pulling away from her and staring into her eyes. "If I sounded like I didn't trust you, it's only because I'm afraid of losing you."

"You won't." She let him pull her close again, only this time he didn't kiss her, only put his hand behind her head and caressed her hair.

Reveling in the bracing, male smell of him, she put her cheek in the hollow of his neck and drank in the comfort of his nearness. He stood strong, like a sturdy tree, and would be there for her when she needed him. She had to believe that, or she'd lose someone she couldn't bear to lose. A sigh trembled from her lips.

"Is everything okay?" he asked, slowly releasing her as if afraid to let her go.

"Everything's fine." Forcing herself to concentrate on the positive, she pushed her doubts as far down in her consciousness as she could. Smiling at him through her tears, she felt hope reappear and blossom.

Hand in hand they walked down the gravel path to the parking lot. The whole world looked different when she truly believed he cared for her, even their inconspicuous black sedan.

They'd been on the road less than twenty minutes when Erin noticed Donovan, who was driving, glancing uneasily into the rearview mirror.

"Is something wrong?" she asked.

"I'm not sure," he said slowly. "Did you see a dark green Ford wagon behind us this morning?"

An icy chill swept over her. Erin stared at him. "No, but I was so interested in our conversation, I might have missed it."

"Our trip to your mother's hideaway has just gotten more complicated." He frowned as he looked in the rearview mirror. "Don't turn around, but I'm sure we're being followed."

Chapter Eleven

Erin ignored her overwhelming urge to turn and peer out the rearview window.

"What're we going to do?" she asked in a small, frightened voice.

Donovan shrugged dismissively. "As soon as we get to the next town, we're going to switch cars."

"*Switch cars?*" Erin stared at him in disbelief. "How're you going to manage that?"

Inclining his head, he glanced at her, the roguish glint back in his eyes. "Since this is an emergency, we'll just have to steal one."

"We can't do that!" She gave him an appalled glare.

"Sure we can, the same way we stole your stepfather's car right out of his own garage." He reached over and gave her arm a friendly pat. "No reason to be concerned. The owner will get it back in good condition."

"*No reason to be concerned?* You've got to be joking. We're in enough trouble as it is." Startled at the sharpness in her own voice, Erin added more softly, "We've already got Patrick, an assassin and God knows who else after us. As soon as we steal a car, the police will be chasing us, too."

"I'll switch license plates with another car," he said. "By the time the police figure it out, we'll have ditched the one we stole."

He seemed so glib in talking about car theft that a sour taste rose in Erin's throat. Had he stolen the car they were driving? He'd told her he got it from the American Embassy.

A chill ran through her. What if he were lying about where he got this car, as part of his scheme to convince her he was a CIA agent? At the time she'd thought it odd that he could obtain a U.S. government car so quickly in the pre-dawn hours. Since she'd waited downtown in an all-night McDonald's while he picked up the vehicle, she had no way to confirm the truth.

Angrily she pushed her suspicions aside, determined to trust him. He was right. In an emergency like this, dire measures were needed. If that meant stealing a car, that's what they'd do. Her mother had to be protected at all costs.

"Are they still behind us?" She prayed he'd been wrong about someone following them.

He nodded. "Sometimes they drop way back, out of sight, but not for long." He glanced at her over his shoulder. "What's the next town on this road?"

Erin studied the map. "Roscommon. About ten miles ahead."

He looked in the rearview mirror. "They've fallen behind again. If there's anything in your suitcase you can't live without, get it now while they can't see us."

Erin didn't have to be told the reason. To fool their pursuers, her suitcase would have to be abandoned with the car. Just thinking of what they were about to do shattered her.

Erin forced herself to concentrate on her mother so she wouldn't get panicky. If they didn't switch cars, they'd risk leading whoever was following them straight to Margaret. And they didn't dare get caught by the police. Locked up in jail, they'd be unable to help her mother, no matter what sort of trouble she was in.

Leaning over the back of her seat, Erin removed a change of underwear and a heavy wool sweater from her suitcase.

Quickly she slipped the bra and panties into the pockets of her coat. The sweater lay across her lap. She'd wear it—and the coat—when they left the car. Pulse racing, she settled back in her seat.

Donovan seemed to sense her fear. Reaching out, he put his free arm companionably across her shoulders. "Think of what we're doing as a game. Then it won't bother you so much."

"A game?" She twisted her head to see if he was serious. Though there were touches of humor around his mouth and near his eyes, Erin didn't think he was teasing.

He inclined his head toward her. "When you're scared you make mistakes. By concentrating on the game, you lessen some of the fear."

"And the game now is to get rid of whoever's following?" To steady herself, she kept her eyes locked on his profile.

His square jaw tensed visibly. "You've got it." He glanced into the rearview mirror again. "Now that we're getting near a town, they've come closer."

"Can you see who's inside the car?" Erin tried telling herself this was only a game, but that didn't stop her heart from doing push-ups in her chest.

"They're not *that* close. We'll stop at the first pub or store that looks like it's got a side or back entrance and leave the car parked in front where they can't miss it."

"What if they come inside after us? In two minutes they'll figure out we've left the place." She couldn't keep the fear out of her voice.

He shook his head confidently. "They don't want us to recognize them, so they won't come inside."

Donovan's attempts to reassure Erin only made her more apprehensive. "Won't they wonder what we're doing in the pub? It's been less than an hour since we stopped for lunch."

"Sure they'll wonder, but there are a couple of very good reasons to stop. The best is using the bathroom."

"But that only takes minutes. If we can't get away from these people, we'll never get to Mom by tonight."

Ahead Erin saw the ruins of what appeared to be an ancient stone church. The crumbling rocks, with their slimy moss coatings, reflected the growing decay of her own confident spirit.

DONOVAN HEARD THE apprehension in Erin's voice and caught her hand in his. As usual, he felt her touch right down to the soles of his feet. When had it started, he wondered, this acute awareness of everything about her—from the fresh outdoorsy way she smelled to the silky feel of her skin beneath his fingertips?

"Remember, they're not after us," he said, squeezing her hand. "They're following us to get to your mother. All we have to do is lose them."

In spite of his confident words, Donovan wasn't at all sure their pursuers meant them no harm. If his theory was correct, O'Shaughnessy already knew where his wife was. He'd sent her away from Glenkillan House either to divert interest from his counterfeiting scheme or to hide crucial evidence.

With no reason to follow Erin to her mother, he must have a more sinister motive for having them tailed—like getting rid of the CIA agent and stepdaughter who knew too much.

For Erin's sake, Donovan forced himself to maintain a reassuring expression. But he suspected the occupants of the car behind them were probably looking for a good place to stage a fatal accident. Donovan intended to ditch the car and get the hell out of Roscommon.

Ahead he saw a broad street lined with old two-and three-story Victorian and Georgian style buildings, their steep roofs and prominent chimneys etched against a gray-blue sky. Slowing, he circled the town square, his eyes searching for a suitable place to disappear inside.

Nothing. Like many main streets in small Irish towns,

this one had few side streets. Behind their car, the green
Ford had come close enough for him to make out two shadowy figures inside. Would they try something in this little
town? Donovan didn't think so but couldn't afford to take
chances.

Beside him, he felt Erin tense. Leaning forward, she
pointed to a sign over a Victorian style storefront about a
hundred yards ahead. John E. Lotts And Sons: Housewares
And Funerary Libations. Below the words was a gray tomb-
stone with a stemmed cocktail glass superimposed diago-
nally across it.

"Mr. Lotts must have an interesting sense of humor,"
she said. "That sign seems to be announcing a pub. There
must be a back exit to an alley or street where they make
deliveries."

"Agreed." As they approached, he eyed the place.
Wooden chairs, porcelain bowls and other paraphernalia
were piled untidily on the sidewalk in front. Through dusty
narrow windows he saw more of the same inside. The bar
must be in back.

"This is perfect." He nodded his head with satisfaction.
"Just the kind of quaint old shop tourists love. They'll
think we went inside to look around."

"Do you really think we'll fool them that easily?"

Hearing the fear in her voice, he grinned to reassure her.
"You bet. They've got no idea how good I am at switching
cars."

After parking at the curb, Donovan made sure Erin's
suitcase was in plain sight on the back seat. He hesitated a
moment before folding the map and sticking it in the pocket
of his sweat suit jacket. Like the suitcase, an unfolded map
left behind would tend to make their pursuers believe they
planned to return to the car. But they needed the map to
find their way to Donegal. Donovan couldn't risk losing it.

Beside him, Erin unbuckled her seat belt and started to
take off her coat. Reaching to help her, he let his fingers
linger on her neck. Then, as he watched her pull her sweater

over her head, he felt his body respond to the lush fullness of her breasts straining against the wool fabric. Damn. The longer he knew her, the worse it got—this foolhardy desire to have all of her.

She hadn't said a word, he remembered, when he asked her to take what she needed from her suitcase. No complaints. No whining. Not like his sisters, whose voices raised like a Wagnerian chorus if they had to leave a lipstick behind on a family outing.

He remembered her scream at the cathedral, the yell that probably saved his life. He remembered how quickly she'd followed him out the window at Glenkillan House—though obviously scared.

Erin wasn't like any other woman he'd known. For the first time in his life, Donovan entertained the barest thought that he might one day be ready for marriage and fatherhood.

Aware of his incautious thoughts, he shook his head, annoyed at himself for having such foolish ideas. No matter how he felt about her, Erin would walk out of his life forever once they were finished with this operation. What else could he expect after he'd brought her mother and stepfather to justice?

EVEN THE PERFUMED SCENT of a candle burning on a counter near the shop's door could not hide the smell of dust and oldness. The aroma permeated the interior of what appeared to be more like a museum than a retail business. Though wearing her sweater and car coat, Erin felt cold and closed in, the shop's walls and clutter smothering her like a gaseous fog. After a sleepless night and a day on the run, the claustrophobic smell gave her a faint, light-headed feeling.

She could see no outside doors beyond the hodgepodge of household collector items. If the assassin rushed through the front door, how would they get away? Where would they run? She felt momentary panic as her mind raced on.

"This place is perfect," Donovan reassured, after a quick glance at her tense face. "The bar must be in back."

A gnomelike man in a white shirt, black tie and red suspenders popped up behind the counter with such suddenness that Erin jumped.

"Yes, the bar is in back," he said, "just follow the carpet."

She looked down. A Persian carpet runner, worn threadbare in places with years of use, led through the maze of old highboys and Bombay chests toward the back of the shop.

With a quick glance toward the door they'd just entered, Donovan grabbed her hand. "Let's go."

As she followed him around a tall armoire, Erin heard the faint tinkle of the street door opening. Donovan heard it, too. He squeezed her hand, warning her not to turn and look. Was it the assassin close behind them?

Her heart in her throat, Erin followed Donovan down a furniture corridor through an arched doorway to a brightly lighted horseshoe bar. Amazingly, since it was midafternoon, the place was nearly full with ten of the twelve barstools occupied. Anxiously she turned and stared behind her, but no one followed them into the bar.

Still anxious, she peered around the place. Everywhere she looked—swinging on strings and tacked to the walls, even plastered on the ceiling—were ads for every kind of product imaginable.

Somehow the whole setup looked unreal to Erin, like a scene from a Broadway play. For a terrifying instant she wondered if she was dreaming, if this bar with its *funerary libations* and oddly shaped signs was part of some horrid nightmare. Donovan's firm squeeze on her hand told her she was wide-awake.

A young version of the gnomelike man out front greeted them from across the bar. Like his father, he was decked out in a white shirt, black tie and red suspenders.

"Sure now," he said, "can I fix you one of our funerary

libations? They're guaranteed to send you straight to paradise.''

Donovan gave him a worried frown. "No, my wife's had a sudden attack of nausea. Is there a back door out of here? She needs some fresh air.''

Right before Erin's eyes, Donovan changed. Without altering as much as a hair on his head, he turned from a charismatic man of the world into a concerned, doting husband. From the worried expression on his face to his slightly bent posture, everything about him fit the part he played.

The bartender's face showed instant sympathy. "Sorry your wife's poorly. Door's at the back o' the bar.'' He nodded behind him. "Just come around then.''

With Donovan still holding her hand, Erin hurried behind him to the door. He pushed it open, and cold air hit her in the face, relieving her mild dizzy spell but not her anxious fear. Would someone come crashing into the alley behind them, the way the assassin had in Georgetown? She breathed deeply, ridding herself of the stuffy inside atmosphere.

"This is starting to be a habit," she gasped, once the door had closed behind them. "We're getting to be experts at running out back doors into alleys." But her light words did nothing to relieve her apprehension. As she glanced around, a new wave of anxiety swept over her.

Like the Georgetown alley, this one was a canyon with wall-to-wall buildings on both sides. If the assassin found them here, there would be no escape.

A few minutes later when they reached the nearest street crossing, Donovan slowed to a more leisurely pace and turned right, away from the main part of town. Erin found herself breathing heavily, more from nervousness than exertion.

On the first intersecting side street the buildings were even older than the one they'd just come through, with peeling paint and broken steps.

"Wait by the side of that chemist's shop," he said, pointing to a local pharmacy.

Quickly Erin did as he asked, then watched with reluctant admiration as he prepared to steal the first unlocked car he found on the street. As in the bar, his demeanor changed completely, this time into what appeared to Erin to be a conscientious public servant.

From the pocket of his sweat jacket he pulled out a pencil, a small notebook and a wide-billed baseball cap. After jamming the cap on his head, he walked along the narrow sidewalk for about half a block stopping at each car and writing down license numbers in his notebook.

Suddenly he bent down to remove a car's front and back license plates with a small screwdriver from his jacket pocket. A few moments later he returned to replace the stolen plates with those of the targeted vehicle.

Erin's heart leapt into her throat when an elderly couple approached and questioned him. He grinned and said something, and they walked away. Though they didn't seem alarmed, Erin half expected to hear the up-and-down scream of a police siren seconds after they turned the corner out of sight. She expelled a giant breath of relief when the license plate switch was complete and he beckoned to her.

Without running, Erin hurried to the car and got in. The interior smelled of stale cigarette smoke. Donovan was already behind the wheel. Gunning the engine, he took off, back in the direction they'd come.

"What did they want?" Erin asked, unable to contain her curiosity.

He glanced toward her. "The old folks? They wanted to know what I was doing. I told them I was recovering a stolen car for its rightful owners."

"And they believed you?"

"Sure. They had no reason not to."

His glib answers bothered her. Had he been lying to her with the same alacrity? "What if the car had been theirs?"

"I would have apologized for my mistake." Pulling the

map out of his pocket, he handed it to her. "We've probably lost our shadow, but to be on the safe side, find a road out of Roscommon other than the one we were on."

Quickly Erin examined the map and gave him directions to a two-lane primary highway leading northwest.

"We're backtracking so we'll lose some time," she explained, "probably not much more than an hour. We'll get back on the highway to Donegal at Boyle."

When they reached the old-fashioned town of Boyle, they stopped long enough to buy a couple of cheap identical suitcases. Erin knew her mother's tastes ran to five-star hotels. Her hideaway was sure to be luxurious. They'd be less conspicuous with luggage. With their limited time, shopping for clothes was out of the question.

Erin didn't let herself think about what would happen after they got there. The idea of spending the night with Donovan flared her vivid imagination into sensual scenes—his lips on hers, hands caressing her naked body. Taking a deep breath, she fought the erotic thoughts, pushing them out of her mind. First they had to locate her mother. If Erin found out she was safe and well, everything else would fall into place.

Night had fallen when they reached Sligo on the west coast with no sign of their pursuers. They had cookies and coffee at a gas station and called it dinner.

Finally, as they drove through Donegal Town and across the narrow causeway to a wooded island on Donegal Bay she announced: "This is it. The Ballyshannon Lodge is straight ahead. That's where Jean said we'd find her."

THE RAMBLING two-story mansion on the shore of Donegal Bay struck Donovan as an investigator's nightmare. Instead of the neat square lines of O'Shaughnessy's Glenkillan House, this place was a tangle of curves and angles.

Inside Donovan knew he'd find narrow passageways, closets hidden behind dark wood wainscoting, and trapdoors leading to underground wine cellars—all features of houses built in the eighteenth century, when this one was probably constructed. If O'Shaughnessy's wife wanted to hide, Donovan—or anybody else—would have a hell of a time finding her. But such would not be the case. He'd been smart to let Erin lead him here. Margaret Sullivan wouldn't hide from her own daughter. A brief moment of smug satisfaction was wiped out by his overwhelming sense of guilt at using Erin so blatantly, especially now that she trusted him.

Telling her to wait by the door, Donovan took a flashlight from the glove box, and examined the license plates of the other cars in the parking lot. None bore the distinctive shamrock emblem that marked all Shamrock Construction vehicles, including O'Shaughnessy's personal cars. But if Margaret Sullivan was as smart as he thought, she would have switched automobiles before she got here.

He returned to Erin, waiting with their empty suitcases by a well-lighted back door. Though the house's main entrance must be in front, facing the bay, the driveway did not extend around the house. Arriving guests obviously entered through the back door.

"Her car's not here," he announced, picking up their bags. He thought he was prepared for Erin's disappointment, but something inside him withered when he saw her glazed look of despair. He wanted to hold her in his arms and smooth away her disappointment.

"Then she's probably not here, either." Erin's voice held a distinct quaver. "She'd never steal a car the way we did, and if she'd borrowed one from a relative, Jean would have told me."

"Maybe she rented a car," he suggested softly, knowing Erin needed a logical explanation more than a sympathetic touch.

"Then what about that stranger?" Her eyes searched his, demanding reassurance. "If he's holding her captive, he'd never have come here. So that's why she's not here."

"Your stepfather *said* somebody saw her with a

stranger," Donovan noted. "You don't know that's the truth. The man who showed up at Jean's was probably sent by O'Shaughnessy, either to check up on her or to fetch her home." Donovan made the suggestion to make Erin feel better, not because he believed it.

"But your mother left Dublin hours before the stranger appeared at your cousin's," he continued. "There's no way he could have caught up with her, especially since he had no idea where she was headed. I'm sure Jean didn't give him a clue." His chest lightened as he saw her expression relax.

"Then you think she might be inside the lodge even though her car isn't here?" Erin's voice sounded stronger.

"Absolutely." He dropped the suitcases. Putting his arms around her, he hugged her to him. Though she wore her car coat, she felt warm and soft in his embrace. "And even if she isn't here, there's no reason to think she's been hurt. She left Dublin under her own steam according to your cousin."

He leaned down to kiss her. Before his lips touched hers, the door swung open. A sweet-faced elderly woman stood in the doorway.

"Welcome," she said, her eyes twinkling as she saw their embrace. "How nice you decided to spend the night at the Ballyshannon Lodge." Her gaze dropped to the two identical pieces of new luggage beside Donovan's leg. To his amusement, he realized the suitcases, as well as the fond embrace she'd interrupted, made the old woman think they were newlyweds.

"You're in luck, you two," she said, with the proprietary air of an owner. "We've got just one room left. It's the nicest in the lodge."

Donovan looked down at Erin's tired face. In the past forty-eight hours she'd been fired from her job, flown across the Atlantic, been locked in her bedroom, walked a narrow ledge to escape, and been tracked by an assassin— all without a word of complaint. Though she'd never admit it, he knew she had to have a good night's sleep, or she'd drop from exhaustion.

"That would be just fine," he said in his best Irish brogue.

Erin stared at him, her eyes wide, but didn't object. Like him, she obviously realized they couldn't go hunting all over County Donegal for two available rooms.

"I'll send someone for your luggage," the woman said.

Donovan picked up their two suitcases, slowly so they looked heavy. "I can manage."

The old woman eyed him with admiration. "Of course you can, darlin'." Turning, she bustled away, obviously expecting them to follow.

Inside, the house was exactly as Donovan expected: a maze of corridors and wide stairways. Was Margaret Sullivan hidden away somewhere in the nooks and crannies of this grand old house?

The drawing room was filled with oil paintings and antiques, and the dining room—all pink and green with a tented ceiling—looked ready for a royal visit. In spite of its angles and curves, the lodge was truly elegant, a fitting place for his first night with Erin.

Now why had that thought occurred to him? Before he could thrust it from his mind, he heard Erin ask if a Margaret Sullivan was staying here. He froze. What would the old woman's answer be?

"YOU SAY SHE'D BE registered under Sullivan?" The old woman gave Erin a piercing stare. Suddenly her light blue eyes, so friendly at the door, turned suspicious. "Nobody with that name stayed here the past couple of days."

"Are you sure?" Erin persisted, resisting the flood of weariness and despair that threatened to engulf her.

Lifting her chin, the old woman nodded vigorously. "Since we have only sixteen rooms, it's not difficult to recognize all our patrons—if they come out while I'm at the desk."

"Then you must know them by sight, as well as name." Fumbling in her handbag, Erin pulled out her wallet. A picture of her mother was in the plastic sleeve on top. She handed it to the woman. "Here. This is what my mother looks like."

The woman stared at the picture, then at Erin. "You say she's your mother? She doesn't look like you."

"I know." Erin told herself to be patient. "But she's my mother, she really is."

"No, I haven't seen her." Handing the picture back to Erin, the old woman appeared to relent. "Some of our patrons eat an early dinner and go to their rooms before the night staff comes on. You might try showing the day clerk this picture tomorrow morning."

"The day clerk?" Erin realized this woman must be the night clerk, probably hired because her folksy chatter and appearance made her seem like family.

While Erin talked to the clerk, Donovan signed the register. Erin noticed that he took plenty of time, enough to scrutinize every name on the top page and the two underneath. After hearing the clerk's words, he straightened and stepped toward them.

"What's the day clerk's home number?" he asked, flashing his beguiling smile. "Mrs. Blake needs to locate her mother right away."

Mrs. Blake? With sudden insight Erin realized he was telling her he'd signed them in with a false name—and as man and wife.

Eyeing Donovan the old woman lifted an eyebrow in an expression that was downright flirtatious. Something about him seemed to turn every woman he met, regardless of age, into a coquette.

"Oh, I couldn't do that, sir. It's against lodge rules to give patrons the numbers of staff."

Donovan reached into his pocket and withdrew a handful of Irish pound notes. Making sure the woman saw the money, he thrust it into her skirt pocket.

"We'd truly appreciate your help," he said, giving her an intimate smile.

Baksheesh again, Erin thought, without a shred of guilt at Donovan's bribe. To find her mother she would gladly have bribed anyone on the face of the earth, and her former smug scruples be damned.

"Well," the old woman said reluctantly, fingering the notes in her pocket, "for two nice young newlyweds like yourselves, I suppose I can be forgiven for breaking a rule or two." Leaning over the small registration desk, she jotted a name and number on a slip of paper.

Hope rose within Erin. Maybe now she'd get some answers.

Chapter Twelve

Erin waited until the elderly clerk had shown them to their rooms before dialing the day clerk's home number. A woman answered. Perched on the bed in the assigned grand suite, she asked for Brian Cairns.

"Who is this?" The voice at the other end of the line was as raspy as worn brakes.

Thinking quickly, Erin said, "Mrs. Dan Blake." It was the name Donovan had written in the register downstairs. "I'm staying at the Ballyshannon Lodge and need to ask Mr. Cairns about my mother. She said she'd be here, but she's not signed in and the night clerk doesn't remember her." Erin gripped the phone tightly as a feeling of helplessness almost suffocated her. Where could her mother have gone? As far as Erin knew, she had no friends—and certainly no relatives—on Ireland's west coast.

"Sorry about your mother, Mrs. Blake." The raspy voice softened a fraction. "I'm afraid I can't help you. My husband isn't home yet."

Erin stiffened. Fear for her mother made her paranoid. Had something happened to the day clerk? "Do you expect him soon, Mrs. Cairns?"

The woman sighed. "He's likely stopped at the Red Fox on the way and won't make it home till after the place closes."

"When's that?" Wearily Erin brushed back her hair. "It's important to talk to him."

"No sense botherin' to call here later. After a night at the Red Fox, he's not fit fer man nor beast till next mornin'." The woman sounded impatient. "You'll just have to wait till he shows up for work."

After thanking her, Erin hung up and turned to Donovan. "He isn't home yet. His wife says he probably stopped at a local pub called the Red Fox."

Donovan dropped beside her on the canopied bed. It sagged beneath his weight. "Do you want to go into town, try to find him at the pub?"

Erin's hopes leapt. Maybe they *could* do something tonight. Then reality hit her, and she shook her head. "By now the clerk's been drinking for hours. His wife said he'd be too intoxicated to make any sense."

"I still think we ought to try." The bed wobbled as Donovan turned toward her. "Maybe his wife's exaggerating." His gaze slid from Erin's face to her breasts to the satin covered bedspread. He slid his eyes upward to meet with hers. A tinge of red colored his cheeks.

Erin's pulse beat faster. Was he thinking the same thing she was? That paradise might be under that spread? As soon as the thought appeared, she hated herself for thinking it. How could she be so crass with her precious mother missing? She took a deep breath, tearing her eyes away from his rugged face. Somehow his shadow of emerging beard made him look more appealing than ever.

"After your flight and last night without sleep, you must be bushed," Donovan said. There was an odd, gentle note to his voice. "Why don't I check out the pub while you stay here and get some shut-eye?"

The sympathy in his voice told Erin she must have misjudged him. Stress and lack of sleep were addling her brain. He was more concerned for her comfort and peace of mind than for the pleasures of the bed. Every time she thought she had this strange man figured out, he turned the tables on her.

An unsettling thought occurred. Was Donovan changing personalities now—from devil-may-care rogue to sympathetic friend? Hadn't she seen how easily he'd changed at the pub in Roscommon? Maybe he was snowing her to get to her mother first. The possibility tugged at the fringes of Erin's mind, threatening to suck away her optimism like killer quicksand. Angrily she thrust her suspicion away, knowing it would interfere with her search for her mother. No matter what game he was playing, she needed Donovan's help.

"If you're going to the pub, so am I," she declared.

Donovan gave an approving nod. In spite of her doubts his slightest hint of praise sent her spirits soaring.

"I thought you might," he said, his voice warm.

Downstairs, the night clerk directed them to the Red Fox, located on Donegal's Diamond, the town square. Since the pub closed at eleven, they had only half an hour to get to town and find Brian Cairns.

"WHO WANTS TO KNOW?" The stocky bartender glared at Donovan and Erin with suspicious eyes.

Donovan peered up and down the scratched mahogany bar. From their casual sweaters, none of the men gathered there looked as if they'd stopped on the way home from work. But the elderly night clerk hadn't dressed in a businesslike fashion either. If her casual attire was the usual work uniform at the Ballyshannon Lodge, any of these men might be Brian Cairns regardless of their clothes.

"I'm Dan Blake and this is my wife." Donovan gave the bartender a serious man-to-man stare. "We're hoping Mr. Cairns can help us locate my wife's mother. She was supposed to meet us at the lodge, but the night clerk has no record."

Though Donovan had spoken loudly enough for everyone in the room to hear, nobody at the bar met his gaze.

But the bartender's expression softened, as Donovan had guessed it would. The Irish were notoriously devoted to their mothers.

"Brian stops once, twice a week," the bartender said. "But not tonight. Did you try callin' his house, then?"

Donovan nodded. "His wife said he'd be here."

The bartender glanced toward Erin, his suspicion changed to sympathy. "Is she an old lady, then?"

"Not exactly elderly," Erin said. Picturing her beautiful mother, she could almost hear Margaret's impulsive burst of laughter at the bartender's question.

"But she's not young anymore, either," Erin went on, embroidering the truth, "and usually doesn't travel alone. We're quite worried about her."

"Can't say as I blame you," he replied, beaming under the influence of Erin's warm smile. "Now that you know he's not here, would you like to call Cairns's missus again—see if she's heard from him?" He nodded toward the end of the room. "Phone's behind the bar."

As Donovan led Erin past a big stone fireplace, heat enveloped them even though the dying fire was reduced to embers. The men clustered at the bar gave them curious glances, but nobody met Donovan's inquiring gaze.

The phone sat on a shelf alongside bottles of Irish whiskey. Pulling the number from her purse, Erin dialed.

Though Donovan got only Erin's side of the conversation, he could tell the news wasn't good.

"So Cairns isn't home yet?" he said, after she'd hung up.

"That's right," she answered. "Since he isn't here, his wife thinks he probably stopped at a friend's."

Donovan could see Erin's frustration and anxiety in the tense look on her face—her brows drawn down, her full lips pressed together. He put one arm around her waist and was disturbed at the tension he felt in her body.

"One good thing," she said, her expression lightening, "his wife says he never misses work. No matter how drunk he gets the night before, he'll be at the lodge tomorrow morning.''

For a brief moment Donovan held her close to his side, letting himself enjoy her softness against him. "Then we'll just have to be patient. Tomorrow morning isn't that far off." Reluctantly he released her.

"Any luck?" the bartender asked as they headed for the door.

Donovan shook his head. "No, but thanks for the phone." He passed the man a ten-pound note. "If you should happen to see Brian Cairns, tell him to call Dan Blake at the lodge." Quickly he jotted the name on a bar napkin.

A broad smile on his face, the bartender took the napkin and promised he would.

OUTSIDE THE PUB, the cold night air slapped Erin's face like a damp rag. Wretchedly tired, she felt icy fingers seep into every pore.

"Baksheesh for the bartender?" she snapped, emphasizing the question. "Do you think he knows where Cairns is?"

Donovan shrugged matter-of-factly. "Maybe yes, maybe no. In any case, a little baksheesh is guaranteed to help his memory."

"Tips? Bribes? Baksheesh? You think they'll buy you anything, don't you, Donovan?" She spit the words out, surprised at herself for feeling so angry at something that hadn't bothered her earlier. She was angry at her mother for dropping off the face of the earth; angry at the clerk for not going home after work the way any normal person would; infuriated with Donovan for thinking bribes could buy anything. Erin tightened her lips.

They stood at one side of the pub on the Diamond, Donegal's three-sided town square. The hotel and storefronts glowed whitely in the lamplight. To the north at the top of the square, she could make out the towers and turrets of Donegal Castle, like something out of a fairy tale.

With his bribes and his changing personalities, Donovan's the one out of a fairy tale, she thought, angry at herself for wanting him.

"You're tired, Erin," Donovan said softly, taking her hand and drawing it through his arm. "Let's go back to the lodge and get some shut-eye."

To Erin, he sounded patronizing again, the way he had when he'd tried to convince her not to come to Ireland. She felt her cheeks burn.

"I'm not tired," she contradicted, jerking her hand away. "And don't think your precious baksheesh is going to work with me, Donovan. Because I'm not taking."

He recoiled as though she'd struck him. "What the hell are you talking about?"

"About us." She glared at him, unable to stop the torrent of words flooding upward. "Don't try to soft-soap me into making me think you're here because you want to be with me when it's my mother you've been after all along. I know baksheesh when I see and hear it. And all the care and attention you've been giving me since I got to Ireland adds up to just one thing: a bribe to make me trust you so I'll find Mom for you." Somehow it had escaped—all the dark suspicion festering inside her.

"No, listen to me, Erin. Baksheesh is money pure and simple. Pounds. Dollars. Legal tender."

"Not entirely," she argued, knowing she was right. "It can be anything given to get somebody to do something they don't want to."

"Are you saying I'm pretending to care for you as a sort of bribe? That my feelings for you are phony?" There was hurt disbelief in his voice.

Knowing how good an actor he was, Erin ignored the pain in his eyes. "Well, aren't they phony?"

"Not anymore they aren't."

Staring into his eyes, she sensed what was coming, but

couldn't force herself to back away. He pulled her against him roughly, almost violently. She told herself to fight, to resist, to break away, but she felt paralyzed. On trembling legs she found herself pressing tightly against his body, all her anger and need welded together in a giant surge of yearning.

When his lips met hers, he tasted salty, like the sea, and Erin floundered, drowning in waves of sensation. She tried to force her confused emotions into some sort of order, but her brain was in tumult. Giving herself freely to her passion, she wound her arms inside his jacket and around his back. His muscles tensed under her fingertips.

"Oh, Erin," he whispered, lifting his head to look at her. "You're what I want, not your mother. If you don't trust me to talk to her, I won't, at least not until this operation is over."

In an odd contrast to her heated longing for him, the tiny hairs on her arms prickled at his words. "If not you, then would someone else from the agency question Mom?"

Sighing, he cradled her face in his hands. "I'm afraid that's unavoidable. But at least it wouldn't be me. When I talk to her, it'll be because she's your mother, not because she may be involved in a counterfeiting conspiracy."

Erin inhaled deeply, breathing in his strong male scent. Her anger gone, she no longer needed him to promise anything, only to feel his arms around her and know he was here with her.

"But I'd rather it be you who talked to her than a stranger," she admitted slowly, knowing in her heart it was so. "You'd be fair with her and let her know what she was up against."

"Of course I would." He tilted her chin up and stared into her eyes. "Are you sure my interrogation won't be a barrier between us?"

Erin nodded. "Now that I know you won't try to trap her…"

"The only one I want to trap is you." There was a burning light in his eyes as he reluctantly released her.

Holding hands they hurried past lovers embracing near the monument in the Diamond's parklike center. The short drive across the causeway to the lodge seemed to take forever. By the time they reached their suite of rooms, they were both breathing heavily, more from anticipation than the sprint up the stairs.

Erin stood by the sitting-room sofa as Donovan turned the key in the ancient lock, the key they'd had to request specially, because lodge doors weren't normally locked. She could feel him watching as she took off her car coat and flung it on the cushions. The dim light glimmered over his rugged face revealing his unleashed hunger. Though the room wasn't overheated, drops of moisture clung to his damp forehead.

He came toward her with flames smoldering in his eyes. When his large hand touched her face and held it gently, her body tingled from the contact. In one forward motion she was in his arms and his mouth was on hers. Again she tasted the saltiness of the sea, but this time she didn't flounder. Winding her arms around his neck, she raised herself to meet him.

His mouth searched hers hungrily and she felt his hands sear her bare back, pushing up under her sweater and bra. As she drowned in his kiss, his fingers lifted her sweater even higher and she felt his hand caressing her bare breast. Shivers of delight flowed through her at his touch.

He was trembling, too. Letting go of her, he yanked off his windbreaker. Taking her hand, he drew her into the bedroom where the king-size bed awaited. Gently he eased her down onto it.

The light from the bedside lamps cast blurry shadows on the papered walls. Eyes wide, she watched him take off his gray sweatshirt. He wore nothing underneath, and his chest muscles glistened in the pale light. Senses reeling, she glimpsed the mat of curly hair on his chest before he lay down beside her.

He pulled her to him. Through the mists of her passion, her mother's smiling face appeared in Erin's mind. Lord have mercy, what was she doing? Though barely able to control the raging fire inside her, she forced herself to push him away. "Oh God, I can't do this, Donovan," she said, her voice choked.

Frowning, he stared into her eyes with such intensity she felt naked inside, her mind stripped bare for him to read. "What's wrong, Erin?" he whispered. "Is it something I've done or said?"

"Oh, no." She touched his cheek in reassurance, her heart aching. "I want you terribly. You must know that."

"Then why?" His broad shoulders were heaving as he breathed.

"I can't do this while my mother's missing. It's like— like dancing on her grave."

"But you can't rob yourself of joy," he whispered, "on the remote possibility something's happened to her."

"But maybe something *has* happened to her." Erin tried to swallow the sob in her throat and didn't succeed. "Tonight while we were in that pub I had the strongest feeling that something dreadful had happened. I can't shrug it off. Even here with you, wanting you, that feeling is all around me..." She tried to steady her voice and failed. If only he would understand.

Very reluctantly, Donovan eased her sweater down over her breasts, the nipples still swollen with passion. God knows he wanted her. The cramping ache in his loins had already started. But tonight Erin needed sleep, not the intimate attentions of a CIA agent. This was the wrong place and time for what his hungry body was demanding.

"You're just tired," he said, trying to relieve her anxiety. "That's why you're imagining a world-class disaster."

"You're probably right," she agreed slowly. "Before

tonight I've never shown signs of being able to read the future, thank goodness.''

The grateful look on her beautiful face made him glad he hadn't pressed her into an intimacy she'd be sorry for.

A tiny smile crooked the corners of her mouth. "I'm afraid the real disaster happened just now, when I pushed you away."

"That was no disaster," he said, "just two people being honest with each other."

"I'm really sorry, and—"

He raised two fingers to cover her lips. "Don't say anything more. Just lie here beside me and let me hold you."

Turning toward him, she rested her face in the hollow of his throat. "You've been so wonderful tonight, Donovan. Promise you won't change again." Her words were muffled against his throat, and he knew she was already half asleep.

Not certain exactly what she meant, he breathed a kiss on her fragrant hair.

But he didn't promise her anything.

MORNING DAWNED WITH drizzly rain. The front of the lodge, where Erin now stood gazing out the tall drawing-room windows, looked across a wide expanse of lawn toward Donegal Bay.

Sensing movement behind her, she turned. A youngish man in a beautifully patterned green-and-saffron sweater hurried across the room toward her. At last! This must be Brian Cairns. She'd left Donovan asleep and slipped downstairs early to catch Cairns as soon as he came on duty.

"You're up ahead of your husband, then, Mrs. Blake," he said.

"Mr. Cairns?" Erin extended her hand.

Eagerly the young man shook it. "No, but I'm pleased to meet you, Mrs. Blake. Since I'm on nights, I don't get a chance to chat with any but early risers like yourself."

"Do you recall seeing my mother?" Erin pulled out Margaret's picture and showed it to him.

He shook his head. "No, but like I said I see only the early risers. Brian's the man you need to talk to. He comes in at eight. If your mother were here, he'd know it."

Sighing, Erin thanked him and went into the dining room. Early though it was, the breakfast buffet was ready with fruit, milk and cereals displayed on a long, linen-covered table. A chef stood by to prepare eggs, waffles, pancakes and a variety of meats.

Erin had ordered when Donovan joined her at her table. Bending, he gave her a light kiss on the cheek. When she smelled his aftershave and felt his smooth skin against hers, a throbbing welled up deep inside her.

"What's the story on Cairns?" he asked, still standing.

"Get your food. I'll tell you when you get back."

A few minutes later after he returned with a plate loaded with fruit, she told him the day clerk was due at eight.

He dug into his melon. "That'll just about give me time to finish my pancakes and potatoes."

When eight o'clock came, they were sitting on an elegant sofa upholstered in silk brocade, their backs to the rain-gray windows, facing the small registration desk in one corner.

At eight-fifteen the late-night clerk assured them that Brian sometimes came in a few minutes late. But he'd be here soon, never fear. At eight forty-five he called Cairns's house. His wife said he wasn't there—hadn't been home all night.

Erin asked to speak to her. "Do you have any idea where he might be, Mrs. Cairns?"

"I've already called his two best mates," sniffed the wife, obviously close to tears. "They haven't seen him. The stupid article must be lying in a ditch somewhere, Mrs. Blake. The way that man drinks, I knew something would happen to him."

After a few words of sympathy, Erin hung up the phone. When she turned to Donovan her mood was as gray as the drizzly rain outside the drawing-room window.

"Well, where do we go from here?" she asked helplessly. "Cairns might not show up for days."

Donovan led her back to the sofa. "We'll let everybody on the day staff take a look at your mother's picture. If she's been here, somebody's bound to have seen her." He paused, thinking. "Another thing we can do is call your cousin. If your mother had a last minute change of plans, she might have phoned Jean."

"Good idea," Erin said, feeling more in control. "What about license numbers? If the lodge keeps a record, we could correlate numbers with people registered. If Mom used another name, we'd at least find that out."

Donovan shook his head. "The lodge didn't ask for our license number. They didn't even ask for the make and model of the car."

Erin's spirits dropped again.

"But maybe somebody checks the lot during the night," Donovan suggested. "If so—"

"Then he might remember seeing the shamrock Patrick puts on all his car licenses," she concluded, jumping up.

They hurried to the registration desk.

The weary late-night clerk no longer appeared as eager to greet them as he had Erin earlier this morning. "Yes, sir?" he said to Donovan without smiling.

"Does anybody from the lodge keep an eye on patrons' cars during the night?" Donovan asked.

The clerk gave him an *are-you-kidding* look. "Nobody's going to bother your vehicle, if that's what's worrying you, Mr. Blake. In an establishment that doesn't even issue room keys unless they're requested, we don't find it necessary to stand guard over our patrons' cars."

With an apologetic glance at Erin, Donovan took some folded Irish pounds from his pocket, holding the bills so the clerk could see how much. "It's worth twenty pounds to me to talk to someone who might have got a look at the license plates in the parking lot during the past few nights."

The clerk's harsh expression softened. "Well, I do like to take a bit of fresh air now and then."

Donovan handed him the money.

Baksheesh again, Erin thought, but this time she felt no anger. Last night she'd been weary and full of doubt. Her suspicion had made her angry at everything and everybody. But this morning the feeling was gone. If the clerk remembered seeing the shamrock, they'd at least know Margaret had been here.

"So," Donovan said, "during the past couple of days, do you remember seeing a plate with a shamrock on the left-hand side?"

"Sure," the clerk replied without hesitating. "I don't see many like that."

"The car my wife's mother was driving had a license with that symbol."

Erin let out a slow breath of relief. "That means she's been here, doesn't it?" she said to Donovan.

He nodded. "No doubt about it. Now we have to figure out where she went."

"If she went somewhere, she didn't go in that car." The clerk made the statement matter-of-factly.

Startled, Erin stared at him. "What do you mean?"

"Car was parked in the north lot where the help parks," the clerk said. "'Twas still there last night."

Erin and Donovan stared at each other and then at the clerk. *"The north lot?"* They said the words together.

"You mean there's more than one lot?" Donovan added.

The clerk nodded. "Not surprised you missed it. There's no road to it from the house."

"Where the hell is it?" Donovan snapped.

"Other side of the house. There's a footpath to it. Car exit leads directly to the main road."

The clerk had barely finished speaking when Donovan grabbed Erin's hand and started down the corridor toward the back door. Heedless of the drizzling rain, they crossed the gravel parking area at a swift pace. After hunting frantically, they finally found the path. Overgrown with bushes, it started on the far side of a wide expanse of lawn and wound through scrubby foliage to the employee lot. The cold drizzle soaked Erin's sweater and jeans, but she barely noticed.

They both spotted the distinctive shamrock emblem on the license plate of a white BMW at the same time. Donovan tried the door on the driver's side. It was open.

How like her mother, Erin thought, not to worry about something as mundane as locking a car. The drizzly wetness on her face turned warm with her tears.

Donovan flung the door open and stepped aside to let Erin stick her head in. Instantly she smelled the subtle odor of the Nina Ricci perfume her mother used. On the seat was a silk scarf Erin recognized.

"This is Mom's car all right," she said, fighting her tears. "She must have been in terrible trouble to just walk away and leave it."

"Let's see if she left anything in the trunk."

Keeping an eye on the path, Erin stood behind him while he tinkered with the lock. As he swung the lid open, she peered around his shoulder.

Donovan took one look and slammed the lid shut.

It was too late.

She'd already glimpsed the crumpled corpse inside, its clothing stained with blood.

Chapter Thirteen

For one horrified moment, Erin thought the body in the BMW's trunk was her mother's. Assailed by a terrible sense of loss and shock, she gulped huge mouthfuls of the cold misty air. When she started to shake, Donovan quickly pulled her to him.

"It's a man, Erin, not your mother." He held her face so tightly against his throat she could hear the blood pounding in his veins.

"Wha...what's a dead man doing in Mom's car?" Her words were muffled against Donovan's skin. "Who is he?"

Gently he rocked her back and forth. "I've got a pretty good idea. Soon as you're feeling better, I'll search the body."

"I'm feeling fine," she declared, trying to pull free so they could find out who he was.

Donovan wouldn't let her go. "Not until you stop shaking."

Clamping her teeth together so they wouldn't chatter, Erin pushed harder. Struggling against him warmed her, and she stopping shivering.

Hurriedly he let her go. "Turn your back to the car and tell me if you hear anyone coming."

Grateful to look away, she swung around, eyeing the narrow path to the lodge. Surrounded by tall bushes, the parking area was isolated. She heard nothing but the small

rasping noises Donovan made when he opened the trunk
lid. A few moments later she heard the lock snap closed.

A shudder swept through Erin. What if the body had
been her mother's? Without being told, she knew who the
dead man was. "Is it Brian Cairns?" she asked.

Donovan nodded. "Looks like he didn't stop anywhere
on the way home last night after all."

She started for the lodge. "We've got to call the police
in Donegal. Mrs. Cairns has to be told about her husband."

Donovan caught her arm, stopping her in midstep. "Listen to me, Erin. We can't tell anybody about this, not until
we talk to your mother."

Dumbfounded, Erin stared at him. The drizzle had turned
to a steady rain. Both of them were soaked. Water dripped
off Donovan's wet hair and trickled down his cheeks.

"This man had a wife and family," she said, aghast.
"And his body in Mom's car means she's in terrible danger. We can't just walk away without reporting it."

"Oh yes we can." There was a tense note in his voice.
"Because if we don't, the police will get involved, and
your mother might very well be accused of murder."

"Accused of murder?" Shock caused the words to
wedge in her throat. "You can't be serious. My mother
would *never* kill anyone. Never!" Erin glared at him.

Taking her arm, he turned her toward the car. Reluctantly, back ramrod stiff, she went with him.

"I'm not saying she killed anyone," he explained
smoothly, his face displaying an uncanny awareness of
what she was feeling. "But think about how this will look
to the police. If she's involved in counterfeiting with your
stepfather, she might have a motive. Who knows what role
Brian Cairns played in their operation?"

"You can't be serious," she repeated resentfully, fighting her own fears. But several other reasons to keep quiet
crowded into her mind. She and Donovan were driving a
stolen car. Worse, as soon as they called the police, the
authorities would alert Patrick, since the BMW was his.

The last thing Erin wanted was for her stepfather to find out anything about her, Donovan or Margaret.

"Listen to me," Donovan implored, urgency in his voice. "By killing Cairns, somebody's just proved he or she means business. We've got to move quickly before somebody else gets hurt."

Wavering, Erin tried to comprehend what she was hearing. "Wha…What can we do?" Her job as an intelligence officer hadn't prepared her for murder. She couldn't seem to think straight.

He went to the driver's side of the BMW and jerked the door open. "First we need to examine this car, see if there's any indication where your mother planned to go next. Then we've got to show her picture to the staff. Somebody other than Cairns must have talked to her."

"Do you think Mom told Cairns where she was going?" Erin drew back, not wanting to get near the car. With its corpse in the trunk, it had suddenly turned into a glistening white coffin.

Donovan shrugged. "The killer must have thought so."

"And he killed Cairns so he wouldn't tell anyone else?" she asked, the chill deepening within her.

"Either that, or he didn't want Cairns to identify him." Donovan scooted across the seat, opened the glove box, and began examining the contents.

"Here's something." He handed her a road map of Ireland. Two towns were circled—Donegal and Westport, about a hundred miles south on Clew Bay.

"Westport? Do you think that's where she went?" Erin tucked the map in her bag.

He shrugged. "It's our best bet so far."

"I guess I don't understand how a killer's mind works," she said, glancing between Donovan inside the car and the overgrown path to the lodge. "I should think the killer would want to distance himself from Mom. Why would he put the body in the trunk of her car?" Water dripped into her eyes from her wet hair. Annoyed, she brushed the soaking wet strands off her face.

After returning the contents to the glove box, Donovan shoved it closed. When he turned toward Erin, his mouth was tight and grim. "The bastard left Cairns's body in your mother's car because he didn't want it to be discovered right away."

For a tense moment Erin couldn't speak. Then the full implication of Donovan's words sunk in. "That means he knew she'd left the lodge and wouldn't be back for the car. Do you think he saw the map?"

Donovan shook his head. "No. He would have taken it if he'd seen it—to keep us, or the authorities, from finding it and guessing where to look for your mother."

Erin's stomach churned with fear for her mother. Donovan was bent low, poking at something on the carpet, when she caught a glimpse of movement on the path.

"Someone's coming," she said softly.

Donovan didn't straighten. "Act natural," he whispered.

It was the late-night clerk. He waved at them from across the lot. "I see you found the car," he called, coming toward them. Prepared for the wet weather, he wore a rain slicker and carried a black umbrella.

Straightening, Donovan settled on the driver's seat. "It belongs to my wife's mother, all right," he said congenially. "She must be here in the neighborhood."

The clerk came toward them and held the umbrella over Erin's head. She blinked, suddenly able to see without the rain dripping in her eyes.

"We're looking the car over," Donovan said, "trying to see if Mrs. Sullivan left any clues as to where she went."

"She'll probably be back at the lodge tonight," the clerk said noncommittally.

"I wonder where this bluish mud came from?" Donovan asked, holding up some dirt for Erin to see. "I'm surprised your mother left this stuff in her car."

Curious, the clerk handed the umbrella to Erin and bent

over to look. When he straightened, he held a clump of hard mud. Cautiously he sniffed it, then crumbled it between his fingers. "With that blue-gray color, it doesn't look to be from around here. I'd say Clew Bay, about a hundred miles south."

Erin's spirits soared. Clew Bay again. That had to be where her mother was.

The clerk looked quizzically at Erin. "Did your mother come from Clew Bay to Donegal, then?"

Automatically Erin shook her head. "No, from Dublin."

Bending, the clerk examined the BMW's carpet again. "Looks like too much mud for a woman's shoes. Maybe a friend or relative came up from Clew Bay to Donegal and drove the car."

Getting out of the BMW, Donovan faced the clerk. "She'll probably be back later. Guess we'll hang around for a while."

"Then maybe I'll see you tonight, if you're still up when I check in," said the clerk.

Erin moved to hand him his umbrella, but he shook his head. "I'm parked here, so I don't need it. Just leave it at the lodge when you're through with it." He swung around, but stopped in midstep.

"Now, if that isn't odd," he said, nodding toward a compact car parked near the BMW. "That's Brian's Renault. Long as I've worked here, I've never seen him leave it overnight, even when he planned to stop at the pub on the way home."

Donovan shrugged. "A friend must have picked him up."

"I'm sure you're right," the clerk agreed. "But if the car's here tonight, and Brian's still missing, I'll have to call the police." He frowned, obviously not thrilled at the prospect.

"I'm betting Cairns will be back before then to pick it up," Donovan soothed. Holding the umbrella, he started back toward the lodge with Erin by his side.

DURING THE NEXT HOUR, Erin showed her mother's picture
to everybody on the day staff, including kitchen help. Nobody remembered seeing her except a bellboy who recalled
delivering a meal to her room two days before. She'd been
alone, at least when the food was delivered. But the next
day when he carried her bags out, a man was behind the
wheel of the car she got into.

He couldn't describe the man. Neither could he remember the make of the car, nor the name she registered under.
But he was able to provide the room number from lodge
records of the room-service transaction. Armed with that
information, Erin and Donovan hurried back to the small
registration desk in the drawing room.

The register listed a woman named Margaret Kelly as
the room's only occupant. The signature was slanted, as
though her mother had tried to disguise her handwriting,
but it was close enough for Erin to recognize. Lord, she
thought, Mom must have been scared to death to hide like
this.

And this stranger who kept cropping up. Erin's neck hair
prickled every time she thought of some unknown man
hovering around her mother like a hungry vulture. Had he
some hold on her? Was he threatening her? Erin's mind
was filled with fear. Lifting worried eyes, she stared anxiously at Donovan. His warm hand covered hers in a quick
reassuring touch.

For a moment she closed her eyes against the sudden
sting of tears. Then, drawing a deep breath, carefully jotted
down the address listed on the register—an apartment in
Dublin. She called her cousin from the phone in their suite.

Jean said she had not heard from Margaret. "What can
I do to help?" she asked in a strained voice.

Erin had a ready answer. "Find out who lives at this
apartment in Dublin." Quickly she repeated the street number and her mother's assumed name, on the off chance the
apartment was listed under Margaret Kelly. "And get the
telephone number, too, if you can.

"You might have to go there," Erin said, "but I'm sure there's nothing dangerous about the apartment or Mom wouldn't have listed it as her address. It might even be a number she made up."

"I understand," Jean said, her voice tight with emotion. "I'll drive into Dublin this afternoon. Is there a telephone number where I can reach you?"

Covering the mouthpiece with her hand, Erin glanced toward Donovan, sitting next to her on the suite's sofa. "She wants to know where she can call to let us know what she found out."

"Tell her we'll be on the road and will check in with her when we get where we're going," he said, his eyes warning her to be careful.

After Erin had repeated what Donovan said, Jean's tone brightened. "Sounds like you have an idea where she's gone."

"Since this is the lodge phone, I can't tell you much," Erin stressed. "I'll call you tonight. Try not to worry."

Their clothes still damp, Erin and Donovan climbed into their stolen car.

"Clew Bay?" he asked, as they headed across the narrow causeway to Donegal. In his mind, that was the only logical place to go.

Erin sighed. "Even if the stranger drove up from there to bring her back, how're we going to find her once we get to Westport? Though it's the main town near Clew Bay, we'll never find her in a hundred years if she's hiding in somebody's house."

Disturbed at her anguished tone, Donovan glanced toward Erin. With her flame-red hair curling damply on her shoulders and her eyes downcast, she had the air of a woman trembling on the edge of despair. While he watched, she took a wet tissue from her jeans pocket. It tore as she brushed at her eyes and nose.

Reaching in the pocket of his jacket, he took out a damp,

but clean, linen handkerchief. Wordlessly he handed it to her.

She blew her nose. "Sorry, Donovan, I'm usually not a crybaby, but this whole thing looks more and more hopeless—starting with a map the killer should have found but apparently didn't and ending with a one-legged man who appears and vanishes like some kind of magician."

Donovan shifted uncomfortably in his seat. Erin's description of the mysterious stranger sounded very much like the one Mike Essinger had used to describe the assassin, Chameleon. Could Chameleon, in one of his disguises, be the man who kept appearing with Erin's mother? And if so, was he in league with her and O'Shaughnessy? Or was he holding her captive, as Erin feared? Donovan was betting on the former.

"Your mother acts scared," he admitted, "but she seems to be free and in good health. The man the bellboy saw in the car wasn't holding her prisoner."

"Maybe she's going along with the kidnapper to keep me from being hurt. Or maybe even Patrick."

Not even a remote possibility, Donovan thought, but he kept his suspicion to himself. Reaching out, he ran his hand up and down her arm. Damn, her sweater was still wet and probably the shirt under it. No wonder her voice sounded quivery. He turned the car heater up another notch.

Erin glanced helplessly at Donovan. "How in the world are we going to find her once we get there?"

"Simple," he said, with an assurance he didn't feel. "Westport is a small town—everybody knows everybody else's business. When we get there, we'll tell the town gossip Margaret Sullivan's daughter is looking for her. Then we'll let your mother find us."

THEY REACHED WESTPORT, on an eastern inlet of Clew Bay, at a little after five o'clock that afternoon. The steady rain continued, a cold gray sheet outside Erin's window.

Instead of stopping at the hotel overlooking the river at

town center, they found a bed-and-breakfast a couple of blocks away. Donovan parked in front of the two-story, steep-roofed house that looked out on the street.

Though the trip from Donegal to Westport was less than a hundred miles, it had taken more than four hours on the winding country road. Tired and hungry and more worried than ever about her mother, Erin had to get something squared away before they went inside. She put her hand on Donovan's sleeve. Dry at last, his sweatshirt felt pleasantly warm to her fingers.

At Erin's touch, he glanced toward her.

"If we expect Mom to find me, I'll have to register under my own name," she said softly.

"For appearances, that sounds like two rooms." The regret in his voice made her heart beat faster.

"Are you disappointed?" She tried to keep her tone light, so he wouldn't see how much his desire excited her.

"Very," he admitted, his gaze holding hers showed undeniable sexual warmth. "But since I suggested letting your mother find you, I guess I can't complain."

His look was so penetrating, it sent a tremor through her.

He eyed her thoughtfully. "If your mother can find us, so can anyone else who happens to be looking. Once the word goes out..."

He didn't have to finish his sentence for Erin to know what he meant. "You think whoever killed Brian Cairns might be here in Westport?"

"I'm almost positive he is," Donovan returned. "Cairns must have been killed because he knew where your mother was headed and the killer didn't want Cairns to tell anyone. Once he found out, it's only logical that he'd come here— if, indeed, this is where she is."

"Then he's a terrible threat to her." Rain dripping down the windshield took on an eerie brownish red hue. Erin clutched her armrest. A frightening moment passed before she realized it was only dirt sprayed by a passing car.

"He's a threat to us, too," Donovan said soberly. "If

we get to her first, we'll find out what she's so afraid of. I'm sure he doesn't want that.''

"You sound like you've changed your mind about her involvement in the conspiracy.'' As Erin watched, he thrust his jaw forward.

"I'm keeping an open mind,'' he said, meeting her gaze. "Whoever's after her might want to steal your stepfather's secrets, or kidnap your mother for ransom, or maybe get even with Patrick through her. Until you talk to her, you can't do more than speculate.''

"I don't have to speculate. I *know* she's not involved.'' With a sigh, Erin stepped out into the rain and crossed the sidewalk to the door of the bed-and-breakfast. With their two empty suitcases in hand, Donovan followed. Erin rang the bell. Nobody answered.

"Maybe they're not home,'' he said.

From her research on Ireland, she knew many of the country's bed-and-breakfast inns, especially in small towns like Westport, were operated by families who shared their homes with tourists. Rarely did they leave the house empty.

"They're probably at dinner,'' she said, ringing the bell again. This time she heard the sound of footsteps inside, and the door swung open. Erin met the level gaze of a young girl with hair even redder than her own. Barely into her teens, she had a generous sprinkling of freckles and the fine skin models dream about.

"We need two rooms for tonight,'' Erin said.

The girl smiled, opening the door wider. "Please come in, then.''

The front door opened into a small vestibule with a living room off to one side, and a long hallway straight ahead flanked on one side by a plain wooden stairway. From somewhere in the house came the clink of dishes and the intoxicating smell of roast lamb. They hadn't stopped for lunch, and the smell made Erin's stomach howl for food.

"Who is it, Molly?'' a woman's voice called.

"People who want two rooms.''

A buxom older version of the girl, with the same carrot-red hair, appeared from the living room. Like her daughter, she wore jeans and a faded plaid shirt with the sleeves rolled up. A white butcher's apron hung around her neck.

Breaking into a wide, open smile, she extended a plump hand. "I'm Mrs. Flaherty. Welcome to our home."

Shaking her hand, Erin knew they'd come to the right place. Their proprietress had the air of someone well acquainted in town. Quickly she pulled out her picture of her mother.

"Have you seen this woman?" she pleaded, her hands trembling. "She's Margaret Sullivan, my mother, and she's dropped out of sight. We think she's here in Westport. I'm worried sick about her."

Erin thought she saw the girl's eyes light with recognition, but, after glancing at her mother, she said nothing.

The mother shook her head. "No, I haven't seen her. Sure and with a face like that, I'd not soon be forgettin' her." She glanced at Erin and then at the picture. Erin expected her to remark how unlike her mother she looked, as the elderly clerk at the lodge had done. Instead she nodded, as if satisfied that she was indeed the daughter.

"We'll be happy to pay extra for the rooms if you'll ask around town for Mrs. Sullivan," Donovan said.

This time his bribe didn't work.

"I'll be glad to ask if anyone's heard of her," Mrs. Flaherty said, "but it'll now't cost you extra." She handed them two keys. "Dinner comes with the room. Bathroom's at the end of the hall upstairs. You'll share with four others." She turned to Molly, "Show them the rooms, darlin'," and then to Donovan.

"One thing," she said. "We'll need to park your car behind the house. If you'll give me the key, I'll have my boy do it."

"Is it right behind the house?" Donovan asked, giving her one of his high-voltage smiles. "If you don't mind, I'd rather park it myself."

"No problem," she said. "Go down the street, around, and up the alley. Don't worry about blocking another car. If somebody wants out, we'll get the boy to move yours."

After Donovan had left, Mrs. Flaherty turned to go.

"Mrs. Flaherty?" Erin queried softly. "Can I speak to you alone and in confidence?"

"Yes, of course." Quickly she shooed her curious daughter out of the vestibule.

"If you hear something about my mother, please tell me privately." Erin felt like a rat for asking, but she couldn't risk her mother's security. "I don't want Mr. Donovan to know."

"You don't trust him, then?" A quizzical look crossed her face. "Too bad, such an attractive man."

Erin wanted to spill out her heart and say that yes, she did trust him, with her life, her love, everything she held dear. But she couldn't. Because it wouldn't be true. In spite of the closeness they'd shared the past few days, a tiny kernel of doubt remained.

AFTER DINNER ERIN and Donovan started out the door to call Jean from a pay telephone, when Mrs. Flaherty emerged from the living room.

"I'm glad I caught you before your walk," she said.

"What's wrong?" Erin and Donovan spoke together, almost in unison.

Mrs. Flaherty put a steady hand on Erin's wrist. "Nothing's wrong, nothing a'tal. It's just that I'll be needin' you to move your car before you go, Mr. Donovan. Or give me the keys and I'll have the boy do it."

Donovan turned toward the back of the house. "Sure thing, Mrs. F. We'll start our walk from the alley."

The woman's fingers tightened on Erin's wrist. "You'll be needin' an umbrella, Miss Meyer. I'll get one for you while Mr. Donovan's movin' the car."

The woman's hand on Erin's wrist felt hot as a branding

iron. Her mind racing, Erin knew Mrs. Flaherty wanted to talk to her alone.

"We don't need an umbrella," Donovan said. "The rain's stopped."

It took all of Erin's self-control not to let her anxiety show. She gave him a *let's-humor-her* smile. "We might want one later. It's been raining off and on all day."

"Okay," he groaned. "I'll be back in a few minutes."

As soon as he'd disappeared through the living room toward the rear of the house, Mrs. Flaherty produced a sealed envelope from her apron pocket. Wordlessly, she handed it to Erin.

With trembling fingers, Erin ripped the envelope open and took out the message inside. Her heart leapt into her throat when she recognized her mother's handwriting. Though scribbled in pencil in obvious haste, the writing was undoubtedly hers. Quickly she scanned the note.

Erin,
Can't wait to see you. A friend will meet you tonight at eleven and bring you to me. The northwest corner of the bridge across the Carrowheg River at town center. Be careful and TELL NO ONE.

Her mother was okay. Erin's relief turned her knees to jelly, and she slumped into a chair next to the desk.

"Are you all right?" Mrs. Flaherty's bright blue eyes widened with concern.

She let out a huge sigh. "I couldn't be better."

"I'm glad it was good news," the woman said. "You stay right there. I'll fetch that umbrella."

Alone for the moment, Erin scanned the note again, memorizing it. The last three words were written in capital letters and underlined. TELL NO ONE. Their meaning was clear as a child's tears. Obviously her mother knew that Donovan was traveling with Erin, and didn't trust him.

Donovan, the man who had been so understanding, the man Erin loved. The man she herself didn't completely trust. Did her mother mistrust him for the same reason Erin did? Because he was a CIA agent investigating a conspiracy? Or did her mother know something Erin didn't? Perhaps that Donovan still worked for Patrick O'Shaughnessy?

If the two men had planned this whole thing to locate Margaret, they couldn't have come up with a more brilliant scheme. Erin was alone, in a foreign country, worried sick about her mother. Then Donovan stepped in, eager to help. With her intelligence background and knowledge of the restricted files, she was primed to believe his farfetched CIA story, complete with conspiracy.

Uneasily Erin recalled that Donovan had been with her almost constantly since she arrived in Ireland. Thanks to her he'd been welcomed at Jean Magee's house. Thanks to her he'd learned about the Ballyshannon Lodge and Clew Bay, where her mother obviously was. What if Patrick had locked her in the bedroom at his mansion purposely so Donovan could rescue her and earn her confidence?

She remembered Donovan's explanations for everything he'd done—from the missing wolfhounds to the open garage door to the unmarked embassy car. His explanations made sense. And she wanted to believe him, wanted to with all her heart. But what if they were all fabricated?

No, she told herself, *you've got to give him the benefit of the doubt.* Until she talked to her mother tonight, she mustn't make the mistake of jumping to unwarranted conclusions.

But if he'd been lying to her all along, she'd have to leave him or lose her sanity. For the first time Erin faced the frightening reality that she loved Donovan and might have to give him up without ever satisfying her yearning for him. And she wanted him, needed him, with a longing that turned her veins to liquid fire.

WITHOUT TALKING, Erin and Donovan walked on the sidewalk beside the Carrowheg River, back toward their rooms at the bed-and-breakfast. Old-fashioned Victorian lamps cast dim shadows on the stone walls containing the river's flow through town. Glancing over the wall at the black water below, Erin wondered how she could be so relieved yet so full of anxiety at the same time.

She'd called Jean from a public phone on the street across the river. According to her cousin, the address Erin's mother listed on the lodge register was an apartment in Dublin. The apartment's tenant wasn't home, but neighbors said he limped. From their description, Jean thought he might well be the man who came to her door asking for Margaret Sullivan.

The one-legged man again. Why had her mother listed his address on the lodge register? Well, she'd get the answer to all her questions tonight. After she'd repeated the phone conversation to Donovan, she'd lapsed into a worried silence. *TELL NO ONE.* Her mother's warning was burned into her brain.

"Is something wrong?" Donovan asked. "You seem preoccupied tonight."

"I'm still worried about Mom," she said, not quite truthfully since she now believed her mother was okay. Stopping, she leaned over the wall. When she felt Donovan close beside her, his body touching hers, she turned to face him. In the dim light his eyes were dark and unsmiling, the eyes of someone she didn't know.

"Who are you really, Donovan?" she murmured, trying to probe his mind. "Sometimes you seem as familiar as someone in my own family. But sometimes, like right now, I feel I scarcely know you."

Instantly his expression softened, changing him into the man she recognized. He drew her into his arms. "We've only been together a few days," he said as she felt his breath on her hair. "It's natural to have feelings like that."

With his body hard against hers, Erin couldn't force herself to move away. "If you're a true undercover agent, your name probably isn't Dan Donovan,'' she whispered in his ear. "Who are you really?"

"I'm the man who loves you," he whispered back, his voice thick. "And everything I've said about my family is true."

He hadn't answered her question, but whoever Dan Donovan was, she loved him. But could she believe him?

Chapter Fourteen

Hand in hand they walked along the river to the town square known as the Octagon, and then to their bed-and-breakfast a few blocks away.

A short while later, as they entered Donovan's room, Erin no longer tried to fight her yearning. Fearing she might never be with him like this again, she came willingly into his arms. And as he held her, she sought to imprint his essence on her memory: his salty-sweet masculine smell, the husky sound of his voice, the feel of his hard muscular body against hers. She nuzzled his neck, kissing the pulse throbbing there.

Then, pulling back, she waited for his familiar roguish smile. But there was no smile for her tonight. Instead, concern chiseled his features.

"Are you sure nothing's wrong?" he asked. "Ever since dinner I've had the feeling something's bothering you."

Trembling, Erin buried her head against his shoulder so he wouldn't see her eyes. She didn't want him to guess she was about to leave him, maybe forever.

"How I wish we could go back to Lake Ree and stay in that nice little inn where we had lunch," she said, her voice muffled against his shoulder. Even as she spoke, Erin heard the futility in her words. Happily-ever-afters weren't in the cards for her. Not with Donovan, a man she couldn't trust.

He stroked her hair. "We *will* go back to Lake Ree. As

soon as this is over, and we know your mother's safe, we'll spend as much time as you'd like there.''

He kissed her then, a comfortable warm kiss that told her he'd be there for her at Lake Ree or anywhere else. And that he was willing to wait for sex until she was ready.

At the touch of Donovan's lips, gentle though it was, Erin's emotions ignited. Hungrily she tightened her arms around his neck and pressed herself against him.

"I don't want to wait for Lake Ree," she whispered. "I want you now. Make love to me, Donovan."

Lifting her chin with his hand, he peered into her eyes. "Are you sure?"

Erin could see him struggling to understand what had happened to change her mind from last night. Oh, she wished she could tell him her mother was safe, that she'd be seeing her soon.

She buried her face in the hollow of his shoulder again. "Let me feel some joy. Please. I want to feel happy again, if only for a little while."

Donovan groaned, tracing her face with his fingers. "I'll make you feel happy, phenomenally happy."

Erin sucked in her breath as all her doubts and questions about him suddenly burst forth in her mind. She shoved them away. This was the man she loved, and she wanted them to be close, at least for a little while, before she left him.

Backing away from him she lowered herself to the edge of the bed. Then she held out her arms to him.

For a moment he watched her, desire and tenderness exposed on his rugged face. Then, reaching up, he pulled the cord on the overhead light, plunging the room into darkness. Through the shadowy space, he came to her. Erin felt his hands on her skin, lowering her jeans, lifting her sweater, his warm, seeking mouth on her breast. Gasping for breath, she pulled him down on top of her, delighting in the firm body pressed against her.

Somehow he'd managed to shed his sweatshirt. The soft

massage of his chest hair against her sensitive breasts sent waves of desire singing through her.

Through the curtained window, a dim streetlight silhouetted his naked shoulders. Erin could barely see his face, but she could feel his weight, heavy and protective on top of her. And she could feel the whisper of his breath against her face, the texture of his body beneath her hands. The skin on his back was like satin to her fingers, his muscles firm, the manly scent of him an aphrodisiac to her heightened senses.

Taking her face in his hands, he lowered his mouth to hers, and kissed her, lightly at first, then with more passion, until she saw exploding stars behind her closed eyes. His lips traveled to her cheek then to her eyes and back to her mouth again, his hunger matching her own, as if he could never get enough of the taste and feel of her.

All at once she was drowning in his kisses and one of his hands was searing a path across her flat, quivering belly to the juncture of her thighs. His fingers slid even lower, to the burning core of her pleasure, and she trembled at his touch, marveling that he knew instinctively where and how to caress her.

Fires raged inside her, sparking yearning so great that she had to clench her teeth to keep from crying out. For a moment her eyes blinked open in the shadowy darkness and the look of sheer wonder on his face made her want him even more.

Donovan's lovemaking was like nothing Erin had ever dreamed of in her wildest fantasies. Without hurrying, he learned what aroused her—how to caress the inside of her thighs with exactly the right motion, how to apply just enough pressure on her hardened nipples to turn her insides to liquid flame.

And with his guidance she explored his muscular body, with no part of it off-limits to her searching fingers and tongue. His skin felt silky beneath her hands. Fed by her ever-increasing passion, her desire grew until it was nearly uncontrollable. Donovan didn't just make love, she discovered. With his body and soul he worshiped her.

He lifted himself above her, and captured first one and then the other of her sensitive breasts in his mouth with a knowing sureness that brought her to the brink of some sweet lunacy. Eagerly she let him take her to the edge.

Finally, after making her cry out for him, he slid into her. Delirious with longing, her passion heightened even more as his hands drew her closer. Moaning, she felt him deep inside her, stretching her body to rapturous pleasure. Erin wrapped her legs around him and abandoned herself to the spiraling whirl of sensations he aroused.

Deep inside her, Donovan lost his carefully disciplined control. He'd wanted her since the moment he laid eyes on her, and now that the end was near, he could no longer command his rebellious body. Yet even as he thrust himself into her, he was supremely conscious of her reactions. Not until she cried out and tightened around him with the desire, did he allow his own release.

Later, as they lay in each other's arms, Donovan felt wetness on his shoulder. Lifting himself to one elbow, he stared down at her face, a blurry white shadow against the pillow.

"Erin, you're crying. Did I hurt you?" But he knew she'd wanted him. Her passion had exceeded his fondest dreams. So why was she crying?

"No—no, you didn't hurt me," she cried. "Don't ever think that." Her voice trembled as she spoke.

"Then what's wrong? Something's been bothering you all night."

She turned toward him. "It's Mom, Donovan. I can't stop worrying about her."

Something about the way she murmured the words sounded insincere. He doubted she was telling him the whole story. But he didn't question her further. She'd turned toward him, her full breasts brushing his chest, and he felt himself harden with desire. Lord help him, he wanted her again.

As he leaned down to kiss her and felt her eager response, all thought of something being wrong vanished from his mind. Now there was only Erin, so warm and ready, waiting for him...wanting him.

QUIETLY ERIN LET herself out of the front door of the bed-and-breakfast and headed toward the Octagon, Westport's town square.

Getting away from Donovan had been easier than she expected. After they'd made love a second time, he'd lain exhausted beside her. As soon as he'd gone to sleep, she'd yanked on her jeans, sweater, and car coat and started on her way to the northwest corner of the bridge across the Carrowheg River.

As she passed in front of the quiet buildings near the grassy town square, she forced herself not to think about Donovan. After their lovemaking tonight, she knew instinctively that he'd never hurt her. But until Erin talked to her mother, she couldn't let herself trust him.

Though it wasn't yet ten-thirty, the sidewalk crossing the Octagon's lawn was deserted as were the two streets on either side of the river. Taking a deep breath, Erin started down the sidewalk. Modern upside-down L-shaped streetlights made the square as bright as day. But beyond, on both sides of the river, old-fashioned Victorian lamps provided only dim light to the adjacent streets.

Shivering, she hugged her car coat more closely around her. The emptiness was unnerving, like something out of an Edward Hopper painting. Nothing moved near the rectangular two-story buildings lined up side by side facing the Octagon or, farther on, the river. Since it curved right at its juncture with the Octagon, the water seemed a dark highway, stretching away from the square into the night.

Skeletal trees, their branches still bare, bordered the stone walls on both sides of the river. Why hadn't she noticed the trees when she was with Donovan? As she approached, the tree limbs seemed to jerk and move, as though somebody or something were lurking in the branches above the sidewalk.

Annoyed by her irrational fears, Erin walked faster. If the branches were moving then cats or squirrels were in them, not goblins or assassins. Or the effect was a trick of lighting—the bright light on the square contrasted with the dim Victorian lamps along the river walls.

Though her rubber-soled shoes made no sound, she thought she heard the click of heels behind her. Stopping midstride, she spun around, her heart pounding in her ears.

Nothing. Nobody behind her. Complete silence.

Don't be a fool, she told herself. *The Republic of Ireland is one of the safest countries in the world for tourists. You can wander around almost anywhere at any hour.* It was one of her favorite lines when she'd been a Pentagon desk analyst briefing diplomatic personnel en route to the area.

But diplomatic personnel didn't find bodies in car trunks or dodge assassin's bullets. Resolutely thrusting such frightening thoughts from her mind, she continued at a steady pace. After she'd crossed a bridge over the river's bend, she reached the sidewalk beside the right-hand wall.

The light from the old-fashioned lamps was decidedly dimmer here by the river's wall, and the trees' spidery limbs—still winter-bare—cast grotesque shadows on the street and sidewalk. Anxiously Erin peered upward, searching the top branches for any sign of life.

Nothing moved.

A car appeared on the other side of the river, traveling in her direction. When it reached the bridge ahead of her, it crossed and started down the street toward her. Instinctively, she swiveled and leaned out over the stone wall, keeping her head down so only her back was visible in the headlights.

The car, a late model black sedan, drove past without changing its speed. Holding her breath, she didn't dare turn away from the wall until it reached the corner, too late to see its license.

When she finally reached the bridge, she was still twenty minutes early. Arriving ahead of time was a big mistake, she thought, glancing fearfully around her. Since no trees grew near the bridge, there were no shadows to hide in.

Suddenly, the nearby Victorian lamp that had seemed so dim before, felt like a spotlight focused on her face. Breathing in quick, shallow gasps, she looked down at the ground so anyone peering at her from the windows across the street wouldn't recognize her. Then she realized her mother had probably selected that location so the friend coming to pick her up would see her clearly.

Who was he? Erin wondered, this mysterious person? Was he the man who limped, the one her mother had seen watching from a distance? If so, how had he changed from threat to benefactor in only a few days?

Maybe he hadn't.

A frightening new thought sent chills down Erin's spine. What if her mother had been coerced into writing the note? What if her kidnapper wanted Donovan out of the way so he fostered Erin's mistrust with the disturbing instruction to TELL NO ONE? Without Donovan, she was virtually defenseless.

Taking deep gulps of the cold damp air, Erin told herself to stay calm. She still had time, if she hurried, to return to the bed-and-breakfast, rouse Donovan, and get back here only a few minutes after eleven. With him keeping an eye on her from their parked car, she'd feel safe.

Before she could start back, another car appeared, heading toward her on her side of the river. She couldn't get to the shadows without facing directly into the headlights. And turning her back to the street would be too obvious.

So she pulled her hood up to hide her hair and lowered her head. Part of her face was hidden, but looking up through her lashes, she could identify the car. It was the

same black sedan that had passed less than half an hour
ago.

Her heart leapt into her throat when it slowed as it drew
near. Who was inside? Her mother's friend? Or her stepfather's assassin?

DONOVAN AWOKE WITH a troubled feeling. He reached for
Erin and found her gone. The sheet where she'd lain was
cold.

She's probably gone to her room, he thought. But nothing would still his nagging fear that something was wrong.

Rising, he yanked on his pants and padded barefoot
across the dimly lighted hall to Erin's room. He knocked
lightly, then tried the door. It was open. "Erin?" he called
softly, pushing it wide.

He needed only an instant to see she wasn't there, and
probably didn't intend to return. Her bed hadn't been slept
in, and she'd left nothing behind to let him know she'd be
back. Running to his room, he pulled on his shirt and shoes
and raced down the hall.

He took the stairs two at a time. A night-light provided
faint illumination in the vestibule. The living room was
dark, but if she was anywhere inside the house, she'd be
here. He whispered her name.

But there was no answering whisper. His uneasiness
swelled to outright fear. Where could she have gone? To
meet someone, of course. Donovan cursed under his breath.
What a fool he'd been not to make her tell him what was
wrong. Obviously she'd been upset about what she planned
to do tonight; that's why she was crying. And now she was
out in the street alone with no weapon, no way to defend
herself. He had to find her. Thank God the car was where
he could get to it quickly.

Donovan crossed through the living room. As he reached
the door toward the back of the house, he felt the unmistakable pressure of cold steel against his neck.

"Well, it's Mr. Donovan as I live and breathe. How good

of you to save me a trip up to your room to get you." It was a man's voice.

Even without seeing him, Donovan knew who he was. "Where's your assassin, O'Shaughnessy?" he asked. "Don't you let him do your dirty work anymore?"

"Shut up or I'll blow your head off," O'Shaughnessy snapped. "And along with it, the heads of everybody in this house. If you don't want to cause a massacre, you'd better start moving."

APPROACHING THE intersection, the black sedan slowed, drew even with Erin. Without lifting her head, she stole a look at its occupants. For a breathless moment they were visible in the light from the old-fashioned streetlamp behind her.

Two men sat in the car's front seat. All the breath seemed to leave her body when she recognized both of them. In the passenger's seat, half turned away from her, sat Patrick O'Shaughnessy. Driving the sedan, his rugged face staring straight ahead, was Donovan.

Stiff with shock, Erin stood cemented to the pavement, her eyes fastened on the car's window. For an instant Donovan glanced her way and their eyes met. Quickly—so fast she might have imagined the slight twitch—he shook his head. Then he stared ahead again, as though he'd never seen her.

Maybe he hadn't.

Don't be a fool, she told herself. Even with her hood up and her head lowered, he must have recognized her. She'd worn the maroon car coat most of the day. And she was standing directly under the streetlight.

Expecting the car to pull over and stop, Erin braced herself to run. She had no idea where to go, only that she had to get away from them. Donovan and her stepfather together—wasn't this what she'd feared all along? He must have awakened and found her missing. Suspecting that she'd gone to meet someone who would take her to her mother, he'd notified Patrick who must have been following them all day.

It was the worst moment of her life.

In the blink of an eye, the man Erin loved turned from protector to betrayer, from defender to executioner. Though she'd never trusted Donovan completely, she saw now that she'd come much closer to doing so than she'd thought. A melange of feelings washed over her as she saw her dreams crumble and die. Swallowing the sob in her throat, she almost wished he and Patrick would come for her and put an end to her despair.

But the black sedan didn't stop. When it reached the intersection, it turned left over the bridge.

Quickly she roused herself. What was she thinking, quietly accepting Donovan's treachery? The only way to beat him and Patrick was to get to her mother first, and that meant not letting herself get caught.

Her heart pounding furiously, Erin watched the taillights until they disappeared. Had she been wrong about Donovan recognizing her? When she met his eyes, she'd been so sure—but in her shocked condition, maybe she was wrong. She *had* to be wrong, she thought wildly. If he'd recognized her, he would have stopped.

Run her brain screamed. *They'll be back.* But she couldn't leave or she'd miss her mother's messenger.

How much longer to wait? She checked her watch. Only five minutes. Stepping away from the lamppost, she moved closer to the trees where she could still be seen but not so easily.

She'd waited only a few minutes when headlights appeared coming toward the bridge. Her stomach tightened into a solid lump of concrete. Were Donovan and her stepfather returning for her?

Squinting, she peered toward the oncoming car. As it came into view, she let her breath out in a long sigh. It was a light-colored sport utility vehicle—a Jeep Cherokee—the first she'd seen in Ireland. Removing her hood, she returned to her position directly under the streetlight.

The Cherokee turned onto the street across the river, then swung around at the bend facing the Octagon. Completing its broad U, it headed down the north side of the river toward Erin. Slowing, it stopped opposite her.

The driver rolled down his window. Without leaning out, he called to her. "Are you Erin Meyer?" His voice, a rich strong baritone, could belong to a trained singer or actor.

"Yes, I'm Erin." She strained to see his face, but the car had stopped just far enough from her so that the driver was in shadow.

"Margaret Sullivan sent me," he said, in an obvious attempt to reassure her. Opening the door, he stepped out. In that instant the light shone full on his face.

Erin couldn't control her gasp of surprise. He had red hair the same shade as hers and his face was oval and rather long, like hers. His nose was a larger version of her own, and his eyes the same color blue.

Amazed at the resemblance, she stood staring at him, unable to speak. He was a man, so of course his features were coarser than hers. And since he was older, he had lines around his mouth, crow's-feet at his eyes, and creases in his forehead where Erin had none.

But even so the likeness was uncanny. For a panicky moment, she imagined she saw a distorted mirror image of her own face. Hardly daring to breathe, Erin found herself staring at a man who looked enough like her to be her real father.

THANK GOD SHE hadn't moved as they drove past, Donovan thought, hunching over the wheel of O'Shaughnessy's Mercedes. If she'd run or even turned her back to them, her stepfather would certainly have noticed.

When he'd driven past, Donovan had seen the stricken look on her face. She'd undoubtedly recognized her stepfather and assumed he and Donovan were working together.

How he wanted to hold her in his arms and reassure her of his loyalty. But that would have to wait until he found a way out of this mess.

At least she was safe, since he was with the man who posed the greatest threat to her. She'd been waiting for someone she trusted—probably someone sent by her mother. Maybe she waited for Margaret herself. If so, O'Shaughnessy and his wife probably weren't working together after all. Lord, he hoped he'd been wrong about that. Clutching the wheel, Donovan had to believe Erin was in safe hands. Otherwise he wouldn't be able to think straight.

"Turn left at the next corner," O'Shaughnessy barked. "Then right after two blocks."

They were still in town, and Donovan drove as slowly as he dared, looking for a good spot to floor the gas pedal and throw his captor off balance. The darkened streets, nearly deserted, begged for a burst of speed. But O'Shaughnessy already had the pistol's safety off and his finger on the trigger. One good jolt and the weapon might fire. Reluctantly, Donovan decided he couldn't risk it. He'd be useless to himself—and to Erin—with a bullet in his side.

"Mind telling me where we're going?" he asked in a conversational tone.

"Just keep your eyes on the road, Mr. CIA agent," O'Shaughnessy ordered. "You'll find out when we get there."

"Don't tell me, let me guess," Donovan said sarcastically. "We're joining your wife and fellow counterfeiters who're somehow going to put the finger on me for some horrendous crime before you kill me."

"Don't try to outguess me." O'Shaughnessy's buttery face melted into a lopsided smile, but he shifted nervously in his seat as though Donovan had struck a responsive chord. "I'm the one with the gun, remember?"

"Believe me, I'm not forgetting," he retorted, hoping to goad his captor into revealing his plan. "I'm sure you'd have put a bullet in me by now if you hadn't been planning to pin something on me.'' Even more positive he was right, Donovan shot O'Shaughnessy a knowing smile.

"You think you're pretty smart, don't you, Donovan?" O'Shaughnessy snarled, his customary veneer of congeniality totally gone. In his light-colored sweat suit—similar to Donovan's—he looked like someone Donovan didn't know.

"Well, let me tell you something, bigshot," O'Shaughnessy added. "You made a big mistake when you took on Shamrock Construction."

"Shamrock's small peanuts compared to the U.S. government," Donovan replied. "We're on to you, buddy. And if you kill me and try to blame me for something I didn't do, you'd better watch your back. You'll have every agent in this sector after you."

As far as Donovan knew, there weren't any other undercover agents in the Republic of Ireland, but the suggestion might make O'Shaughnessy nervous.

Donovan cast a sidelong glance at him. Seemingly unfazed, O'Shaughnessy was eyeing him the way a spider eyes a fly that has carelessly become caught in its web.

"Step on it," he said laconically.

Obediently Donovan upped the speed to ten kilometers over the maximum allowed on the winding two-lane road. They'd left Westport and were headed west. After a few turns Donovan knew they were paralleling the southern coast of Clew Bay, a large shallow body of water dotted with hundreds of small, treeless islands and surrounded by a mucky sandy shore—the apparent source of the mud on the floor of the BMW Erin's mother had left at the Ballyshannon Lodge.

He gripped the wheel more tightly as a frightening new thought struck him. Brian Cairns, the day clerk at the lodge, was killed many hours before Donovan and Erin arrived. O'Shaughnessy—and his assassin—were the most logical suspects. Somehow—probably through the BMW license—they'd traced Margaret Sullivan to the lodge, and found out where she was headed from the luckless clerk. Then Chameleon had killed him so he wouldn't identify him and O'Shaughnessy. But why even ask the clerk where she'd gone when the circled map pointed the way?

In his mind, Donovan saw the map, left so conveniently in the BMW's glove box. Why hadn't Cairns's killers found it?

Stiffening with impotent rage, Donovan knew the answer. O'Shaughnessy himself had left the map to be sure he and Erin came to Clew Bay. Once they'd arrived, he planned to kill Erin, her mother, and Donovan and blame their deaths on him. He and Erin must have been followed again after they left the Ballyshannon Lodge. That's how O'Shaughnessy found them so quickly at the bed-and-breakfast.

His gut twisted into a hard knot. It seemed likely that Chameleon waited for O'Shaughnessy where they'd found Erin's mother. Donovan knew she would never have left him tonight unless she intended to join her mother. Was she headed straight into a monstrous web where a killer spider would be waiting?

Chapter Fifteen

The red-haired man had barely stepped out of the car when Erin ran toward him.

"Quick!" she gasped. "We've got to get out of here."

Without a word he jumped back inside the Cherokee. Before Erin could fasten her seat belt, the Jeep lurched ahead and made a left turn across the bridge.

"What's wrong?" He glanced toward her with eyes so like her own that she seemed to be looking into a mirror. "Did something happen before I got here?"

"Yes," she said, still breathless from her near encounter with Patrick and Donovan and her run to the Jeep. "My stepfather's here in Westport. He's with a man named Donovan who works for him. They drove past me only five minutes ago."

"Mrs. Flaherty said Donovan was with you." The stranger's rich voice reflected stunned disbelief.

"He was—until I left to meet Mom." Erin swallowed the sob in her throat. "I just saw him in the same car with Patrick."

He swore under his breath. "Which way did they go?"

"Up this street. The same way we're going." Stretching her seat belt, Erin shifted uneasily. Because of her selfish insistence on allowing Donovan to come, her stepfather now knew where they were. A terrible bitterness tightened her throat. Somehow Donovan must have managed to in-form him of their whereabouts every step of the way. She swallowed hard remembering the sincere look in his eyes when he swore he wasn't working for Patrick.

The man beside her cursed again. "O'Shaughnessy's got eyes in the back of his head." Speed increasing, he swung around a corner, throwing Erin sideways against the door.

"Just where do you fit?" she asked, pushing aside her guilty feelings. She had to find out who this man was. "We look so much alike, you've got to be a relative. Are you my father's brother, or maybe a cousin?"

For a long moment he was silent. "Yes, we do look alike, Erin," he said finally, "more so than I'd guessed." His voice choked. "For now, you can call me Uncle Michael."

Uncle Michael? Erin sensed he wasn't telling her the whole truth, but why would he lie? Awkwardly she cleared her throat. "Then you *are* my father's brother?"

"I'm Michael Riley, your mother's friend. My brother died a long time ago."

"Were you the man watching her in Dublin? The one who came to my cousin Jean's house asking for her?" Anxiously Erin stared at the profile so like her own.

"Guilty on both counts." There was no trace of an Irish accent. Had he grown up with her father in the United States? If so, what was he doing back in Ireland? Sensing his uneasiness, she struggled to control her own anxiety.

"Then you drove with Mom from Dublin to Donegal?" Erin asked, as casually as she could manage. "My stepfather said friends saw her with a man in a town outside Dublin."

"O'Shaughnessy was lying," he asserted emphatically. "She drove from Dublin to the Ballyshannon Lodge alone."

She sighed. "He claimed she'd been kidnapped."

"A lie to throw you off the track." There was an angry note to his voice. "When I missed your mother at your cousin's, I drove to Clew Bay, hoping she might go to my home here.''

His home? The way he said it, he sounded as though he'd lived in Ireland all his life. Then why no accent?

"But she didn't go to your place," Erin countered. "She checked in at the Ballyshannon Lodge.''

"Right. But she *did* phone me from there," he said. "I drove from Clew Bay up to Donegal and got her.''

For Erin, a couple of pieces fell into place. A surge of excitement shot through her. "And while there, you moved her car to the remote parking lot, hoping my stepfather or one of his spies wouldn't see it for a few days—until you could decide what to do.''

"Right again. How the hell did you figure that out?''

"We—I—saw the Clew Bay mud on the BMW's floor." A pang went through her as she pictured Donovan's face when he looked up at her and the night clerk, a clump of dried dirt in his hand. With a determined shake of her head, she forced the image away.

Beside her, her uncle sighed loudly. "Then that must be how O'Shaughnessy tracked us to Westport. Through that damned Clew Bay mud. I was in such a hurry to get to your mother, I didn't wipe my feet before I moved her car.''

"No," Erin said, with sudden insight. "The day clerk must have told Patrick where Mom was going." Of course that's what happened, she thought, a great load dropping off her shoulders. Donovan hadn't informed Patrick of their whereabouts after all. He couldn't have. She'd been with him almost every moment. So why was he with her stepfather in the Mercedes?

"The day clerk at the Ballyshannon Lodge?" Her uncle's voice was incredulous. "What's he got to do with this?''

Quickly Erin told her uncle about finding the clerk's body in the trunk of her mother's car. "Donovan—the man

I was traveling with—thinks he was killed to keep him quiet.''

"Why would your mother tell a clerk where she was going?" Even more incredulous, her uncle glanced sideways at Erin. "She didn't even know herself till after she'd called me."

Erin drew a long breath. "Maybe he simply figured it out from your car license when you picked her up. Or maybe Mom thought I wouldn't find the map she left in the glove box with Westport circled so she told the clerk."

Her uncle gave her a piercing glance. "What map?"

The alarm in his voice made her catch her breath. "The road map of Ireland in the glove box. Mom drew circles around both Donegal and Westport."

Her uncle shook his head. "That map had nothing circled, Erin. I made sure when I checked the glove box before we left."

"Then who did it?"

"O'Shaughnessy," her uncle said grimly, confirming Erin's worst fears. "He wanted to be sure you and Donovan joined your mother. It seems he'd like to see you both dead, Erin, along with your mother." He stepped down hard on the accelerator. "She can clinch the case against him."

Her stomach churning with dread at her uncle's words, Erin clutched her armrest. The Cherokee was going much too fast for this narrow road. But with Patrick headed in the same direction, they had to get to her mother first.

They roared around a curve. "She stumbled onto some pretty incriminating records," her uncle went on. "Robert, the butler, who's part of the counterfeiting operation, figured out what she was up to. She got away before Robert could tell O'Shaughnessy or she'd probably be dead now."

"If Patrick and Donovan get to your house before we do," Erin said, putting her fears into words, "can they get inside and hurt Mom?"

The road straightened, and her uncle inched the Jeep's

speed up another notch. "It's not a house, Erin, it's a castle. I—"

"A castle!" she interrupted. "Then you must have a staff—someone to protect her."

"Not really," he said, dashing Erin's hopes. "Most of the building is closed off. Right now there are only six people working full-time—none of them know beans about weapons."

"At least Mom's not alone." Erin studied her uncle's profile. In the reflected light from the Cherokee's dashboard, she could make out his aquiline nose and straight forehead, so like her own that shivers ran across her shoulders.

"I left orders for the doors to be barred," he said, "but it's a big place with lots of entrances. Somebody who wanted to sneak in, probably could."

In her mind's eye, Donovan appeared in the window outside her bedroom. Erin sucked in her breath. "Donovan can sneak in anywhere. He says he's a CIA agent investigating Patrick's counterfeiting, but I'm sure he's lying." An odd mixture of admiration and fear rippled through her. "He climbs walls and breaks into places like a professional cat burglar."

For a long moment her uncle hesitated. "Why are you so sure Donovan still works for O'Shaughnessy?" he asked finally. "Your mother thought so, too, after Mrs. Flaherty said he was with you and that you didn't trust him. That's why she insisted you tell no one I was picking you up."

Her uncle paused long enough for Erin to recall her anxious request that her landlady withhold information from Donovan about her mother's message.

"If he's a CIA agent, maybe he's only pretending to be loyal to O'Shaughnessy," her uncle went on. "Does O'Shaughnessy have any idea he's an agent?"

"Yes," she said softly. "Donovan told me Patrick knows."

"Then there's your answer." Erin heard the satisfaction

in her uncle's voice. "O'Shaughnessy would never trust an agent."

"I have only Donovan's word for all this." Erin's heart sank as she realized how completely she'd been taken in. "He's the one who said he was an agent and that Patrick knew. Maybe the whole story was a lie."

"And maybe it wasn't," her uncle persisted. "Since you're an intelligence officer who could spot a lie, would he make up an outlandish story like that without some sort of proof?"

Quickly Erin told her uncle about the assassination attempts in Washington and the restricted CIA files. Her voice quavering, she repeated the words she'd heard Donovan say so many times. "According to him, baksheesh can buy you anything."

"Can it buy Mr. Donovan?" Her uncle's tone was insistent.

"An hour ago, I would have said no," Erin whispered, close to tears. "But now, after seeing him with Patrick, I'm not sure. God help me, I'm not sure of anything." Erin had never been so miserable, or so frightened, in her life.

The man beside her seemed to sense her fear. "I'm not going to let anything happen to you or your mother," he assured her with quiet emphasis. "They'd have to kill me first."

Her heart overflowing with gratitude, Erin turned toward him. "Thank God you were here for us when we needed you, Uncle Michael."

She heard a choked sound, as though he were swallowing something caught in his throat.

Leaning forward, she waited anxiously for him to say something. But he didn't. Instead, he quickly turned off the blacktopped road onto a narrow, unpaved lane angling toward the bay's shoreline.

As the Jeep lurched over the rocky road, Erin gripped the armrest, engrossed in the scene ahead. In the beam from the headlights, she saw the sandy mud of Clew Bay, stretched out ahead of them like mucky gray quicksand. Did his castle lie across the muck, perhaps on one of the low treeless islands rising blackly from the tideflats?

Then the road curved around a low hill, and she spied the castle, a dark shadow of turrets and towers looming three-stories tall against the night sky. Only the lower floor of the middle section glowed with light, the rest barely visible in the darkness. Erin's heart swelled. Her mother was inside, probably eyeing the approaching headlights with the same eager anticipation Erin herself felt. The anxious worry, the waiting, the bone-chilling fear—they'd be over soon.

"Hang on," her uncle said.

A moment later the Jeep's wheels spun in the muck, caught, and carried the vehicle forward across the tideflats.

"How do you get to the castle when the tide's in?" Erin asked, viewing the muddy expanse in the headlights' circle.

"We take the lane around behind," he said. "Cutting across the flats'll save us a few minutes."

Hearing the urgency in his voice, Erin stiffened. They weren't home free yet, not by a long shot. "We've seen no sign of Patrick and Donovan. Do you think they know Mom's here?"

Her uncle didn't hesitate. "O'Shaughnessy has eyes and ears everywhere. Once that clerk told him Margaret Sullivan was headed for Clew Bay, he'd have no trouble deducing she was at Castle Clew, the Riley ancestral home."

"Yes, I'm sure Mom told Patrick about my biological father," Erin said, trying to control her mounting dread. "So he'd recognize the name *Riley*."

"O'Shaughnessy might have beaten us here." Her uncle's voice was tight and drawn. "Listen to me carefully, Erin."

The Jeep left the rocks and muck of the shore and started up an incline toward the massive front door. "If we run into trouble and you need to hide," he instructed, "there's a door under the largest oil painting in the dining room.

The door's built into the molding and hard to see, but if
you push on the molding, it'll swing open. It leads into
tunnels that exit at the bay.''

Pulling into a circular driveway, he braked to a stop.
"I've had lights put in the tunnels for safety, but watch
your step and stay close to the wall. There's a dangerous
drop-off." Walking with the slight limp of a one-legged
man, he got out of the Jeep and came around to her side.
"Don't go near the tunnels unless there's an emergency."

Erin jumped out of the car and headed toward the house
with her uncle a step behind. They reached the massive
front door. Heart in her throat, Erin stepped back while he
twisted a key in the lock. Hope and fear warred within her.
Would her mother be waiting? Or Patrick and Donovan,
with weapons drawn?

At her uncle's push, the door swung open. Carefully he
peered inside. Erin caught a glimpse of wide staircases on
either side of an elegant entryway, of an elaborate crystal
chandelier hanging from a ceiling three-stories high, of a
gleaming black-and-white tile floor.

But her mother wasn't there. Nobody was. After glancing
to his left and right, her uncle went in. Erin followed.

Suddenly the enormous wooden door slammed shut behind them. Every cell in Erin's body screamed with alarm.
In her peripheral vision, shadows moved toward her,
lengthening and shortening in the light from the chandelier
swaying overhead. She jerked swiftly toward the movement.

Her body stiffened with shock as she saw who lurked
there in the space left by the closed door. It was Patrick
O'Shaughnessy and a man she didn't recognize. But her
blood ran cold at the sight of him. With his bones prominent in his cadaverous face he seemed more skeleton than
flesh.

The assassin, Chameleon. It had to be he, in another of
his infamous disguises. She could hardly believe a man
with the face of Adonis could turn himself into such an

inhuman creature. In his hand he held a lethal-looking revolver.

But where was Donovan? Not here. Had her uncle been right about his innocence? Petrified with terror she glanced from the assassin to Patrick. Her stepfather, his big body dressed in unfamiliar gray sweatpants and shirt, seemed a complete stranger. Brandishing a pistol, he leered at Erin, a smug smile on his florid round face.

"Welcome to Castle Clew, stepdaughter and Mr. Riley. Would you please come with us?"

"No!" roared her uncle.

Erin sensed his movement rather than saw it, a vicious kick that smashed into Patrick's hand. Her stepfather screeched with pain, and his pistol clattered to the tile floor.

"Run, Erin," her uncle yelled, pointing toward the long hall ahead of them.

The precious few seconds provided by her uncle gave Erin her chance. Running for her life, she dashed past her uncle, past Patrick and Chameleon who were facing him, to an open archway off to one side of the hall.

Behind her she heard a weapon fire. It had to be the assassin's gun. With only a short distance to his target, he couldn't have missed. Her newly found uncle must be dead.

Panic-stricken, Erin dashed through the archway. The assassin's next shot would be for her.

THROUGH A BLANKET of swirling black fog, Donovan fought to wake up. Breathing deeply, he struggled to his senses. Hazily he remembered the bag they'd put over his head, the suffocating smell of chloroform. He'd tried not to breathe, but finally he couldn't hold out any longer.

His head hurt like hell. Through the throbbing pain, he forced his eyes open. Blackness. But when he waved his hand before his face, he could see it. There must be light coming from somewhere. Under the door. A faint glimmer as though from a long distance. If there were windows, they must be covered with heavy curtains. Not the slightest flicker of light from outside revealed their presence.

Where was he? Lying on a hard surface, like a wooden floor. In the air around him, he could smell the acrid odors of paint and new plaster. O'Shaughnessy and Chameleon must have dumped his unconscious body in an area of the castle under renovation. As soon as Donovan had seen O'Shaughnessy's associate, waiting for him in the castle, he'd known it was the assassin. Nobody but a man in disguise could so resemble a skeleton and still be a living human being.

Why hadn't they killed him? Because they must want him alive. He'd been right with his guess in the car: O'Shaughnessy planned to blame him for whatever devastation he would cause tonight. Donovan couldn't bear to use the word *murder,* even in his mind, because Erin and her mother would surely be the victims. And he'd be accused of the crime. Blaming him must be why they hadn't tied him. The ropes would leave marks on his arms and feet, marks the authorities would recognize.

Slowly he sat up, then patted his pockets. Empty. Damn. He still wore his sweatpants, sweater and jacket, but they'd removed everything from his pockets, including his tools.

Standing, he tried the door. Locked, of course. And the double bolt lock felt smooth and new to his practiced fingertips, the kind of device he couldn't open without tools. How the hell was he going to get out of here? Some light would help. Fighting to stay calm, he moved his hands across the plaster around the door, hunting for the light switch.

There it was. He flicked it up and down. Nothing. The electricity must be off in this part of the castle. So was the heat. It was cold as Hades.

Rather than waste time hunting in the darkness for something to pry open the door, he put his shoulder to it and pushed. It didn't budge. Next he aimed a kick at the center. In his rubber-soled shoes, he did no damage.

Find the windows, Donovan told himself, groping his way across the room. Perhaps they'd offer an escape. After he'd felt along the wall opposite the door, he realized there weren't any. He was in a closed-in room, about ten by twelve, probably a closet or storage chamber.

He clenched his fists in impotent rage. How the hell was he going to get out of here? Breathing deeply, he was even more conscious of the strong odor of paint and turpentine. Renovation supplies must be stored here.

Moving carefully, Donovan groped around until he stumbled over a metal canister. There were others sitting in the same general area. Propped against the wall behind the paint cans was a wooden ladder. When he lifted it, he discovered the ladder was satisfyingly heavy. He'd use it as a battering ram.

His first lunge at the door jolted but didn't crack it. His second lunge smashed the ladder, leaving the top dangling uselessly from the base. But the door had splintered all the way through. A shaft of dim light poured through the vertical crack.

Ripping the ladder's dangling top off, he thrust at the door with the base. Time after time he continued, until finally a small opening appeared. More dim light filtered into his dark prison.

But the door was solid, made of hardwood. His escape was taking forever. With every minute that passed, the danger grew. Since her mother must be somewhere in the castle, Erin was probably headed here right now. She'd soon arrive, if she hadn't already. The thought of her in danger made him scour the room with savage intensity, looking for something to get him out.

In the dim light provided by the crack in the door, Donovan's probing eyes focused on something that might be useful. Amid the paint cans sat one containing brushes and a couple of screwdrivers used to open the cans.

Eagerly he seized one. Using the screwdriver as a lever and the unattached ladder top as a hammer, he removed the

pins from the hinges and forced the door wide enough to
squeeze through.

After peering up and down the dark hall outside, he
started toward the light at one end at a fast trot. When he
heard the first shot, he started running.

AS SHE RAN, ERIN'S FEET seemed weighted with rocks. Her
lungs bursting, she darted through the open archway. Her
quick movement saved her life. The bullet meant for her
ricocheted harmlessly off the black-and-white tile floor.

Behind her she heard footsteps and a shout. "Don't let
her get away." The voice was Patrick's.

She found herself in a peach-colored drawing room.
Without slowing her pace, Erin sprinted across a magnifi-
cent Oriental carpet toward the nearest door. Though table
lamps had been turned on, casting a soft glow over the
stylish upholstered furniture, no one was in the room.

After the longest minute in her life, she reached the door,
yanked it open, and slammed it shut behind her. Breathing
hard, she clung desperately to her fragile control. Had Patrick and the assassin seen which way she went? Maybe not.
The room had several exits. But they were getting close.
Through the closed door she detected the lighter sound of
their footsteps when they pounded off the tile onto the
drawing room's wood floor and then muffled thuds as they
crossed the Oriental carpet at its center.

"You take that door, I'll try this one." It was Patrick's
excited tenor voice.

So they didn't know where she was. Frantically glancing
around for the quickest escape route, Erin's eyes passed
over a long table with chairs neatly lined up alongside—
then to the nearest door.

Praise God, she was in the dining room. Thanks to her
uncle, she'd found it. That's why he had pointed in this
direction.

Instantly she spotted the painting her uncle mentioned.
Twice as large as any of the others, it featured a mare and

her foal in a verdant pasture, with the spires of Castle Clew looming in the background.

With panic welling in her throat, Erin darted to the painting. Standing directly underneath it, she pushed on the molding nearest the painting's center. Nothing happened. Sliding her hand down, she shoved again. Still nothing.

Ordering herself to keep cool, she shoved yet again. Something clicked and the hidden panel opened inward.

"Over here!" Behind her she heard Patrick's excited shout. "Let's get her." He'd seen her open the tunnel door.

WHEN DONOVAN SAW the corpse sprawled against the wall in the castle's entry hall, he knew right away who it was. He must be the one-legged man Erin's mother had seen. With one pant leg empty and his head slumped on his chest, the body appeared to be a redheaded life-size rag doll. What had happened to his artificial leg? It wasn't near the body.

Though certain the man was dead, Donovan knelt down to check his pulse. Pale blue eyes that were very much alive stared into his. Startled, Donovan jerked back.

"I'm not dead, at least not yet," the stranger wheezed in a halting voice. "O'Shaughnessy's saving me for later. Said he wanted her—Margaret—to watch me die. They yanked off my damn leg and took it with them to slow me down—as if I could run with a bullet in me."

"Who are you?" Carefully Donovan removed the stranger's dark suit coat. The white shirt underneath was wet with blood, but the wound did not seem to be bleeding excessively.

"Don't waste time on me. You've got to stop them, Donovan. They're after Erin."

At the sound of her name and his own, Donovan stiffened, his blood turning to ice water. "She's here? Where did she go?"

"That way." He waved a limp hand toward an arch off the hallway. "O'Shaughnessy and his hit man're behind her."

His voice weakening, he paused to catch his breath. "Through arch to lounge to dining room. Door to tunnels hidden in paneling under largest painting. Press molding."

Donovan lurched to his feet.

"Wait," the stranger whispered. Donovan bent down to hear him. "The passage has a dangerous drop-off where the tunnels meet. Stick close to the walls and watch your step."

After laying the injured man down with his own coat over him and Donovan's jacket under his head for a pillow, Donovan whirled and took off. He needed only a few seconds to find the dining room. Next to it was the kitchen. He needed a weapon and the kitchen was the place to find one.

Impelled by an awful sense of urgency, he yanked drawers open until he found what he was looking for—an eight-inch butcher knife, and a vicious-looking meat cleaver, its cutting edge glistening bright silver in the strong overhead light.

CARVED OUT OF SOLID ROCK, the low, narrow tunnel bristled with sharp outcrops. The first time Erin stumbled on the uneven floor, she hit her arm on a jagged stone and had to bite her lip to keep from crying out. If she hadn't been wearing a coat, she'd have been gashed by the impact.

At least the passage curved frequently so she was out of sight of her pursuers, and they couldn't get a shot at her. But they were gaining. Gasping, she panted in terror. She could hear them behind her, not bothering to muffle their curses and animal-like grunts. The tunnel was like a sound chamber, amplifying their voices.

"We're going to get you, stepdaughter," Patrick yelled. "You might as well sit down where you are and wait for us. It'll be easier for you." His voice echoed hollowly down the tunnel like some surrealistic monster's.

Erin's blood ran cold when she heard a hissing noise and

realized the frightening sound must be coming from the assassin.

"Let me get her before you kill her, boss." His words were vicious as poison. Obviously said to scare her witless, the threat added wings to her feet.

How far were they behind her? Fifty yards? Two hundred? She couldn't tell from the reverberating sound.

"You hear that?" Patrick shouted. "If you keep running, I'll let Chameleon have his way before I put you with the others."

The others? Obviously that included her mother, Donovan and the household staff. What did her stepfather intend to do with them? The answer was so frightening, a sob rose in her throat. If he didn't intend to murder them all, he'd never have revealed himself to her—and probably to Donovan. How could she have thought Donovan would betray her? Patrick must have taken him captive, along with her mother and the staff. Erin prayed to God they were still alive.

Slow down, she told herself as she ran to the next curve. So far she hadn't seen any drop-offs, but after her uncle's warning, she was taking no chances. With every curve she inched her way around the wall, close to the jagged surface. And with every curve, her pursuers got closer.

Hugging the wall she rounded a curve. Erin's heart lifted. Ahead she saw a division in the passage. Maybe there was a chance for her after all. They wouldn't know which way she'd gone. Hoping she wasn't headed into a dead end, she took the left fork.

She heard their oaths when they reached the division.

"We'll have to split up," Patrick said. Though he lowered his voice, Erin still heard him clearly.

God help her, they were only one curve behind.

Chapter Sixteen

Chameleon was coming for her.

As Erin inched her way around the next curve, she heard him close behind, hissing like a fanged reptile.

"I know you're there, just around that wall."

Erin took off toward the next curve. Dodging the jagged rocks in her path slowed her down, and she knew Chameleon caught sight of her before she could squeeze herself around the wall. Glancing back she saw him, a grotesque parody of a man, edging around the curve behind her.

With his skeletal face and dark clothing, the assassin could have risen from some stony burial ground. Somehow knowing a comely face lay hidden under that ugly disguise made him seem more horrid—because the cover-up reflected the twisted demon inside him.

Like Erin, Chameleon stayed close to the wall where it curved. When he spoke again, there was no trace of the hissing sound he reserved for her.

"Boss?" Though the assassin didn't raise his voice, it sounded almost as loud as Patrick's shouted answer. "Yes, I hear ya."

"She's in this corridor."

"Good. Take care of her..." Patrick's voice echoed through the tunnels, an otherworldly omen of catastrophe.

Stark terror jolted through Erin. She couldn't help trembling as she visualized her own death at this gargoyle's hands. No! She couldn't let him catch her. Taking a desperate deep breath, she murmured a prayer, determined she would not be caught.

Darting toward the next curve, she eyed the thin electric cord connecting the bare lightbulbs on the left side of the tunnel. Spaced about fifty feet apart, they provided only dim light. But if she broke the cord, even that light would be gone, and the tunnels would be plunged into total darkness.

Anything would be better than her present situation. Or would it? In the dark Chameleon could creep up on her, and she'd never know until he grabbed her.

Shuddering, she imagined his fingers slithering across her face until his hands coiled around her throat. Her skin crawled with revulsion.

Erin didn't kid herself. She'd never escape once he got hold of her. Worse, in the light he could aim and fire his weapon. Though the darkness was terrifying, she'd be better off if he couldn't see her.

She reached for the cord and gave it a good yank. It didn't break. The lights flickered but didn't go out. To snap the cord, she'd have to find a jagged rock. But she had no time. Chameleon was on the backside of the curve, only feet behind her. Her heart ready to explode, she swerved around rocks in her path, sprinting as fast as she dared to the next curve.

"Erin, don't let them catch you." The voice echoing down the tunnel wasn't Patrick's or Chameleon's. It sounded so much like Donovan that at first Erin thought she was hearing things—that her confused mind was conjuring up a miracle.

Then the voice spoke again, and she knew she wasn't wrong.

It couldn't be, but it was—Donovan's voice echoing through the rock corridors.

"Keep running," he yelled.

Hearing him, Erin almost sobbed with relief. She didn't question where he'd been or how he'd found the tunnels.

No longer did she wonder if he was involved in some elaborate scheme with her stepfather. He was here to save her, and she loved and trusted him with all her heart and soul. Nothing mattered but the two of them together. And to touch him again, she had to keep running.

"Take the left fork," she screamed, and couldn't believe the resonant tones that vibrated through the rock corridor were echoes of her own voice.

"I'm coming," he yelled, to let her know he'd heard.

Hugging the wall on the next curve, she listened for Chameleon, but heard nothing. Was he sneaking up on her even now?

At the sound of Donovan's voice, all the small noises connected with the assassin's pursuit had ceased, as though he'd stopped to wait for Donovan to appear. But Erin was sure he hadn't stopped. He was just moving more quietly so she—and Donovan—wouldn't hear him. Neither the demon nor his master spoke, probably hoping to surprise Donovan.

"Both Patrick and Chameleon are in the tunnels," she yelled to alert him. "Patrick took the right fork and Chameleon the left. The assassin is close behind me."

"I hear you," Donovan cried. Already he sounded nearer, but the echo disguised distances.

There was no drop-off around this curve. But ahead lay the longest stretch of fairly straight corridor she'd encountered. It was low and so dark she could barely make out the next turn. Bending, she threaded her way through the jagged rocks. Mindful of her uncle's warning about the drop-off, she scrutinized the space ahead, slowing her pace with each shadowy dip in the tunnel's floor.

In the distance she heard the slap, slap, slap of Donovan's shoes against bare rock. From the sound, he was jogging toward her, moving more rapidly than she or Chameleon since he wasn't inching his way around each curve. Her heart sang with hope. He'd be here any minute. Was that why the assassin was making no noise?

Glancing over her shoulder, she saw Chameleon's black

costumed figure edge around the shadowy curve behind her. In the dim light, she couldn't make out his skeletal features, only the blurry whiteness of his face.

Erin flinched, expecting to feel a bullet slam into her. But he turned from her and backed away from the curve, staring at the direction he'd come, his weapon drawn.

"Donovan! Watch out!" Erin screamed, panic rioting within her.

There was no reassuring shout of reply, no change in the rhythmic slap, slap of the approaching footsteps.

Before she reached the next bend in the tunnel, Erin peered over her shoulder again. Chameleon had backed to a position midway down the corridor. Ignoring her, he stood facing the curve he'd just rounded. With her eyes glued to the tunnel floor, Erin resumed her careful pace down the rocky corridor.

She didn't see the drop-off until she was right on top of it. Camouflaged by the tunnel's curvature and rock formations, it dropped twenty-five feet or so to a rough stone bottom.

Sweat dripping down her back, she eyed the black hole. Though fifteen to twenty feet in diameter, it was almost impossible to see. If she hadn't been watching for it, she'd have fallen for sure.

Across the drop-off, two other tunnels curved away from the abyss, one leading downward, the other up. The upward passage must be the right hand fork Patrick took, joining the left here at the booby trap.

Echoing through the system, she heard her stepfather's voice. "It's me, O'Shaughnessy," he yelled to Chameleon. "Don't shoot." Her eyes glued on the opening to the tunnel opposite her across the abyss, Erin waited for him to appear.

Then, out of the corner of her eye, she caught a movement off to one side. Turning her head, she saw a gray-suited figure come around the bend Chameleon faced. Donovan! In the dim light she saw him, wearing the gray sweatpants and shirt Erin had last seen him in.

"Watch out!" she screamed.

A second later, Chameleon fired. But Donovan didn't fall. Raising his hands in a helpless gesture of submission, he stumbled forward, mouth opening to speak. Chameleon fired again, the sound reverberating through the tunnels. With the second shot, Donovan slumped to the rock floor.

Unable to move, even to breathe, Erin clutched the wall, her eyes wide with horror and a terrible longing for what now could never be. Hit by two bullets fired at point-blank range by a professional killer, Donovan must be dead. And with him all her hopes and dreams.

In the space of a few minutes, she'd plunged from a pinnacle of complete trust and love for this man to a valley of emptiness and loss so acute she wanted to die. And death lay only a few feet from her. A sob in her throat, Erin swung around toward the assassin.

For a precious half second she stood facing Chameleon, her full body exposed, a perfect target. But the assassin, bending over the body, didn't glance toward her.

Her mind spinning, Erin bit her lip until it throbbed like a pulse. The pain brought back her reason. What was she thinking of? Donovan had just sacrificed his life for her, yet here she stood, ready to submit without a fight. As long as there was breath in her, she wouldn't—couldn't—give up. Returning to the wall, she began to inch her way around the drop-off.

In the tunnel opening across the chasm, a man appeared. Instinctively she flinched. Patrick! With no place to hide, she was finished. He could kill her with one quick shot. Trying to shrink into herself so she'd be a smaller target, she stared across at him.

Even in the dim light, Patrick looked taller and slimmer than Erin remembered. And his hair was darker. Much darker. She blinked. The man across from her wasn't pointing a weapon at her. He was waving.

"Erin!" he called. It wasn't Patrick's voice. It was Donovan's.

A cry of pure joy broke from her lips, and hot exultant

tears trickled down her cheeks. Donovan wasn't dead. He was alive, standing across the abyss from her, smiling, waving.

But how? Suddenly, her heart overflowing, she understood. When Patrick first heard Donovan's voice, he'd returned to the left fork in pursuit. But Donovan hadn't gone down the left fork after all. The footsteps she'd heard had been Patrick's not the man she loved.

Somehow, someway, Donovan had figured out the two upper corridors came together here at the drop-off. So he'd taken the right-hand corridor hoping to overtake Patrick and link up with Erin. But he couldn't call out and tell her what he planned or he'd ruin his surprise.

Well, they'd been shocked, all right, so confused that the demon had killed his own master. Thank God! Maybe now Chameleon would go away and leave them alone.

"Erin!" Donovan yelled again. "Behind you."

Fearfully she looked back over her shoulder.

Chameleon stood there, his weapon in his hand, close enough to touch her. Shuddering, she tried to move away, but she couldn't. Her feet seemed frozen to the rocky ledge.

Leering at her, his eyes sunken in their sockets, the assassin reached out and grabbed her arm.

"I'm going to get you!" he snarled. "You're going to suffer for all the chaos you've caused. Then I'm going to kill you, a lovely slow death." He gave an evil laugh, showing yellow, jagged teeth in decaying flesh.

Erin's heart seemed to stop beating. She tried to shrink away, but his grip on her arm was too strong.

From across the chasm she heard a loud roar of pure male rage. Quickly Chameleon swung around to face Donovan across the drop-off.

For an instant, as he turned and lifted his arm to fire, his hold on Erin loosened. She saw her chance and jerked ferociously away from him. Off balance, the assassin missed Donovan, his bullet ricocheting harmlessly off the rock wall behind him.

Before he could fire again, something bright flashed

through the air. Erin could only stare in horror as a silver meat cleaver struck Chameleon squarely in the chest. She heard the soft thump as the knife buried itself deeply in his flesh, saw his mouth open, his sunken eyes turn glassy in the dim light. The gun dropped from his hand, clattering noisily into the abyss.

An instant later, the assassin's skeletal body toppled forward. He seemed to dangle forever, floating in a crazy free-fall. Then his body disappeared in the darkness below. She heard a hollow thud as it struck the rock floor.

Somehow Erin managed to get her leaden feet to move, managed to inch the rest of the way toward Donovan who was coming toward her. With a sigh, she fell into his reaching arms.

"Erin! Darling, are you all right?" Then he held her so close she could hear the blood pounding in the veins in his neck. "Did he hurt you?"

Through chattering teeth she managed a shaky "No." But in spite of Donovan's arms around her and her eye-witness of Chameleon's demise, she couldn't believe he was really gone. Peering around Donovan's shoulder, she half expected to see his skeletal face emerge from the black hole where his body lay.

Carefully Donovan swung around until her back was to the hole, but that was even worse. Now she could imagine the assassin crawling up the chasm's stone wall and creeping toward them from behind.

"Let's get out of here," she whispered, shaking. "I've got to find my mother."

"I'm sure she's okay," Donovan assured her, tenderly kissing her forehead. "She and the household staff are locked up somewhere in the castle."

"How can you be certain?" Erin peered at him searchingly.

"Because your stepfather as good as admitted he intended to massacre them and make it look like I did it. He's the one who circled Westport on the map to make sure we'd know where she'd gone."

Understanding flooded through her. "Uncle Michael said neither he nor Mom marked the map, so Patrick must have done it. But how did he manage to find you so easily at Mrs. Flaherty's?"

Donovan took her hand and led her carefully toward the passageway leading down to the bay. "We must have been followed from the Ballyshannon Lodge—probably by the same people who tailed us from your cousin's. O'Shaughnessy wanted to make damn sure to get us cornered in one spot so he could kill us all and blame the deaths on me."

"Maybe he's already murdered Mom." A terrible new fear rose in her throat.

Putting his arm around her waist, he walked with her down the narrow passage toward the bay. "If he'd already killed her and the staff, he would have killed me, too. And he told the injured man in the entry hall he wanted him to witness their deaths."

"Uncle Michael?" she gasped. "He's still alive?" Erin's heart filled with gratitude. "He was shot trying to save me."

"He was alive when I left him. I'm no doctor, but his wound didn't look fatal."

"But why didn't they kill him?" Erin asked. "After he kicked the gun out of Patrick's hand, Chameleon shot him. That's how I got away."

Hugging her closer, Donovan stared down at her. "O'Shaughnessy told him he'd be killed in a time and place with your mother watching. As if that would make her suffer. Almost as though…"

"Almost as though they were lovers," she concluded for him, guessing his thoughts.

Erin increased her pace. All at once she couldn't wait to see her mother's welcoming smile, to hear her explanation in her own melodious voice. She and Donovan were so close to finding her, so close—

"You got here in the nick of time," she said, managing a wry smile. With his arm still around her waist, they left the tunnel and started across Clew Bay's sandy mud.

"The same way you arrived at the cathedral in the nick of time to save me," he replied. "Hey, we're getting pretty good at this." He pulled her closer to his side.

"So how did you know about the tunnels?" Erin's feet sank into the Clew Bay muck, but she didn't care, not with Donovan unharmed beside her, and her uncle still alive in the entry hall. Now if her mother were just okay...

"Your uncle told me about the tunnels," Donovan replied. "Thanks to him I knew where you'd gone and that the two tunnels joined at the drop-off."

"Uncle Michael again," she breathed. "He said he'd give his life for me and Mom."

Donovan's arm tightened around her as they started up the incline toward the castle. "He meant what he said. If he hadn't kicked the gun out of O'Shaughnessy's hand so you could get away, we'd all be dead."

THEY FOUND ERIN'S UNCLE lying in the entry hall where Donovan had left him.

"O'Shaughnessy and his hit man are dead," Donovan announced. "As soon as we find Erin's mother, I'll go for a doctor and the police."

Her uncle's blue eyes, so like her own, glistened with unshed tears of happiness. "Hurry and find your mother, Erin. She's probably locked in one of the upstairs bedrooms. If O'Shaughnessy's done anything to harm her—"

He reached into his pocket and took out a key ring. "The keys to all the doors are here." He dropped the ring into her palm. "Now, please hurry."

Mounting the stairs two at a time, Erin and Donovan climbed to the third floor.

Breathing in shallow, quick gasps, she called out. "Mom, it's Erin. Are you up here?"

She heard no answering cry, only the dull thump-thumping of feet pounding against wood. Even as they stood at the head of the stairs, the sound doubled, tripled in intensity.

"Quick! It's coming from over here," Donovan said, turning toward the right side of the upper hallway.

The door was locked. Donovan reached for the keys in Erin's hand. After trying a couple of them, he found the right one and pushed the door open.

Erin's heart overflowed as she followed him in.

There was her mother lying side by side on the wood floor with several others, their mouths taped, their hands and feet tied. All appeared to be alive.

Carefully Erin removed the tape from her mother's mouth while Donovan worked on freeing the household staff.

"Where's Kevin?" her mother cried, even before Erin started untying her ropes. "Why isn't he here with you and Mr. Donovan?" Dressed in blue jeans and a bulky sweater, she didn't seem to have even one dark curly hair out of place.

Erin dropped to the floor beside her. "Who's Kevin? The only other person in the house outside of the staff is Uncle Michael." Pausing, she studied her mother's dark blue eyes. "Unless you mean Patrick. And you must know he planned to kill all of us, including you."

"O'Shaughnessy's dead," Donovan volunteered. "Shot by his own hit man."

Her mother's mouth drew down in a frustrated frown. "It's not him I was referring to, Erin. But I thank God that awful man's gone. How he could have fooled me so completely, I'll never know."

"Then who *are* you talking about?" Erin wondered if her mother's horrible ordeal had confused her mind. She set to work undoing the knots binding her mother's wrists. Obviously tied by an expert—Chameleon—they were almost impossible to loosen.

Silently Donovan drew a knife from his shirt front and handed it to her. It sliced through the rope as easily as through a loaf of stale bread. In a moment her mother was free. Instantly she sat up. Leaning against the bed, she gathered Erin near her side, her arm around her shoulders.

"I'm talking about the man you called your uncle Michael," her mother said softly. "He'd not your uncle, Erin. After all these years, I've found your father. Or rather, he found me."

Erin's mind reeled. "My father? What do you mean, Mom? Dad died last year."

"Not the dear general, Erin. Your birth father, Michael Kevin Riley. You've already met him."

"But that's not possible." Erin stared in shock at her mother. She had to struggle to keep her voice calm. "Kevin Riley died in Vietnam." Her throat felt choked and dry, full of dust. Dimly she was aware of movement around her, of the other people in the room talking, stretching, hugging one another. But nothing could interfere with her concentration on her mother's sapphire blue eyes.

"You must forgive me for the lie I told so long ago," she begged, her voice quivering. "I did it for you, because I didn't want you to think your father abandoned you. After a while, I came to believe the lie myself."

All the poisonous resentment Erin had felt for such a long time came bubbling to the surface. "But he did abandon us, Mom. He left you pregnant and me without a dad. He—"

Her mother put a finger across Erin's lips, silencing her. "He lost his leg to a land mine only a few days after he arrived in Vietnam. That precious man thought he'd be useless to me without his leg." She smiled fondly, the way she used to smile at Erin when she'd done something foolishly brave. "That's why my letters were returned unopened, not because he'd died."

"An honorable man doesn't let his child live without a father," Erin argued stubbornly. Glancing around she saw they were alone in the room. Instinctively she knew Donovan had left to get help.

"Your father didn't find out about you until after I'd married George Meyer," her mother replied. "After checking, he found out what a fine man George was and decided he'd be a good husband and father and the best thing he could do was stay out of our lives.''

"How convenient for him." Erin didn't hide her sarcasm.

"Not really," her mother said, smoothing Erin's hair with her hand. "Like some guardian angel, he's watched over us all these years," her mother said, with stars in her eyes. "Even though he'd sworn himself to silence so he wouldn't interfere in our lives, he was always there for us, ready to step in when we needed him."

Her mother's eyes shone with a light Erin recognized. She still loved Kevin Riley, even after all these years. "Your father sensed that I'd seen him watching me in Dublin. He didn't want to scare me so he told me who he was. That was only a few hours after you and I talked on the phone. We planned to have coffee the next morning."

She gave Erin a mischievous smile. "It was all perfectly innocent. We just wanted to get caught up." Her expression sobered. "But later that day I found out about Patrick's counterfeiting and knew I had to get away. When I didn't keep the appointment with your father, he got worried and tried to find me at Jean's, where the household staff said I'd gone. Then, since he'd given me the phone number and address here at the castle, he drove straight to Clew Bay from Dublin, on the off chance I might be in trouble and come to him for help."

"I know," Erin said. "On the way here from Westport he told me how he'd rushed to the Ballyshannon Lodge after you called."

Her mother's eyes misted. "Dear girl, your father would have given his life for us."

The floodgates opened as Erin pictured the injured man lying downstairs. Standing, she helped her mother get up. "He almost did, Mom." Her voice wavered.

Her mother's face turned the color of chalk. She clutched Erin's arm. "How? Where? Tell me what happened."

"Downstairs about an hour ago. He kicked the gun out of Patrick's hand so I could get away." Erin spoke slowly, trying to soften her words. "Uncle Michael—er—Kevin is going to be okay, but he was wounded by Patrick's hired assassin."

Her mother's shudder seemed to shake her entire body. "Shot by that awful skeleton man?" She dashed for the door. "I've got to get downstairs."

DONOVAN HEARD THEM coming when they were still on the third-floor landing, Erin's calm lilting soprano voice answering her mother's excited contralto. During his few minutes alone with the injured man, Donovan had learned he was Erin's biological father.

Now, as he squatted next to Kevin Riley, he heard his name whispered.

"Donovan?" Riley said, his voice weak. "Prop me up against the wall so I don't look so puny when she first sees me."

Opening Riley's shirt, Donovan examined the wound. The bleeding had slowed to a trickle. Carefully, Donovan raised him to an upright position and draped his coat over his shirt to hide the blood. A tall slender man with broad shoulders, Riley was heavier than he looked.

Erin's mother hit the bottom stair running. An instant later she was kneeling beside Riley, holding his face in her hands.

"Oh, Kevin, are you all right? If he'd killed you, I don't know what I'd have done." Her eyes brimming, she caressed his cheek with her fingers.

"I'm fine, Peg. It's only a flesh wound and Donovan says the bullet went clear through so it's nice and clean." His eyes locked with hers.

She lifted his shirt and gasped. "This doesn't look like a flesh wound to me." She glanced at Erin. "Get me a clean cloth and some hot water."

Her attention turned to Donovan. Suddenly her voice took on the strident tones of an imperious drill sergeant. "Where's the doctor, Mr. Donovan? Why isn't he here?"

For one of the few times in his adult life, Donovan felt

awkward. "I tried to call a doctor, but the phone line's been cut," he explained lamely.

Erin's mother glowered at him. "Well, there are cars in the garage. Why are you still here?"

Donovan cleared his throat. "I didn't want to leave Mr. Riley until you and Erin got here."

"We're here," she returned abruptly. "Now go for the doctor. And Erin, why are you standing there with your mouth open? Get me that hot water."

Erin eyed her mother anxiously. "You've been through an awful lot in the past few hours, Mom. Let me take over while you get some rest."

Her mother's glance was positively glacial. "Nonsense! Your father needs me." But when she glanced up again and gazed into Erin's eyes, her expression softened. "You need rest far more than I, dear girl. You're the one who's been shot at and chased by two maniacs. Call one of the servants to help me."

Now it was Erin's turn to throw a glacial glance. "I'll do no such thing!" Kneeling beside her parents, she felt the comforting pressure of her mother's arm around her shoulders.

"Thanks for coming to my rescue, Erin," she said softly. "Now, if you really want to help—"

"I'll get the hot water," Erin replied. No errand had ever seemed sweeter.

HOURS LATER, after the doctor had come and gone, Erin and Donovan walked hand in hand across the castle lawn in the rosy light of an early Irish morning. In an upstairs bedroom, Erin's mother hovered protectively over the man she'd never stopped loving.

"Did your mother tell you how a disabled American Vietnam vet ended up with a castle on Clew Bay?" Donovan asked, as they reached the lawn's edge. Beyond, the water was creeping up, slowly covering the mucky sand. Erin could smell the salty fragrance of the incoming tide.

She flashed him a quick smile. "The uncle he's named

for left him the castle a couple of years ago. When Mom moved to Dublin, Uncle Michael—er—Dad followed her. Since he was in Ireland, he decided to renovate the castle and turn it into a hotel. Dublin and Clew Bay are only a couple hundred miles apart so he figured he could keep an eye on her and still oversee the work at the castle.''

Donovan kept his gaze fastened on the many islands dotting the shallow bay. ''Where'd he get the money? Turning a castle into a luxury hotel is a hell of an expense.''

''Computers,'' Erin said. ''He got in on the ground floor and did pretty well. And now he's got backing for the hotel from some well-known companies. Mom's all excited about it.''

''Then she's going to stay here in Ireland?''

''I'm sure she will as long as Dad's here,'' Erin replied, the word *Dad* now rolling easily off her tongue. ''She says her place is with him.''

''How do you feel about that?'' Donovan asked. ''Do you think a woman's place is with her man?''

Erin thought she heard subtle laughter in his voice. But when he turned toward her, he wasn't smiling. His intense searching look made her heart do flip-flops.

''Let's put it this way,'' she said, hope spiraling within her. ''I think people who love each other should be together.''

''If we're going to be together, we need to make some important decisions about our jobs.'' His husky voice held a challenge. ''I gather you're not too happy with yours. Well, after the way the agency's handled the Shamrock Conspiracy, I feel the same way about mine.''

''What about your freedom?'' she asked, dumbfounded. ''You're the one who's against commitment.''

''Not anymore,'' he returned quickly, casting a sidelong glance at her.

''Since when?'' Erin held a trembling breath, waiting for his answer.

''Since I met you. I want us to be free together.'' There was a sincere fervency to his voice.

She let her breath out in a long sigh. "Would you really quit your job?"

Donovan snapped his fingers. "Just like that. I'm a different man from when I gave you that bunk about freedom, Erin. No man in love wants to be truly free if freedom means being without the woman he loves."

Turning to her, his face lit up with a glow to rival the dawn sky. "Why don't you resign your commission and we'll both go to work for your dad at the castle? Clew Bay's a great place to raise a tribe of young Donovans. Think what fun they'd have playing hide and seek in the tunnels."

"We'd have to fill in the drop-off," Erin responded without a second thought. "It's terribly dangerous."

Donovan grinned at her. "That sounds like you accept my proposal." Relief filled his voice.

Eyes wide, Erin stared at him. This couldn't be happening. Could all her dreams be coming true at once? In the space of a few hours she'd rescued her mother, witnessed the resurrection of her birth father, and heard the sincere proposal of the man she wanted to spend the rest of her life with. What more miracles did life have in store?

"Yes, oh yes," she said joyously, her heart filled with love.

In the east the pale pink sky bloomed to a rosy yellow, paving the smooth surface of the water with gold. For the rest of her life, whenever she saw Clew Bay in the early morning, Erin would remember this special day and its three wonderful miracles.

HARLEQUIN®

I N T R I G U E ®

COMING NEXT MONTH

#425 THE CASE OF THE BAD LUCK FIANCÉ by Sheryl Lynn
Honeymoon Hideaway
Megan Duke loved Tristan Cayle before they ever even met—due to an Internet romance. But now Tristan stands accused of already being betrothed—to two wives. And Megan's life will depend on whether she can trust Tristan....

#426 FAMILIAR HEART by Caroline Burnes
Fear Familiar
Racing to recover animal trainer Brak Brunston's missing panthers, law officer Ashley Curry couldn't resist his strong, savage appeal. Brak was a man Ashley wanted to help...and to love. But would she have to turn him in to the law?

#427 HER DESTINY by Aimée Thurlo
Four Winds
He'd saved her from the flames, but it was Sheriff Gabriel Blackhorse's own heat Lanie Matthews feared. It seemed a mysterious gift from a passing peddlar had put Lanie's life in danger...and her fate in the hands of the very man she was determined to avoid.

#428 SWEET DECEPTION by Susan Kearney
To find her cousin's murderer, lady P.I. Denise Ward needed billionaire Ford Braddack, husband to the victim, who was about to remarry. So she abducted the unsuspecting groom on his wedding day, in *his* limo, spirited him from the country in *his* jet. She planned for everything—except falling in love with Ford.

AVAILABLE THIS MONTH:

#421 SWORN TO SILENCE
Vickie York

#422 ALIAS: DADDY
Adrianne Lee

#423 ONE TOUGH TEXAN
M.J. Rodgers

#424 THE CASE OF THE VANISHED GROOM
Sheryl Lynn

Look us up on-line at: http://www.romance.net